ALONE

Carlota Gurt

ALONE

*Translated from the Catalan
by Adrian Nathan West*

Europa
editions

Europa Editions
8 Blackstock Mews
London N4 2BT
www.europaeditions.co.uk

This book was translated with the help of a grant from the Institut Ramon Llull

LLLL institut
ramon llull | **20** years

Translation by Adrian Nathan West
Original title: *Sola*
Translation copyright © 2023 by Europa Editions

A catalogue record for this title is available from the British Library
ISBN 978-1-78770-443-5

Gurt, Carlota
Alone

Art direction by Emanuele Ragnisco
instagram.com/emanueleragnisco

Cover design and illustration by Ginevra Rapisardi

Prepress by Grafica Punto Print – Rome

Printed and bound in Great Britain by Clays Ltd, Elcograf S.p.A

C O N T E N T S

To you,
for temerities and scars,
for prodigies,
for the marvels that await us.

Whoever lives alone is either a god or a beast.
—ARISTOTLE
(OR BOTH)

ALONE

APRIL

When the road turned into the woods, the wind started to blow as if anxious to hurry me home. I advanced beneath a derangement of trees and clouds, past eyeless trees that watched over me when I was born. In the rearview, nothing but the veil of dust my machine raised. Here, cars are factories of haze that keep you from seeing what's behind you, and when you hit a pothole, the whole world trembles.

Finally, it appeared on the hill, smaller and more desolate than I remembered. I'd have liked to park right there and run over open-armed, even naked, climb barefoot up the fifteen stone steps, but I saw a man with a shaggy dog waiting for me at the top, and I had to reserve my bucolic spirit for another time.

It was Manel, obviously.

He rushed over to me, all smiles, with the animal behind him, crestfallen, tied with a rope. I hardly got out of the car before he started talking, and he hasn't quieted down since.

You used to be pretty as a pea, he repeated two or three times, eyes lost like someone uttering a phrase of deep significance. Then he went off about don't you remember me and I didn't look anything like my mother, and how close they used to be when they were kids, and he winked at me several times throughout. What a woman, your mother! he exclaimed, then he turned wistful and made a gesture as though whipping a magic wand through the air and added: *zub-zub*.

Inevitably, returning here meant encountering the tragic

onomatopoeia of my adolescence, the one teachers, classmates, and shopkeepers repeated to me when I was fourteen and my mother did an ad for Minipimer hand blenders, and I had to put up with it the way you put up with a sibling who gets all the praise; the onomatopoeia that invoked the device's super-power—grinding up everything with its magic touch—the onomatopoeia and the gesture that grotesquely filled my dreams, along with my father, who had died not long before.

Zub-zub, Manel says, and I remember our solitude, my mother's and mine, shut up in our little apartment in Horta, with the whole world deceived, thinking my mother had a magic wand and an ineffaceable smile and whirled humming around the kitchen as she did in the ad, solving every problem with a *zub-zub*. But no. Nothing hummed in our dining room except a silence we didn't know how to fill. And the hand blender, it hummed too. Hummed and ground everything into nothing.

Manel said *zub-zub* and I laughed at the joke, as I did at fourteen and later at twenty, at thirty, as I still do, embarrassingly, at forty.

As we climbed the stairs, he offered his barroom philosopher's musings about youth and how time flies. I counted the stairs, as always. Fifteen, same as when I was a girl. Reality keeps count.

He opened the door, but I wasn't listening to him, I was too busy looking: outside, the washbasin with the rusty tap, the rotten wood of the porch; inside, the cracked tiles, the carpet of dust fallen from the ceiling, the light switches, so old I was reluctant to touch them, afraid they'd give me a shock. And in the background, Manel, on a tear: *You'll love it here, you'll see.* I don't know if he was pulling my leg or he really believed it.

He gave me endless instructions I couldn't repeat if my life depended on it: be careful opening the windows, there's a trick to turning on the water heater, you need to jiggle the lock. What he didn't tell me was what to do with the memories creeping across the floor, climbing the walls, the ceiling, whether it would be best to nurture or exterminate them.

Truffle followed us the whole time, six inches away. I tried not to think about the fleas and ticks she must have. Every time I saw her rubbing herself on the chair, the curtains, the bed— the bed!—I walked over as though at random and discreetly sent her on her way. She exudes a canine stench that suffused the air; it's night now, and I think I still smell it, it's seeped into my pituitary gland.

After half an hour, he finally left me alone. I paid him for the first four months, just as we'd agreed. He opened the envelope and counted the banknotes with a look of satisfaction. *It's not that I don't trust you, but it's best to avoid misunderstandings, right?* He couldn't help but remind me that if he gave me a deal, it was because of my mother, because they'd known each other and because my mother should never have sold the place, who would ever think of doing such a thing, etc. If I needed any-thing, all I had to do was say the word. I just nodded devoutly, like a nun.

Then he looked at me with those beady eyes of his and said, *You don't talk much, do you?,* and like an idiot I just mumbled some incoherent nonsense. Maybe I should have marked off my territory more, I've got the impression now he must have thought I was a little dim.

He reached out and we shook hands as though closing an important deal. Then he said, *You've got the same little girl's hands.* A little girl, sure, I've caught him more than once already eyeing my breasts up with a grin that covers his whole face. If I tell Guim, he'll say I'm exaggerating, that I always think every-one's looking at me.

But he was.

I thanked him for everything. It seemed like a bad idea to piss off the owner on the very first day.

He was already walking down the stairs when he turned

around and threatened me: We'll be seeing a lot of each other, he said, because when he drives the sheep out to pasture, he usually stops at the trough down from the house. I nodded like a lamb thinking how I could clog it at the source, destroy it so I wouldn't have to see him too often. Nice as he might be, I've come here to be alone.

He departed on foot, sluggish and bow-legged, singing in an unsettlingly pleasant tenor voice: *And he told me, when you get older, never trust the calm . . .* I found not a trace of the famous resemblance to Rock Hudson my mother had spoken to me of.

Then I realized my car was the only one there. I could have taken him to the village. Walking, he'd need an hour, maybe two, by car it's just twenty minutes, but I didn't feel like making the trip with him riding shotgun and talking the whole time. I must be a bitch. The poor man, he hasn't done anything to me, he rented me the place for peanuts, but my heart just wasn't in it. The state I found the place in was a little demoralizing. I'd gotten ahead of myself. Back in Barcelona, everything seemed so easy.

Lashed by the wind, I unloaded the car and left my entire life in a pyramid of boxes in the alcove. I walked hurriedly through the house making a list of all that I needed, cleaning products above all, and at every step, I had to shake off the memories that leapt at me: my father's armchair, the painting of sunflowers, the vegetal shapes carved in the wooden headboard.

Not now—there will be time soon enough.

I had to take off before the shop closed. In the village, everything closes early. As soon as I walked in, I saw the framed advertisement for the hand blender on the wall in the back: my mother, Sorrius's local celebrity. Town hall could start the canonization process with the miracle of the *zub-zub*—they could call me in to attest that with a single motion it could grind anything to a paste. I would affirm it was true.

Can Boronat is the typical shop that has it all. And if it doesn't, then too bad. Mercè, the shopkeeper, already told me Sorrius doesn't have a butcher or a pharmacy or a newspaper stand.

"The shop, the bar, and the garage, dear. If you need anything else, you'll have to go down to Vilamitja."

Mercè's familiar to me. Maybe just because she looks like the universal woman from the country: ruddy, ever-smiling, hefty like someone who feasts on too much sausage, wavy blond helmet-hair and a bust perfect for breastfeeding children or lovers with Freudian hang-ups. A Russian matron. Queen milkmaid. Or maybe I just remember her subconsciously from when I was little and I used to run through the village, she was probably one of those girls who gave you candy and sang songs and bounced you on her lap, whether you liked it or not. I don't know if she knows who I am. She didn't ask and she didn't start up with the routine about my mother and the house. It's for the best.

But right before I left: *I close on Thursdays and Sunday afternoons, hon,* as if she knew I wasn't just passing through, and then, when I was already outside: *Tomorrow morning there's a market in the square.*

When I got in the car, the sky was covered in black breasts—mammatocumulus clouds. I still hadn't made it out of the village when raindrops as big as quail eggs started bombarding me. They shattered angrily against the windshield, their rhythm frenetic, as if they wanted to drive the wipers insane. I leaned in toward the glass like a myopic grandmother. Again, the road that never ends. Between the machine gunfire of the rain, my concentration behind the wheel, and the car's rattling, I arrived in a daze.

When I got out, I thought I could hear a metallic plunk mixing with the rain sounds, and a current of cold air encircled my ankles like a Roman cuff. Here, the storms are living, not like the ones that spill impotently on the asphalt of the city.

I climbed the stone steps outside two at a time, it didn't stop me from getting soaked. Once at home—at home, I say!—I didn't feel the gentle warmth you notice when you're suddenly safe and the outside world can't get you. No, I noticed the damp. Hostile. It's a dead house, I'll have to resuscitate it.

Fortunately, Manel was thoughtful enough to leave me some wood for the fireplace. I had to struggle for half an hour, but finally I've gotten it lit and curled up next to it with a feeling of victory.

Just now I tried to call Guim. All day I've just sent him one message. But it turns out I don't have service anywhere in the house.

More tomorrow.

MAY

When I woke up, I didn't know where I was. At first I thought I was in my apartment in Barcelona, but something didn't add up: the light coming from the right instead of the left, the bed—too short, as if shrunken—the dark scent of the air, the catastrophic silence. For a few moments, I was afraid.

It was strange to imagine that my mother and father slept in this bed forty years back, that I was stretched out on the same mattress where I was conceived, the same bed my father would let me share on special occasions when my mother had already gotten up.

A vital vertigo overtook me. I'd have submitted to it, if only to grasp this memory of my father and show myself I still think of him often, but I felt the urge to flee it. I stayed in bed, petrified for some time, observing the crumbling beams, the cobwebs in the corners, the wicker chair with the seat that caved in years ago, the loose clay tiles forming little waves, as though resting on a liquid surface.

It creeped me out to sit up, raise my bare foot, and place it on the cold ground, as if when I touched it everything might disappear or the sea of tiles might swallow me. Or maybe it creeped me out because I've realized this is serious, that stepping onto the tiles means signing a contract with myself. Of course, I finally dared it, I couldn't just stay in bed forever.

I threw open the shutters. How green the green is, how

luminous, how living, and all of it for me, with the sun further off, peeking out over the crowns of the trees. Not a trace of the storm sent to welcome me yesterday. Drowsing in the sheets has made me winsome, I think, or maybe my father's still on my mind. All at once, there was no room inside me, my body was too small for so much soul. I opened the window and took a breath. I looked all round to make sure no one was there—how silly!—and uttered a series of meaningless cries, concentrated air erupting from inside me.

I shouted till I was empty, I must have been carrying all those cries around for years. In the end, the bastards from the publisher might really have done me a favor by giving me the boot. Today, for the first time, I have the sense that those offices were my private platonic cave. How right Guim was when he told me to cut and run! Then it strikes me I'm exaggerating, deceiving myself, because I loved the job in the early days, and maybe it's just that anger makes it easier to kiss it all goodbye.

I had a scant breakfast, not very good; I was impatient to get properly set up and start work. I cleaned everything in a rush. I should have told Guim to come help me; it was a mountain of a task, but I'm like a little girl who wants to tie her own shoes, even if it takes a half-hour and the whole thing turns into a mess.

I opened all the windows, the balcony in the living room, the doors. Light has machine-gunned the house. The sun pierces the rooms like the swords plunged through a magician's magic box, and I am the woman inside, contorting to perpetuate the illusion. A torrent of air has swept away the scent of damp.

The first part was the worst: the dust. Atop the furnishings—the chiffonier, the vitrine full of gewgaws—a sheet of grime lay solidified through time. Time, which turns everything solid and grimy. I screwed up my courage, scrub brush in hand, and with every stroke I scraped away mummified shavings that might well contain scraps of skin from when I was six, or my father's eyelashes—how many botched wishes—or hairs from my mother's brows when she used to pluck them with a hand mirror, sitting stiff at the dining room table, or maybe boogers from that kid (Llorenç? Lluc?) who used to stick me with them when we were the same age and he killed time digging around in his nose.

I scrubbed with verve, fingers cramping now and then, gripped the brush as tightly as if scraping grout from the folds of my mind, polishing my memories, sprucing them up.

I wasn't tired once the dining room was done, to the contrary, I felt more energy and eagerness than before. I ran to the kitchen and the brush moved on its own, and look, there was the basin I knew by heart because my mother used to wash my hair in it with a pot of water heated on the stove. How dirty we were back then! It still has the bird-shaped crack, a little bigger now, opened a little wider; when I was a girl, I thought it was a canary like the ones my grandmother kept crammed in cages squalid with viscous turds, but my mother said no, really, are you out of your mind, it looks like a giant tick, and then she'd always add: Ugh, don't make me think about it. And if we argued too long about which of us was right, my father would whisper in my ear that it was neither a canary nor a tick, it was a swallow on the verge of taking flight. And when I finished scrubbing the sink, I thought the years had proved him right, maybe it really was a swallow after all.

In this hygienic stupor, I lost track of time, and after the kitchen, I applied myself frenetically to the two bedrooms and the bathroom, the filthiest room of all.

As I scrubbed and wiped with a damp rag to trap whatever dust that tried to escape me, all I could think of was a tiny Mei cleaning the most recondite and soiled corners of a brain. Now and again a burst of air shot in and I felt everything turn spongy, my thoughts took wing, and there was this image of a brain and me, an ant, with a brush. Yes ma'am, I said to myself, you're here to clean, all right, clean the filth that's clotted inside you just like all this grime.

Time stretched on: at twelve I had cleared away all the dust from the habitable part of the house. For now, I won't touch the cellar. Just thinking of the narrow stairway provokes a ridiculous claustrophobia, a little girl's claustrophobia, the same one I felt when my mother used to make me go get her a handful of onions, a bottle of wine, brandy for special occasions, and I had to plunge into that fetid darkness.

No, I'll save the cellar for another day.

It struck me it would be good to go to the village and have a snack at the bar the woman from the shop (Maite? Mercè?) told me about. I wanted to gossip a little, study the aborigines, see the stooped old women emerging from Mass, take a look at the market, call Guim, the poor thing, I still haven't managed to talk to him. When I get back I'll roll up my sleeves again. The light coming through the balcony tempted me even more and I could see myself with a vermouth and some chips sitting in the sun in the town square.

But I get in the car and it won't start. I left the lights on, as always. I won't tell Guim this time so I can save myself the sermon. Fucking storm. I had to make do with a beer and a couple of anchovies at the foot of the steps.

Actually, the setback did me some good. No need to waste even a minute. I came here to work and maybe going out for a bite and a drink was just one of my excuses to avoid doing what I have to do, what I want to do, what I've decided to do. We already know your escapist side, Mei.

With every sip of beer, I saw more and more clearly that I had to clean the house today, no excuses, to ready it to be my working sanctuary. I put my shoulder to the wheel again without even finishing my beer, prey to an unease that refused to let me savor it. My apprehension and I embraced the broom and mop, and we didn't rest until everything was immaculate. Everything but the cellar, I mean.

When I finished, it was dark out, and I flopped down in the armchair, which is no longer *the* armchair, but *my* armchair. I covered it with an old sheet because the upholstery was ugly and couldn't be cleaned just like that, and I rolled up exhausted but proud as an empress.

The house, like the armchair, looks different now without the layer of dead dust covering it. I've made it mine. I'm still unsure whether to take down the painting of sunflowers over the fireplace; it's a constant reminder of who I am, and that might suit me, even if now it's odious to be reminded constantly of who I am.

Either way, I'd feel bad sticking it in the cellar or a wardrobe, with all those months it took my father to paint it!

The Day Before

You will count the stairs and there will be fourteen.
Terrifyingly fourteen.

Last night, my novel possessed me, and I woke up bright and early to start working on it. At times I have the sense that I don't want to write a novel, but that there's a novel that wants me to write it.

I gulped down a piece of toast with marmalade standing on the edge of the sink to keep from wasting thirty seconds sitting down at the table. I'll write a kick-ass synopsis, I was thinking the whole time, a wide-ranging synopsis, I've been turning it over for so many days it couldn't be any other way.

I've set up the computer and printer on the desk next to the living room window to be able to see all that insolent green when my determination flags. I've arranged my pencils, erasers, and pens on the edge of the table, taken from my purse the pad where I've written down all my notes these past two months, ever since Guim chewed me out: You need to write your ideas down or they'll vanish from your head.

I sat down in front of the screen and pressed the power button. It was a solemn moment. All that was missing was an engraver to chisel into the stone sill of the balcony:

HERE REMEI SALA MUNT BEGAN
WRITING *ALONE*
MMXVI AD

I opened the word processor. The cursor blinked over the

white pixels. I wrote *Synopsis,* and I saved the document in a new folder. Today everything is a first.

Then I looked up. The sight of the broken-down car dispersed all those ideas of mine which up until now were so well wrought, and I heard the little voice: you-have-to-go-to-the-mechanic, you-have-to-go-to-the-mechanic. I turned a deaf ear to it and wrote the first sentence, the one I'd spent the whole morning pondering until it was perfect, but once it was there, it didn't seem so striking. I started to regurgitate the synopsis as it came to me, in a gush.

But—ah!—when I opened the notepad, Guim overwhelmed me, because it was he who gave it to me; objects, always objects, with the memories that lie incrusted in them. I struggled to get him out of my head. How I needed to call him, and would we miss each other, and how the day he gave it to me I thought he was ridiculing my literary aspirations.

I started hitting the keys harder to drown out the little sabotaging voices. I typed at top speed as if that would deliver me from those mental disturbances, repeating to myself over and over, You're going to write the most kick-ass synopsis of all time, even if I knew it wasn't true, I just kept saying it, This synopsis is the shit, it's the best synopsis you could ever write.

The car and Guim tried to sneak in through the cracks in my brain, but I blocked them out with nouns and verbs and adjectives that hurtled toward my fingers to try and propagate themselves across the screen. Now and then, I forgot everything, and was able truly to dive into my world of words.

It was there, buffeted by concentration and distraction, that I finished. It's not perfect. Not yet. But I've done it, and that's what I had to do, much as I'd have liked to compose the most kick-ass synopsis of all time.

I've finished the first version.

I will write a novel. I will write it because *I* want to.

Swelling with pride at a job well done, I threw on my hiking shoes and took off for the village to resolve the issue with the car.

To tread an earthen path is to become conscious of each step: to feel the crunch of the gravel compressed underfoot, the little sharp-edged pebbles that get stuck in your soles. The feeling that the path is a living thing, not an unchangeable surface, secure and permanent like a city, where the sound of steps is grey and empty. Or dead. Here everything moves, everything changes.

It's spring, the entire forest was humming. I thought it might be a beehive, but the humming wouldn't let up, it wished to hypnotize me. And it worked. I let myself be lulled by the sylvan soundtrack, and on one stretch I even dared to close my eyes and walk forward blindly, my fear of tripping and falling mingled with suppressed euphoria. My head emptied out, I stopped thinking about *Solitude* and Mila, who worried me so much all the sudden, because I had to work on my protagonist, and I'm still unsure whether I ought to change her name to distance myself a little from the work that inspires me and that might wind up being more a burden than a mainstay. But there with my eyes closed, none of this existed. There was only me, levitating through the forest.

Every time I opened my eyes, I found some corner I had overlooked on my drives. A boulder sputtering a rivulet of crystalline water I haven't dared taste, a slope above a strangely geometric depression, as though left behind by an alien spaceship many years back. But I couldn't stop: I had to make it to the mechanic's before he closed, however dispiriting it was to think of something so prosaic in that moment.

When I'd been walking for an hour, the landscape grew suddenly unfamiliar. Standing before an enormous pit, I told myself, if you'd driven past this, you'd remember. Maybe I passed some crossroads with my eyes closed or was in a trance when I opened them. That thing my beloved Erfind used to say to me comes into my head: that we walk through life with a blindfold over our eyes, and by the time it falls off, we've missed all the interesting twists and turns. I was cursing myself when a hoarseness swallowed the humming of the forest.

A car appeared rumbling down the road, threatening to crash at any moment. I motioned for it to stop. A Crusoe of the forest lowered the window. Bony, hair unkempt, skin weathered from hours spent out of doors gathering coconuts and waiting for a vassal to come rescue him, oceanic eyes.

"Sorry, is this the way to Sorrius?"

It is, he said, but if I want, he can take me, because I'll need another hour to get there on foot.

I, customarily so distrustful, got into the stranger's car without a thought, but as soon as I shut the door, I was anxious. What if he was a maniac?

Now he's going to pepper me with questions, I thought. But he looked straight ahead and didn't open his mouth and seemed not in the least discomfited by the silence. I, on the other hand, was. From the corner of my eye, I saw his wrists, thin like those of a starving prisoner, and the thoughtlessness of the smile on his lips. And what hands, they could grab a small person like myself around the waist as if I were a coffee cup. Or break her neck. After three turns I couldn't take it anymore and I started telling him all the things I didn't want him to ask me: who I am, where I live, why I'm here, the novel, and I even confessed that the mistress of the Minipimer who presides over Can Boronat is none other than my mother. I don't know why I'm so determined to do the opposite of what's expected of me.

"We'll be neighbors, then, because I live five minutes from the old Munt place," he said.

In the end, I was the one who interrogated him. Some

spectacle. It was like I was taking a statement. Name? Profession? Place of residence? Answers: his name's Flavi— how weird—and he's a beekeeper. When he dropped me at the entrance to town, he gave me a jar of honey.

The garage was already closed. I didn't get upset, I don't have a right to demand anything more of today: I've written the first version of the synopsis and that's enough. I've strolled down the streets in the village, not a soul, even if I could sense presences behind the curtains of the windows and balconies— cracks, slight undulations giving them away. I found myself walking with cinematic aplomb through that desert of stone houses, acting for an invisible public, all that was missing was my sheriff's badge and my pistol.

The bar was open though. The patio empty under the merciless sun. Relieved, I went inside like someone taking refuge in a cave. Just one customer at the bar. Black leather and glossy metalhead hair that needed a bottle of conditioner per week. How foul the thought of his hairy thighs sweating in those leather pants! He looked me up and down with the gaze of a farmer mulling over a sow for purchase, and his crossed eyes made him even more repulsive. I ignored him and ordered a sandwich of pork loin and cheese. I couldn't stay inside, the scent of coffee was too strong, mingled with the scent of memory, of when my mother used to leave me there an hour or more while she was off running errands. Or so she said.

It was around two when I sat at the only table in the shadow of the plane tree. Everything immobile, an unnatural silence, it was as though I'd suddenly gone deaf. The sun burned the flagstones.

Now you'll wake up in your room in Barcelona and tell Guim that you dreamed you were at the bar in Sorrius but that the village was uninhabited and the bells were ringing on their own. Everything was all too strange: me there in the square, the church steps observing me, the fountain that used to drip decades before, Ms. Antònia's window, someone else's now, I guess, since she was already a mummy when I was five years old and she taught me to thread needles and cross-stitch.

I called Guim. I doubt he can make it here within the month, this morning they hired him to illustrate Durand's new book, but the deadline's tight, publishers always make you rush.

"But I can't turn down illustrating Durand, right? Even if it is a poetic nebularium. Jesus, what a drag! A thousand drawings of clouds. I'm running into a wall, I mean, they're all the same. Cirrus, nimbostratus, stratocumulus. I haven't even started and I'm already over it!"

Durand, he kept repeating every ten words. And afterwards, these motherfucking clouds. But the woman's got talent. I reminded him that this always happens, that he's blocked at first and then he turns out the most precious illustrations ever, and I told him not to worry if he can't come, that way maybe we'll miss each other, we could use that.

We stopped talking.

I'm sure he too was thinking of that last fuck the night before I left. Idiotic: we spend half a year basically celibate and then the day I leave we're hot to trot. He started blabbing, to avoid turning sentimental and then not knowing how to get out of it. It turns out Carles will be moving in for a few days, he hooked up with that girl from Terrassa, we told him he didn't know what he was getting into, and of course it all went to shit. Our stock of Bordeaux is going to feel it.

I told him about my adventures over the past two days. He cracked up at my description of Manel, but right away:

"Don't make fun of him, he did you one hell of a favor."

He's a specialist in making me feel miserable.

I wound up eating my sandwich with the phone pressed to my ear, we couldn't figure out how to hang up. So I'll call you when I come back down to Sorrius, I told him, and then he remembered he wanted to ask me about the shop where I buy the cinnamon tea, and then it was one thing after another until eventually he told me: Look, I've got to work. Then I asked him if he'd look and see if I left the annotated edition of Víctor Català's *Solitude* on the nightstand, I'd swear I brought it with me but I can't find it anywhere.

I imagined him walking to the bedroom in those brown slippers I abhor. I closed my eyes and saw our hallway with the charcoal portrait he made of me a long time ago and won't let me take down, the green doorframe, our bed, unmade I suppose. I couldn't help asking him if he really was wearing the brown slippers and him: Now you're gonna ask me if I'm walking around without underwear on or with my hand down my pants or what? It made me laugh. He's an expert in that, too. When we hung up, my phone and my ear were smoldering. And no, I didn't leave the annotated edition in Barcelona, it must be lost in the junk in the entryway.

I didn't tell him I've started working. He didn't ask, either. Probably he doesn't dare. He knows I shut down when pressed. After so many years together, we're familiar with each other's weak points. We've made our peace with the rats that live inside each other, now and again we let them stretch out on the couch and vomit up all the garbage they've consumed, colossal bits of life they've picked up in the sewers of the soul. I still think you can't completely know a person. Guim thinks you can, of course, he loves to play devil's advocate with me, and I always tell him, Look at what happened to Ester when she had her kid. Maybe if we'd had children, we'd have split up too, or maybe even . . . Maybe we'd be different people.

When I went to pay, the cross-eyed rocker was still at the bar, and he said:

"You're Mei, right?"

I really must be dreaming, I thought. Turns out the gleaming rocker is the kid who used to stick me with his boogers when I was little. I beat a retreat like legs-don't-fail-me-now between his how-time-passes-you-haven't-changed-a-bit and my improbable we'll-catch-up-sometime-gotta-run.

This time the garage was open. We arranged things right away. We got in his van. I thought he'd fob me off on the kid that looks like his apprentice, but he wanted to go himself, to snoop, I'd reckon. It's not every day a newcomer shows up around here.

When he sat behind the wheel, his blue coveralls with the grease stains almost popped open. He's got an unbelievably immense belly, round, like a balloon man. I couldn't say if it was as hard as it looked or so soft you could sink your head into it. The whole way, my eyes kept leering at it against my will.

I squeezed up against the door to avoid any "accidental" contact between him and my knee when he changed gears. This constant mistrust of mine exasperates me, but I can't do anything about it, it just comes out like that.

I observed the landscape, but the mechanic—Julià? Joan? Josep? J-something, that's for sure, honestly I'm a disaster with names—the mechanic, either way, was in the mood to talk, and we went over what I now see will be the perennial topics of the zone: how I don't look a thing like my mother (which, keeping in mind that my mother was a babe in her younger days, could well be taken as an insult), whether *the Cubano* gave me a good price on the place, and wasn't I scared to be alone in the middle of the woods? I've cultivated a curtness softened with smiles, oh, of course he made the *zub-zub* joke as well.

He slowed down, gave me a stern look, and started to tell the story of the girl they found here in the forest ten or fifteen years ago.

"Not a stitch on her," he said, and then, worried I wouldn't understand this elevated phrase, added, "Nekkid."

He fell silent, waiting for me to say something, to ask

something, or maybe he wanted me to break down so he could comfort me, but my lone response was *Ah* and so he went on with the story he was clearly eager to tell, about how the Cubano was the one who found the "poor thing" and how the police came and everything, they'd been looking for her for weeks, apparently.

"Thirty-three years old, and now they got her locked up in the nut house," he concluded, dragging out the syllables with his eyes like fried eggs. Maybe he's pulling my leg, trying to scare a city girl who doesn't know what's what.

Fortunately, the house soon peeked out among the trees, exalted by a ray of sunlight. I saw clearly that I'd chosen a good refuge and I was filled with the wish to jump out of the car and leave the mechanic hanging with his stories.

He hooked the cables to the battery, and in five minutes everything was done.

"Don't shut the motor off for twenty minutes," he said, offering me his porcine hand.

I squeezed it tight, shaking it ridiculously up and down as if I could somehow demonstrate through this gesture that I am a strong, brave woman.

"Next time, you can just call," and I explained to him I don't have coverage here and if I went all the way to the village on foot, it wasn't just for laughs. As soon as I said this, I regretted it. It's not his business. But I'd already said it.

Julià-Joan-Josep left and at last I went inside. The armchair was waiting for me, and I collapsed into it. It feels made to measure, it's softening to the shape of my body.

N ow that I'm never in a rush, I make myself formidable breakfasts. Toast, marmalade, cheese, fruit, fresh-
squeezed orange juice. And Flavi's honey, of course. I
lay it all out on the table so neatly that I feel bad when I start
eating and in doing so disturb the still life. Guim, who always
called me a slob, wouldn't recognize me. Am I all at once another Mei? Maybe it's thanks to this breakfast that I have the
mental strength to devote myself for so many hours to planning
the novel. Or maybe the opposite's true and I need a strong
breakfast to withstand the harsh rhythm I've imposed on myself.

Every day, when I slice the oranges, I tell myself that my
novel—the idea of my novel—is still an orange and that I need
to squeeze the last drop out of it, turn the whole thing into
juice, and go on squeezing harder and harder until my arm
hurts. Then, when I drink the juice, it will feel like I'm ingest-
ing a miracle serum.

The day before yesterday, I started laying out cards with
the scenes that I've already thought up. The most complicated
thing will be to find a place to put them up, the stone walls are
irregular and the cards will wind up bent, always on the verge
of falling or blowing away. That I can't stand. At last, I decided
to stick them to the door of the wooden armoire, which is the
smoothest surface in the room. Hopefully the sticky tack won't
leave a mark.

Now, when I enter and they're all there neatly arranged, I

see myself as a cheap parody of Vulkanov. I'm about to set up an altar with his photo to pray an Our Father there every day to keep him always present.

I've also been thinking about the story of the madwoman the mechanic told the other day, I keep turning over and over how to fit it into the novel. If I do it, I'll have to go back over the synopsis for the umpteenth time. For now I've made a note about it and stuck it in the upper righthand corner with other dubious scenes.

Once in a while, I get these flashes of when I used to work for the publisher and I can feel the rage seething inside me: Toni rushing me to look over the galleys and then not bothering to include my edits—*you're splitting hairs, Mei*—as if that weren't exactly what the job of editing entails; when he ignored me about Maran's wonderful novel, which made a huge splash with that snobby publisher, and then he wouldn't even admit it, *Come on, Mei, that's not how it was*; with furious nostalgia, I recollect now my desk by the window and the view over the square that erupted with the shrieks of children at half-past-four; the elation when the first copy of a new book came in and I used to smell it; the doubts when we chose a cover photo; my ups and downs with Toni; that long argument about the picture of the girl dressed in white doing a balancing act (it looked like an ad for maxi-pads), though the book did sell pretty well, I admit, and a volume of short stories at that; the cup of black tea that accompanied me every day; the feeling of being useful, professional, valued.

I forbid myself to think of it anymore. That Mei no longer exists.

Enough.

If I keep going at this rhythm, my brain will dry up. I need to find a way to emerge from the mental labyrinth of the novel, my ideas are starting to crumble from so much handling. They say green animalizes us, disconnects the abstract brain.

I went outside for a walk.

I ventured down a path bordered by ferns that licked at my calves. I didn't think of Mila even for a second: I was too preoccupied with not falling, with not getting pricked by the butcher's broom, the vampiric blackberry brambles that think of nothing but stealing a drop of your blood. I need a machete, I thought, screw Mila and screw the novel.

After a while, my eyes got used to the green the way you get used to darkness. The asparagus on the verge, formerly camouflaged, bowed down to me now, begging me to pick it. My ears caught the frequency of the auditory landscape and I started to distinguish the hissing of the squirrels observing me alarmed from the treetops: Who's this then? Who's here causing a ruckus in our house? The plants quivered, beasts running away from me. I sped up. What the hell will I do if I run smack into a boar?

The feeling I was being stalked excited and frightened me in equal measure. When I made it to an open field, I broke out laughing as though I'd accomplished something big, and I stretched out into the grass on the forest's edge. Little clouds shuttled across the sky, I couldn't help but think of Guim and his Durand. I'll tell him to bring me the text, maybe it will be useful here, help me become fluent in nebulese: who can say whether nature might not be shouting something to me in its indecipherable language, something I'm failing to grasp.

The novel had vanished utterly from my mind. I was just another stone, a smiling stone unimpregnated by literature.

Time evaporated beneath the boiling sun. That must be why the air deforms in the heat, it's the optical effect of temporal evaporation. Attributing it to the refractive index is merely a consolation, a human conceit to avoid the painful truth that time is volatile, that it's disappearing right before our eyes.

And then:

"Xana!"

Now I've lost it, I thought. My father's the only person who ever called me that. "Good night, little Xana," he used to say, and he'd put me to bed with a sponge cake kiss.

I turned my ear to the sound.

"Xana, come over here!"

Was it Manel? What the fuck? How could Manel know this private word of ours? You've gone gaga, you must have gotten stuck by some venomous weed, I kept telling myself.

And another time, closer now:

"Xana!"

I couldn't take it anymore, I got up: behind the trees, Manel with a scad of shorn vassals. He had a rolled-up magazine. A porno mag? Cynic.

"You lost or what?" he shouted.

Me:

"Are you looking for me?"

He discharged a long series of chortles.

"What, your name's Xana now? I'm shouting to that one over there busy ignoring me," he said, pointing to a sheep strayed from the flock. "But if you like, I can call you Xana too, dear."

He decided to send Truffle to gather up the stray, he almost had to push her to get her to go. There was no point in my remaining stretched out there now that I was no longer alone.

"I was just going. See you around, Manel," I said, not waiting for a response before departing.

The path uphill was longer than it was downhill. After ten minutes, I sat down panting to take a rest on a mossy rock. The forest was my lair now, the animals my allies, but then I remembered what my father used to say: never trust nature, always keep your eyes peeled, and once more, I asked myself whether, the day he killed himself scaling the cliff, he had failed to keep his eyes peeled or whether nature had played a nasty joke on him. And the fantasy that there exists in a parallel universe another Mei and another father, now old, who toast bread in the fireplace once a week. Who knows how everything would have gone. Useless thoughts, but inevitable ones.

It turns out the shopkeeper does know who I am, and she didn't hesitate to ask me how it's going in the woods. She aimed her very blue eyes and her very affable face at me, and I had no choice but to respond, evasively, sure, but responding: it's so nice, so peaceful, the countryside here is beautiful, that kind of thing. Her:

"You're a brave girl!"

I think she said this with authentic admiration.

"Word gets round," I said, and she replied that in her case, nothing needed to get around much, home was enough.

What home? What was she getting at? Seeing my disconcertment, she added:

"I'm Manel's sister!"

I nearly dropped the half-dozen eggs I had in my hand. How could two people so opposite emerge from the same womb?

Noting no ill will in her, I've turned her into my informant. Now I know the nearest library is in Vilamitja and that the opening hours are bizarre, meaning whenever you go there, it'll most likely be closed. She insisted on writing them down for me on a slip of paper, though I already know I'll never set foot in there.

"Writers must need to read a lot, no?" and I was taken so off-guard by the fact that she knew why I'd come that I couldn't ask her how she'd found out. I must have told Manel the day I got the keys or maybe before, the day we talked on the phone to settle on dates and prices.

While she sliced off ribeye-thick portions of boiled ham for me, she got on a roll: who would I dedicate the book to, how I was the first writer in the village, because you were born here, right, how wonderful! And of course there was the inevitable *what's it about?* To which I replied, A lot of things, *life,* basically. How embarrassing to hear myself mouthing such pedantic and vacuous bromides.

"Life," she repeated, as though it were a word of incalculable import, and her naivety made her strangely charming.

Before paying, she insisted on giving me some almond cookies as a welcoming present, apparently an old woman in the village makes them, and as she sang their virtues to me, she used the occasion to tell me girl, you're so skinny, you need to eat, it's a pain sometimes to cook for just one, no need to tell me, for writing, the brain needs fuel, and nothing's better for it than some good macaroni. She came out from behind the counter and hugged me softly.

"If you need anything, you know you can just ask, right?"

She saw me off like a proud mother standing in the doorway of the shop, and I was like Little Red Riding Hood, setting off for the forest knowing she'll find the wolf there but still not cowering.

I sat on one of the benches by the river on the other side of the road to kill some time until I knew Guim would take his break.

Spring thaw. The Muntanya descends abundant and moaning endlessly and low: that must be the plaint of winter liquescing and dying off. I threw a few pebbles in it, as I did when I was a girl, to hear the plop when they pierce the surface of the water. Plop, the murmuring river. Plop, the indifferent Sierra Pobleny. Plop, a magpie posted on the other bank looks at me like a painting in a museum. I'm the one who's out of place here, not the magpie.

The gurgling called out to me, obliged me to sink my feet in the water. A shock of cold. An electric signal ran from my big toe to my brain, but I held out, closing my eyes, running the sole of my foot over the smooth stones. The cold hurt. I opened one eye, the magpie was still there, picking at something on the ground. A barefoot woman and a bird eating worms: how strange life is. Woman and bird. Street art. In the middle of Sorrius, a Miró with the disturbing brushwork of De Chirico.

I returned to the bench as the breeze accentuated the cool on my wet skin. It was twenty to one. Sitting there, again, the sensation of unreality, of not being able to believe that I am the person here, free at all hours of the day, my only task to write down whatever comes to mind or nothing at all if that's what I feel like.

A car passed once in a while. The sound of the motor like a wave crashing and receding. I asked myself who it was, where they were going, what the fuck they were up to on this derelict road on a Friday at midday. And who am I, too, and where am I going, and what the fuck am I up to.

At one on the dot, I called him, eager to talk; isolation is great and all, but the chitchat was welling inside me. Right away I realized it was a bad time, it was getting late, he had plans to eat with Carles in the square, he said. For a moment I thought I'd caught him watching porn, like that time I came home from work early and saw him jacking it to a chick with two in her mouth while a guy with a hypertrophied tool pumped her from behind.

"You wouldn't happen to know where my green sweater is?"

I guess the thing about him eating out was true.

"Dude, this is the one day I come down into civilization and call, Carles can wait, no?"

But we both know he detests impunctuality, it shows a lack of respect and so on and so forth. He wasn't paying attention to me, he must have been dressing or looking for his metro card, which he always loses and then he goes all hysterical, as if just buying another were an intolerable waste of money. When I asked him, "How are things with you?" he didn't realize I was talking to him, I could hear him fidgeting. I dropped it.

I stayed there with my verbosity eating me up inside, bummed that I had no one to unload on. The same old thought came back to me: if I've got no one, it's my fault, I'm unbearable; and the other little voice persuading me the problem's them, the others, they're from another planet and they don't understand anything. It's already been said: only on earth can you be an extraterrestrial.

I couldn't do anything this afternoon, I didn't feel like it. I sat in the armchair reading Hoffner to steep myself even further in contempt and despair for humanity.

He's good, the bastard.

THAT DAY

You must want a sagging reverence
and your human drippings lapped up.

169 Days Earlier

Since the one mirror here is so spotty and stands in the bathroom—the darkest room in the house—when I look into it, I don't recognize myself. I look like a wild beast, and without the cruel clarity of modern mirrors, my skin looks taut. I like her, this Mei staring back at me from the beyond.

I had two productive hours with the keys banging out a polka. But the further I progress, the more I doubt whether the text holds up, the characters are sufficiently rounded, the action dosed out in such a way that it maintains the tension. I realize the whole thing is just a long explanation, that the protagonists don't evolve, that it's pointless. This novel is a mistake; someone will tell me so eventually, and they'll be right. Then, as the doubts sink into my skin, I start typing harder so the continuous quaking of the keys will cause my insecurities to drop away.

I went out at mid-morning for a walk. I headed in the other direction, yet unexplored. Overcast sky—again, Guim and his Durand: I need that booklet, it feels like life or death to me now—the ideal weather for taking a stroll without the sun burning your ideas to a crisp. The forest is thinner in this area, here and there you see cultivated fields, lakes of wheat you can swim through in the middle of the nothing, and occasionally you come upon a few rocks piled up at random, dolmens sunken by the centuries, perhaps, but determined not to disappear so we won't forget where we come from, how just a few days back we were running naked through the forests and now we think we're something special with our internet and our Cabernet Sauvignon.

All at once, a white figure with a covered head appeared at the top of a hill. I stopped to observe this apparition. The astronaut turned and started walking toward me, waving as if we'd known each other our whole lives. Today we conquer the moon, my dear, we'll walk weightlessly through life, get in my ship, I can't find the entry hatch, here, put on this spacesuit so you don't fly away. (And Mila, three days after arriving, running, almost floating, through the field in front of the hermitage, amid lunar gravity, with her hair in the wind on her new, small, disappointing planet.)

Imbecile: it was the beekeeper. Beneath the pines, rows of grey cubes. He must think I'm spying on him or something: the ditz from the city standing in the middle of the road gawking and not even trying to cover it up. I didn't dare run away, he would have seen me and it would have looked awful. As he came over, he removed his gloves and the hat with its mesh.

"How's it going?"

How's it going, he says. I deployed cliches like an automaton: great, lots of work, it's such a privilege to be here. He looked at the sky, expecting an answer from it.

"You in the mood for a rice with vegetables and mushrooms at my place? It's lunchtime and it's about to start pouring," he proposed, pointing toward a cabin I had completely overlooked. Insistent: "If you say no, you can bet you'll wind up soaked."

The thunder that echoed through the outcrops of the Sierra Pobleny wound up swaying me. I walked along by his side, neither of us uttered a word, I looked at the sky like a dimwit, as though I could somehow read something in it. Durand, where are you?

The cabin he lives in is minute. A single room with a kitchen, a table, a fireplace, and a huge worn-out sofa. A stairway goes up to the attic, where I can make out the feet of an old-timey double bed, four feet wide max. But oh, the walls were lined with books from floor to ceiling, stuffed with volumes, some turned on their sides to avoid wasting space.

Flavi started taking off his white coveralls. I thought he'd strip down then and there, and I didn't know where to hide. Of course, he had on clothing underneath. Sometimes my head just doesn't work right.

While he cut the onions and set the yellowfoot mushrooms to soak, ignoring my want-some-helps, he asked:

"So, how's the novel coming along?"

I grunted in response, then added:

"I see you're a bookworm, too. What do you like to read?"

He jutted his chin upward, goading me toward the shelves:

"Take a look. Europeans to the right, Catalans by the door, Americans in the red one, essays behind the sofa, everything else to the left.

Holding the glass of red wine he'd just handed me without asking, taking little disinterested sips, angling my head to read the spines, even if doing so wasn't necessary, I walked along the shelves. Some yokel. He's got a shack in the middle of the forest with a better library than mine.

"And you, what do you like to read?"

The rice took its time. While we waited, we drained more than half a bottle of wine. If Guim saw me glugging down this ripple, he'd kill me: son of a winemaker, and a French one at that. Still, the wine was better than I expected, watery, raw, but drunk cool, it went down well.

At some point I started talking about Rezzoli, yeah, love her, but I laid it on too thick, as if she were the greatest writer of all time when I know she's not all that. Now he'll read her and think I don't know jack about literature if I really believe she's the best thing the last century had to offer. He started with Burnts, who's good all right, but he doesn't do that much for me, even if saying so among the literati is a sacrilege.

Between one thing and another, we didn't eat until half-past three. But damn, that was some rice! I plowed through two plates, and him:

"A bag of bones like you must do a lot of reading and writing to burn all that off."

And I laughed without the least trace of embarrassment, mouth open, grains of rice in the interstices between my teeth. It had been so many days since I'd laughed! I don't know how to laugh like that all alone, cutting lose, without thinking you're losing your marbles.

Outside, it had been raining for two hours, and the light that seeped through the crooked window just begged for a fireplace and a wool sweater. And then: what if he wants me to go? If he has things to do?

"I ought to head out," I said, not very convinced, and he was like no, where are you going in this rain, and he refilled my wineglass as I sensed the warmth in my belly and settled back down.

After he opened the second bottle, I told him I'd taken him for an ignorant hayseed.

"Perfect, that's the plan, go unnoticed and do my thing. Around here, there's no other way of surviving."

The questions mounted inside me: Who are you? Where'd you come from? How do you make your living? Why are you smiling? How do you get by? I muffled them. I told him I was a philologist and went into the whole thing about the publisher—*Don't ever buy a book from those sons of bitches*—and from him nothing, like he didn't understand (or didn't want to) that conversation means exchange, first I give then you do. All I could get out of him is he's from Barcelona and studied humanities, maybe with a concentration on Greco-Roman culture, but even then I wasn't sure, just like I wasn't sure if he'd ever done something with it professionally. I decided to take another tack.

"Flavi, it's a funny name, no?"

Once again he sidestepped me.

"Seems I was born stoic."

It was getting dark, I had to leave. He insisted on accompanying me, It's nighttime, you're going to get lost. We downed a shot of ratafia while he gave me a couple of books, among them one by Burnts that I now have to read.

Amid an ambiguous light, we started advancing down the trail. To my left, the toothed profile of the mountain range bit into the twilit sky.

Flavi, who must have noticed I loved looking at the mountains, told me his favorite of the peaks was Blunted Crest.

"You're not going to tell me you don't know the legend?"

I had to admit my ignorance. *Once upon a time,* he started and I let the tale carry me away, like when my cousin used to tell me scary stories and I'd spend the next few weeks terrified and sleeping with the blankets pulled over my head.

It was hard to concentrate on what he was saying: the night came upon us all at once, and between the arduous path and the alcoholic effluvia throwing my balance out of whack, it was all I could do not to fall on my face. He, on the other hand, didn't look where he stepped, walking like someone who's gotten up at night to piss and moves through the dark hallway conforming to an unconscious mental map traced out through countless repetitions.

The legend had to do with a shepherd, a guy named Gilbert, who was either a pervert or the local gossips thought he was, I don't know which, I only got bits and pieces: *he liked the company of animals, shrubs shaking in the breeze, goats uttering blood-curdling shrieks.* Now and again, Flavi would throw out some word that jolted the philologist in me—*he got lost in the swale*—and he'd take a dramatic pause to let me digest it.

Then the thing got all twisted up with some bitch named Rosalia or maybe Roser who fucked with poor Gilbert at all hours, humiliating him and playing tricks on him. She ridiculed him in front of his friends, telling him to clean up the plucked petals of the daisies he'd brought her. And the poor bum did it, crying tears of love.

But then one day this nasty female promises him that if he breaks off the top of Needle Crest for her, she'll let him stroke her ankles as many times as he likes. So there's Gilbert with his pickaxe climbing for days, weeks, months!, ready to mutilate the peak, *and his scabs drained pus day and night.*

(At this point, I'd resigned myself to walking through the darkness, blind amid the dense shadows. I wasn't quite with it. My ear had sharpened along with the sensation of danger; I heard sounds different from the ones I hear when I go out in daytime, of anthropophagous witches stirring their pots, the nic-nic of rats with phosphorescent eyes gliding between my ankles).

Flavi carried on till the finale: one stormy night, Gilbert was at the top of the Needle, and just as he raised his pickaxe a bolt of lightning struck the top of it. There was a monstrous crack, as though the earth itself had split apart. The lightning took mercy on poor Gilbert and blew the top off the peak. The poor boy got scorched, of course, and no one ever saw him again. But since then, on stormy nights, you can often hear his axe striking the rock, and in the morning a wind comes down from Blunted Crest and strokes the ankles of the women it finds in its path.

With that, we'd arrived at the house. I thanked him excessively for accompanying me there and for the rice and the very pleasant afternoon we'd spent together.

Inside, I noticed a strange scent, animal. It seemed to come from the cellar. I'll have to go down there.

168 Days Earlier

I woke up a wreck. Don't drink the cheap stuff, that's what Guim would say. But how nice it was to hop on the sleigh and let myself slip away: wine, chitchat on the sofa, ratafia, that mix of childish fear and adult alarm on the way home. It was nice. I decided to drown myself in a tank of green tea.

Cup in hand, I stood in front of the wardrobe. I looked at the cards from a distance, as if they were one of those pictures that change when you take a step back. The ones on the right were crooked. They must have come unstuck, I told myself while I straightened them out so they would fit in my rigid mind. But when I sat down at the table, I noticed things weren't exactly as I left them. Maybe it was the pencil touching the mouse, where I never leave it, or the pile of papers, perilously close to the edge of the table. I noticed once more the animal stench from when I first arrived.

Bam! The idea pounced on me: Manel must have come to the house when I wasn't here. The smell, the crooked cards, the things out of place or at least maybe out of place, I wouldn't bet my life on it, you know.

I walked to the vestibule to look for clues, a hair, some revealing detail that would confirm my theory. I examined the doorknob, scrubbed it with a rag just in case. I scrutinized the ground. In the bedroom, I couldn't avoid the image of Truffle rubbing against the sheets where they hang down.

I went outside to get some air. The sun cleared my head a

bit, after the wine it wasn't screwed on straight. Let's be honest: what need would Manel have, and even more, what interest, in breaking into my house and rifling through a few papers? Don't be paranoid, Mei.

Such were my thoughts when I started to feel bloated. Those two plates of rice you scarfed down yesterday. And then, But you didn't even have dinner yesterday. So what the hell's up with the bloating? Ah, my period! It always catches me off-guard, in the worst situation, without pads or anything, in light-colored pants if possible. Guim says my lack of interest in remembering when it's on its way is my subconscious rebelling, because deep down I'd prefer to be a man, Freudian penis envy, classic case. Imbecilities.

Either way, bloating. I make my menstrual count: it came the day I went to lunch in the port because any excuse is a good one to go to La Medusa, even the three-month anniversary of being on the dole, commemorating the Friday, January 15 when the son of a bitch from the publisher sent me out on my ear and thanked me for my years of selfless commitment with a severance stuffed in an envelope. The Medusa and the aftertaste of the splendid Chablis we drank, and me coming back from the bathroom blushing, hee-hee, ha-ha, we need to go to a supermarket ASAP or it's going to be like *The Shining* in here.

Bang!

So my period should have come four days earlier. Four.

All at once, everything glows brighter than before, a torrent of frozen light filters through my pupils. A sidery effervescence in my belly. I run inside to consult the calendar, inspect the dates: the puny envelope from January 15—nice present for New Years, you bastards—and then the lunch in April, exactly three months later, my panties soaked in blood. January 15, the envelope. April, the bloodstain. And then I see myself making love to Guim the day before coming here, as if our lives depended on it, pure desperation borne of absurdest abstinence. And today: today, May 17. Four days late. Four.

What do I do?

I stay in the house, the stone exterior will help me stanch the flood. I walk back and forth, bouncing off the walls. The yellow of the painting of sunflowers turns impertinent. I sit in the armchair.

Maybe I should call Guim. But what do I tell him? Guim, I need to tell you something. Or not. Guim, I'm scared. It's been four days since . . . And to top it off, this bloating. I feel my belly and a fearsome vertigo clutches me as I think something could be growing inside there and I didn't even know.

Go figure. Years of trying. Years. Three, four? Years, and now here it is! At the very edge of natural probability. Forty-two. It's not so old. But. Then the weight of disgrace fell on me: yesterday, the wine and ratafia. I've spoiled it before it's even begun.

Two hours it took me to calm down. The hangover didn't help, a cloudy mind is no good in moments like this. Naturally I couldn't work, either. The expanding wave of possibility, of this possibility, inevitably annihilates all other endeavors.

I didn't know whether to laugh or cry, and I remained there poised like a tightrope walker between the two extremes. I finally managed to compose myself, to get hold of thoughts that were hell-bent on gliding off the slope in the midst of the blizzard. It's four days, Mei. Just four days. It could be a delay. Maybe your cycle is starting to change. Maybe it's a million other things. Don't go overboard, I told myself, stirring honey into my tea, sitting beneath the fig tree.

Don't go overboard.

But once you've slipped, it's out of your control.

Despite yesterday's dose of linden blossom tea, I only slept fitfully. I kept waking up, obsessed, and wedged my hand between my thighs to feel around for anything, for a moisture that might give something away. A couple of times, I had to turn on the lights to see if I'd left a stain, however small. Nothing. Just a persistent bloating. Am I doing it to myself?

I got up before eight and made myself a big breakfast to keep my body busy; my mind refused to be distracted, no matter what I offered it. After breakfast, another piss, and to myself: pregnant women piss a lot, right?

I lower my panties. I stay there looking at them, hypnotized. I could stay like that all day, sitting on the toilet scrutinizing them like a fortune teller reading coffee grounds.

I sat at the desk, turned on the computer. The farce of getting to work on my novel made it no further. Guim. I have to call him, I told myself. And then, But why bother him if nothing's yet sure? He's got a job to do and you'll just make him lose his concentration. No, wait. And then, once more, the cycle started over from the beginning: I need to call Guim.

And the perverse idea of telling my mother she was going to be a grandmother, after having to put up with all her pestering that came back to me in the form of nausea: sniping about selfish women who don't have children, the constant subtle gibe about how I was so focused on my work, reminding me of how much my father would have loved being a grandpa, oh how we loved children (and for a laugh, she added he probably would have knitted the kid a scarf), venomously condescending insinuations, fraudulent benevolence masking veiled accusations regarding my supposed infertility, frigidity, insufficiency, always making me feel like a bad woman, a bad daughter, a bad future mother. Honey, everyone does what they can, don't let it get to you. I grew rabid as I thought of telling her and shutting her up, as if being a grandmother would amputate her femininity, do away with her airs of a snotty dowager. Again, I lower my panties and look. Not in the bathroom, no, in the middle of bedroom or living room or kitchen while I wait for the lemon blossom tea to steep. Nothing.

I had to do something to keep from losing my mind. I grabbed the mop and bucket and went down to the cellar, determined, without a trace of the horror from before: today I'm too busy battering down that other horror, the horror of blood.

The steps are just as narrow as they were decades before. I was careful going down them. The last thing I needed was to tumble downstairs and break a leg or split my head open and have them find me chewed up by rats three weeks later. I turned on the light, a bare bulb hanging from a mummified umbilical cord. I remembered it being bigger, the cellar, but the stench is the same or worse than before.

I opened the window level with the ground and, hushing the voice that insisted I lower my panties again, started cleaning in a fury. If a mouse emerges, I'll beat its guts out with the broom. Wipe with the rag, sweep up the dirt, wipe again with the rag, sweep up more dirt. This merry-go-round's better than the other one, the Moebius torture.

I put on the dishwashing gloves to move the cardboard boxes piled up in the corner. Inside, would they be Manel's things or even father's? Maybe his pictures. I didn't dare open them to keep from getting off-track: in my state, nostalgia won't cut it.

What a waste of time, cleaning the cellar if I won't ever go down there, I kept repeating, but still, I ran the sponge over the walls as if I needed to turn the place into an operating room. Or a birthing room.

And my panties. Suppressing the urge to lower them for the millionth time. The dark spot of damp on the wall just wouldn't go away. Spots that won't vanish, spots that won't come. Five days, just five days. You need to call Guim. Now.

Fortunately a little air was blowing in through the window, otherwise I'd have fainted from the thoughts clogging my mind and the smell of the bleach I threw all round to cover the stench of damp. Exhausting myself was my own mental bleach.

But uncertainty didn't take long to start gnawing at me again, and there I was walking back and forth, caged in the house with my doubts, a zebra shut up with a lion. And even if I went outside, the same feeling was there of being chained, of being incapable of escaping the radius drawn out by the idea of pregnancy.

So I decided to leave to test the chain and see if I could break it or if it was horribly elastic, and in passing, I'd go to the store to buy myself a gross of lemon blossom. Before sitting behind the wheel, I looked at my panties again. Then I took off.

Maybe you should take a pregnancy test. Take the car down to Vilamitja, go to the pharmacy, clear up your doubts, but something told me no, I was exaggerating, it was just five days late, I needed to get a hold of myself, you can't consult the oracle until things become clearer, more conclusive, otherwise you'd just be showing your weakness. And then there was Guim. I couldn't take a pregnancy test without him, without at least telling him so—that would be another betrayal; and so going to the pharmacy would mean calling him first.

It wasn't time yet, definitively.

I parked in front of the shop. I jumped out of the car and slammed the door shut, but the chain binding me to the idea of pregnancy, the chain stretched from the house to here, didn't snap; it's made of an unbreakable alloy of titanium and chewing gum.

Mercè was working in the back. When she heard the tinkle of the doorbell, she hurried to me, wiping her hands on her apron. So girl, it's been days since I saw you, are you not eating or is it that you're cheating on me? You look healthy, the mountain's doing you good. They used to send TB patients up here, you know, on account of the pure air.

And I thought maybe yeah, I had some kind of mental tuberculosis, and now I told myself that if I did look fit then then it must have to do with my growing belly. One more proof on the scale, which was starting to really tip. But don't get all wound up. Not yet.

"Listen, yesterday I got these sausages in straight from Pamplona. Take a few."

She shows me what look like bloody umbilical cords.

"Uh, I don't know, Mercè . . ."

"I gobbled down two whole ones all by my lonesome yesterday while I was watching my stories on Channel Five. Do you keep up with *Criminarium?*"

"I don't have a TV at the house. But it doesn't matter, I'm not big on TV, honestly."

"Poor thing! I don't know what I'd do without the TV. But when you go back to Barcelona, you've got to watch it. You ought to stick a murder in your novel, that always works. Yesterday they killed a six-year-old girl. I was biting my nails the whole episode. You'll never guess who did it."

"I mean, right now . . ."

"The grandmother! And everything planned to a T, don't you know. Some world we live in, right? So what? Two sausages?"

"Sure, I'll take them."

"By the way, did you get Manel's note?"

What? What note? What the fuck was she talking about? This guy's leaving me little notes? No, I say.

Then Mercè grabs a mallet and breaks the chain, or at least knocks it out for a good while. Yesterday, she says, Manel needed the generator and went to the house and since you weren't there he went in and grabbed it, because it was urgent, you know, the Martínez's chicken farm had lost power and the chickens, the chickens you know have to be watched over at all hours, the temp and all, they're delicate, right. I told him he should have waited a bit, it's not right to enter someone else's house, but dear, an emergency is an emergency. It was nothing, in and out right away, O.K.? So you say you didn't find the note?

I stutter no, but no worries, it's true, an emergency is an emergency, anyway the place is his, but inside me I see Manel walking through the house, rifling through my drawers, reading the notes for my novel, notes no one else has read and that now he knows, and his greasy dog rubbing itself against the furniture, the bed, the armchair, leaving infectious particles in its wake.

I turn around and pretend to look for something on the pasta shelf. Mercè blathers about yesterday's weather, but I only hear her in bursts; rain, she says, lightning, prudence, while I grab a packet of spaghetti and read the fine print as though the nutritional information harbored some alchemical secret, as if a pack of spaghetti could be more than wheat. My mind's racing at a hundred miles an hour. Calm down, I tell myself, the poor guy just went in for the generator and left. I tell myself that, but I can't believe it.

While I pay, I ask her if Vilamitja has a pharmacy.

THE DAY BEFORE

*Will you tear out your milk teeth
not to see them, Mei?*

I found Manel's note on the table, to the left, on top of the notepad. I don't know how I didn't notice it. In an unusually civilized hand, I read:

Remei, since you're not here, I came in for a second to grab the generator.

Manel

Yesterday I overdid it. I'm upset, my panties are determined not to say anything no matter how often I consult them. After breakfast, I got dressed and went out.

Walking is the best way to clear your head. So they say.

At half-past-nine, the universe is already rolling ahead full steam: frenetic humming, photosynthesizing leaves, asparagus shamelessly offering itself on the roadside. And me there in the middle, an eyesore, a foreign element strolling down the paths and trying to mimetize with these surroundings in my muddy hiking shoes and my earth-tone fleece. Green all around, and now and then the stench of animal, excrement, rot.

I focused on not thinking about the subject at hand, keeping my mind blank, or green, but you'd just as well try to keep a hungry dog from a pile of bones. I tried to channel all my energy into my steps. Now one, now another. Breathe. The clear sky. There must be a technical name for it, the absence of clouds, right? One step after the other. The crackle of pebbles under my soles. Six days now. Hush. Another step. I take a deep breath, particles of forest colonize my lungs. My panties. Another step. Exhale little by little, like blowing on the face of a fevered baby. A baby. One more step. A precise movement of the ankle, of the foot rising, advancing, and landing further off, bearing all the weight of my body. Make of myself a perpetual motion machine.

In the distance, Flavi's cabin appears. I hadn't thought about it again. I could go there and spill my guts, ask him to come home with me and wait for the result of the pregnancy test. When I take it. When I decide to look what's happening in the face and go to the pharmacy to buy the oracle. Anything not to be alone in a moment like that. How sad it would be to keep all that joy or sorrow to myself after finding out the result. But no. I can't ask him for something like that. I don't know who he is. We aren't friends. Or maybe we are, a little: the rice, the wine, the ratafia, the sofa, the overrun bookshelves, Burnts, Rezzoli, the laughter escaping him, the walk back in the dark, a shiver. Friends, maybe a little.

Tomorrow will be seven days. If tomorrow morning I don't have any news, I'll go down to Vilamitja, walk into the pharmacy, and come back with a racing pulse and sweaty palms. I'll get home, leave my bag on the floor, sit in the armchair, and read the instructions fervently. Twice, to leave not the least room for doubt about what the test signifies. I'll go to the bathroom, lower my panties again. A spurt of prophetic urine. And I'll examine the result. Alone. In front of the painting of sunflowers.

Or maybe I'll be impatient and I'll go to a bar in Vilamitja. I'll read the instructions over a lemon blossom tea and hide out in the bathroom with its smell of piss and its obscene graffiti and receive the notice in a dive with unspeakable music. But at least I'll be surrounded by people, half-automatons, maybe, but people. And I won't call Guim till I have an answer. It's all I can do. He'll understand.

But that will be tomorrow.

Now what I have to do is take one step, then another. Turn on the path that borders the creek and head upward. Take a big sip of water, open my trachea. Clean the apple in the raging current. Sink my teeth in as I contemplate a leaf riding the waves like a suicidal raft. That's all.

Find a corner upholstered in green. Open the book and read without interruption until my head tells me enough. Then freeze my feet in the creek, munch some cookies, stretch my legs and dive back into my reading until the seconds and minutes dissolve and time is narcotized, all to keep from having to go back home and stand before the doubts awaiting me huddled under the bed. Then the realization: it's six P.M. already. Get up, distressed, and walk, first one step, then another.

On the way home, I was in peace. Ideas sorted, plan traced out: tomorrow *fumata* in Vilamitja etc. Enough worrying about it. Get through the hours between now and morning and take off downhill. Everything was decided. Or so I thought till I arrived at home.

From the distance I saw him there sitting on the steps. My deliria had gone to find him in Barcelona. I ran to him. I was struggling to breathe. I threw myself on him with a knot in my throat. I sniffed his neck; I could smother myself in his scent. And him, What's going on, Mei? You O.K.? And since I didn't respond, Guim hugged me tight, squeezing my back, my shoulders, my ass, making sure no part of me had been taken from him, and I dug my nails into his spine. I could have stayed like that till the next day.

Ideas sorted, plan traced out: everything shattered. But it's better this way.

"What happened, why'd you run over all upset?"

The two of us there in front of the house. Was I dreaming? In everything there was an air of terrifying unreality, as if

I wasn't me and Guim was the only one who realized it, as if I could look in the mirror in that instant and I'd see someone else. And him, Talk, Mei, you're scaring me. But my thoughts were all clotted. The spot that wouldn't appear. How to tell him? After a moment, I managed to string together my ideas: we should go inside, I'd explain everything, don't fret, it's nothing bad. He acceded, now completely out of sorts.

He grabbed the things from the car and we went inside. I ran straight to the bathroom: sorry, gotta piss. One last lie before vomiting it all up. A last lie to shut myself up in the bathroom, lower my pants, and look at my panties.

Zilch. Immaculate.

I went back to the living room. Guim was opening a Bordeaux—my Bordeaux, how well he knew me—and serving it in the Riedel glasses he brought along from Barcelona (three, in case one of them broke, Mr. Foresight).

"Sit down, I need to tell you something."

He hands me a glass and proposes a toast, says we haven't seen each other in days. He proffers a smile so fragile that I'm afraid it will crack, a Riedel smile, and he didn't bring a replacement. Maybe he thinks I'll tell him I'm in love with someone else or I don't love him anymore or who knows what. He's afraid I'll shatter his life. He proposes a toast to put of the moment when I'll tell him what I have to say and there won't be any going back. We raise our glasses, clink, take a sip, me a small one, I barely wet my tongue, just in case. He notices. He knows I like this Bordeaux. Now's the time. Click.

"Sit down, Guim."

And he sits down without putting up the least resistance. He sits in father's armchair, which is now my armchair, even if he doesn't know that; he knows nothing, not about the chair and basically not about Dad. I sit on the stool, leave the glass on the end table. My hands are sweating, I wipe them on my pants.

"Something's happened. Ugh, that sounds awful. Actually

nothing's happened. Not yet. I wanted to call you but then I didn't want to call you because I would have upset you and since actually nothing has happened, I thought maybe it was better to wait. You know I always hesitate. But don't take it wrong that I didn't tell you anything till now. There's no service here and . . ." Guim clutches his glass, if he squeezes any tighter he'll break it. I have to tell him. Loud. Tell him outright: "My period's late."

The phrase is like a tranquilizer dart shot into a mammoth: it paralyzes him. The words with all their weight have fallen over him and crushed him. A statue of Guim. One two three, freeze. Whereas I, after unburdening myself, feel light and with a longing to laugh like mad. I laugh hysterically, giggle, chortle, repeating the incantation.

"My period's late, can you believe it?"

Guim looks serious. I see the thoughts piling up in his pupils, his brain working at full clip trying to generate a response. I take his hand.

"It's not for sure yet, it should have come six days ago. No guarantees, but six days are six days, right? Don't get all excited yet, I've already spent two days concentrating on trying to keep my excitement at bay but I just can't anymore. In don't even want to think about how thin those walls are, and the armies of excitement are invincible. I'm so happy you came. Well, say something!"

"I see you still talk like a book."

He takes a sip of wine. His wrist is trembling. I'm indignant at his reticence.

"Monda . . ." he finally murmurs, as though hypnotized.

It's been years since he called me that. Monda. I don't even remember where it came from anymore. Our trip to Donosti, for sure. Monda. Did it come from *món,* world? From back when I was his world? Was it from Spanish, Italian? Monda. Why did he call me that all the sudden? Mondo—that's what I used to call him.

I get up from the footstool: the joy inside me demands movement. I hop, bend over, kiss him on the lips. Bordeaux lips.

"Relax, don't worry. I understand. It's too much, just hearing it all of a sudden. Now, when we no longer expected anything. And maybe it won't be anything. Should we go to Vilamitja to the pharmacy?"

I look at the clock. Too late, it'll be closed when we get there. It flashes through my mind that we could leave, go to Barcelona, the two of us, take the test and resolve our doubts and fuck it. It's here. We're both neck-deep in it now.

But Guim says:

"No, let's have dinner. No need to rush."

No need to rush, he says, him, the king of haste.

"Right now I don't know if I'm happy or sad or scared or pissed off or disappointed. Or all those things. Maybe all of them at once. Lucky I brought two bottles."

He's joking, that's a good sign, the spell is taking hold.

I take his hand and drag him through the house without shutting up even for a second. I show him the bedroom and we stretch out on the bed, me in Mom's place, him in Dad's. This bed's fucking narrow—and I hug him—look at the ceiling, you see how it looks like an ear of wheat between the beam and the wall? I look at it everyday. And him:

"Hmmm, to me it looks like a broom made of heather with a crooked handle."

We run back to the office and I show him the cards on the wardrobe. I tell him I'm working hard, Guim, all the time, I'm going to write a novel that'll knock you on your ass, I can do it. He looks at everything surprised, like a father discovering an unsuspected talent in his son.

"I knew it, I knew you'd do it," he says.

I tell him I've turned Mila's story on its head, now she's the one in charge, this novel will complement the classic one, the two stories will fit together to make a single one, like an apple split down the middle.

"Apples turn brown though," Guim notes, and I don't want to know why he's made this impertinent comment.

We go down to the cellar and I brag about how I cleaned it. He doesn't look like he finds it a great accomplishment. But it is. I take him to the kitchen, where the dishes are still dirty from breakfast. I open Flavi's jar of honey, dip my finger in, and let him taste it.

"The neighbor makes it. He looks spaced out, like a crusty old hippie, but the bastard's got a library like you wouldn't believe. We'll go there tomorrow and I'll introduce you. The other day he invited me to his house for lunch, no big deal, just a coincidence because it was starting to rain, and . . . oh right, now that I'm thinking of it, you need to bring me Durand's book! I urgently need it to survive here, it's gonna be my Assimil course for understanding the sky, *New Nebulese With Ease.*"

"Sure, I brought it to you, the original, in French, of course. For now there's no translation planned. It's a lovely text, you'll love it, you'll see. I even made you copies of the photos they sent me for inspiration."

"Oh, sweet! Thanks! *Le nouveau nuageais sans peine.*" I give him a chipper kiss. "Anyway, back to the neighbor: he made a kick-ass rice. You'd get along with him, he likes Burnts, same as you. You ought to see him in his beekeeper-astronaut costume, with his hives and all. He says one day he'll show them to me up close, but I'm not so sure about that. Those outfits probably have holes in them and the bees can creep in and once they're inside you better hurry out of it to keep them from stinging you. I don't know, maybe I'll say yes, it sounds cool. You should meet him."

Guim follows me, smiles now and again. He's a remote-control human. What I say to him doesn't reach his brain, which is busy processing the subject of my panties, but I don't want to look to see whether or not there's a spot. That's enough waiting for the *fumata rossa*. Words spurt from me uncontrolled, words I'd been cellaring for him. Mei Cellarmaster's Select, get drunk on me. Mei Old Vines.

"Come on, let's eat, I was so wound up I skipped lunch."

And he told me he'd brought a truffled sheep's milk cheese with foie and other nonsense I like. I hug him and repeat how happy I am he's come and why doesn't he just move into the house right here, we could find a corner for him to work in, even if I know this is a bad idea: I couldn't concentrate the same if I had him around the house.

Guim was still silent, and some of my euphoria diminished. We made dinner. I take two tiny sips of Bordeaux and then tell him I don't dare do more. Just in case. Now everything is just in case.

"Don't worry, I'll take care of it," he threatens, draining his glass and filling it back up.

I decide we'll have dinner in front of the fireplace. Guim's always been cold-blooded and today the weather's cool. While I light the kindling, he lays out everything on the plates. I ask him how the illustrations for Durand are going. He grunts.

"It's been two weeks, you must have made some progress, right?"

"Yeah. No. A little," he says. His eyes, like his words, avoid me.

"What about Carles? Is he still at the apartment?"

He says no, he left a few days ago, seems like he's getting back with the ditz from Terrassa. I can tell he doesn't feel like talking, but I do, and once again I go off about the novel and tell him that soon I'll be able to start the first chapter, I just need to sketch out a few details, but I haven't been able to do anything for two days because I'm overwhelmed waiting for the spot in my panties. I also talk about Manel and how he came into the house when I wasn't here and how I've had bad vibes since then. And besides that, there's a creepy story about how they found a crazy woman in the forest buck naked and the Cubano had something to do with it.

"Who?"

"The Cubano, I don't know, the mechanic called Manel that."

Guim feigns interest, ohs and ahs when I expect it, finishes the first bottle. His eyes look at me and don't see me, because they're looking inward, a look like a well. Words fall in, but they never reach the bottom. Basta.

"Guim."

I go over to him. I take the glass from his fingers. He looks at me. I don't like how he's looking at me. With sorrow. He's about to tell me Santa Claus isn't real.

"Guim," I repeat, but I don't know how to go on, and then he says it:

"Are you sure?" And he puts his hand on my back, as if he were offering me condolences.

And now I really don't know what's going on. What the hell is he asking me? Are you sure you're pregnant? Are you sure we want a kid?

"What about you, are you sure?"

"I don't know, Mei, it's not that easy."

"What's not that easy?" I interrupt. "Having a kid's not that easy? Obviously it's not easy, we tried to do it for an eternity, and no, it was not easy *at all.* Actually it was impossible. But now it might be easy. You don't want it anymore, or what?"

He grabs his glass again, takes a long sip to make time to think of a response. He tips it back in slow motion to stretch out the chewing gum of seconds.

"Let's not argue, O.K., it's still not anything yet. Maybe your period will come tomorrow and that will be that. We don't have to turn it into some drama. Let's wait, and in the meantime, let's talk about something else, O.K. About clouds! This

Durand thing is gonna land me in the madhouse! If you want, I could give you a three-hour lecture on the types of clouds. Mammatocumulus," he says, then squeezes both my breasts unfunnily, like they were bicycle horns.

"Don't be gross," and I pull away.

"Gross, how lovely, sometimes I forget Miss Philologist can use real insults."

"If you don't like how I talk, you can get fucked. Always pointing out my defects. You could say something nice to me now and again."

"Not this again, Mei. That's not true."

"Anyway, you think I'm capable of not thinking even for a minute about what I've told you? Sometimes you're so . . ."

"So what?"

"Finish the phrase yourself."

"Don't start."

He refills his glass again. I turn around to go to the bathroom, but first:

"You shouldn't drink so much, it's not going to fix anything."

I leave the room with a resolute step, the ground shakes. I shut myself up in the bathroom and lower my panties. Inside my head I shout to them, Say something, goddammit! I take a deep breath, wash my hands with cold water, I wish it was frozen and I could leave my hands under it until they hurt, or cut my leg off to stop feeling the ache in my head. When I go back to the living room, Guim is walking back and forth from armchair to fireplace and drinking. Wine stains his lips, it looks like he's gone down on a menstruating cunt.

"What are we trying to be, Guim? A childless couple getting old, with obsessions that get old too? I want to get pregnant, I want us to have a kid, I want to have a kid with you. For once in my life I know what I want!"

"So you know what you want?" he stings me with an exaggerated life.

I don't give a fuck if he's tipsy, I'm not letting that impertinence slide.

"Sometimes you're a moron. You want to make fun of me? Yeah, I do know perfectly what I want. I want a child and I want to write. You think that's funny? Because I don't—not at all. And you'd better not roll your eyes like an idiot."

"Oh, right, the great author! Who's spent ten years rattling on about her novel and still hasn't managed to write a page of it. Because if I've understood you right, you've been here for three weeks and haven't written a line, or . . .? And that's what you call knowing what you want. Come on, Mei, I'm forty-three years old. If we have a kid now, I'll be sixty when it turns seventeen. It's not the time, Mei. It's over. It just can't be. And you don't even know yet for sure. Come back down to earth and start thinking about what to do when your unemployment's up."

Everything it occurs to me to say is too soft, too little. My thoughts are burning inside me. I want to hurt him.

He keeps going, my silence stoking him: I shouldn't try and fill the void from losing my job with a child. Don't make a mistake, he says. Don't make a mistake! But his voice comes to me muffled, as if I were underwater and holding my breath and he were shouting to me from the shore. It's this pulsating rage, it doesn't allow me to hear a thing. Its violent throb is deafening.

"Get out and leave me in peace. You come here just to ridicule me because you can't stand me knowing what I want. You'd rather I went on being fragile little Mei so you could play the male protector, no? Well look, I'm just fine here and I don't need anything from anyone, I've been putting up with your paternalism for way too many years, and I don't need it. Let alone your paternity. What do you think, that I can't take care of myself? Go!"

Guim isn't laughing anymore. He empties his glass slowly and sets it on the ground.

"As you wish," he says with mock gallantry. "Stay here with your fucking neighbor and suck his dick if you like him so much."

"How about I look for two neighbors I can suck off right now, I'll tape it and you can jack off to it at home, you imbecile."

Guim goes into the bedroom. Now he'll stretch out on the bed and fall asleep, I think. I know him, now the move will be to act like it wasn't such a big deal. Sleep and get up tomorrow and give me a kiss like it was nothing.

But no, he grabs his bag and heads for the door. Before shutting it behind him, he turns:

"You'll call me in two days when your period comes and you feel like shit."

I still say nothing, I say nothing until I hear the car start up and the night devours it. And then I shout, a burning bar of iron pierces me from one end to the other.

Mondo.

All night tossing and turning in bed, falling into a light sleep inhabited by cliffsides and countdowns, my right hand a shield over my belly. Between dreams, my ear pricked up and I half-imagined Guim knocking on the door or heard him shouting outside, *Mei, open up*, and then I'd wake up for an hour or more, certain that the next day I'd find him next to the house, asleep in his car. I saw him approaching with that penitent pose he adopts when he knows he's gone too far.

And goddammit, I'll let you in!

Then, once more, doubt: Could he be right, could it be too late, what do you want, Mei? What are you hoping for? Besides, his reaction's normal. You didn't prepare him before you told him.

Even so, treating me like that, like I was soft-headed, naïve, like having children and writing were larks because I'm forty and bored, no different from signing up for a baking class. He's so condescending sometimes. How can I erase what he said to me? Still, so many years, so much trust, so much intimacy. However much I might tell him otherwise, I do need him, he's the boatman who allows me to navigate the lagoon.

Another roar outside. I held my breath to listen better. It's got to be Guim. Will I open the door for him, or no? And: This anxiousness is no good in your state, it's not good for him. Because all at once I knew that what I had inside me would be a boy. Then I nodded off again and saw streams of blood, a mouth dripping velvet Bordeaux from the corners and the spongy ground palpitating like a placenta.

The hours crept along the walls of the bedroom and I, increasingly exhausted and enraged, ground my teeth until my jaw started to swell. As seven approached, I couldn't take it anymore. I ran outside, and blinded by oneiric luminosity, I looked at the steps, the path at the foot of the house, the first stretch of road.

Deserted.

A shrub moved and a fox emerged. It looked at me immobile, defiant. Like me. Both of us dying from fear. Me with my black hair unsettled by the night, the fox with its orange pelt flagrant. Maybe it's female and pregnant, too. It looked at me as if it wished to say something but didn't know what. Come! I shouted, and it fled without hesitation.

At that moment, everything that had passed through my mind those past few hours came together in a single mechanism. A goddamned epiphany. I also knew that Guim would come back at some point that day and that when he does, I don't want him to find me.

I ran back inside, stuffed a few things in a backpack, and walked toward the woods scribbling notes in a notebook with the feeling that if I didn't, my ideas would vanish forever.

Past the split oak, I headed up a narrow trail. Straight stretches and twists. A trail shaped like an intestine. Time and time. I let myself be carried to a spring that emerges from a crack in a blackish rock, if I balled up I could have fit inside it. Maybe it's concealing a room, a stone womb where I could feed on literature and protect myself from the world. I didn't dare go in.

In a round clearing in the shadows of pines, I sat and tried to compress what was roiling in my mind into a sequence of letters. I started my countdown, and everything emerged like a tapeworm that had to be pulled out of me by force. The fox, the stream of blood, the girl on the edge of the cliff.

I was hungry, but I was afraid to stop writing, to stop and not be able to continue, to cut the tapeworm when it was halfway out and leave the rest of it inside me. The sun was high, burning the crests of the trees. I was almost done, and Don't stop now, you're there. At no point did I ask myself whether this was shit or fantastic, it came out of me, that was enough.

With every paragraph, turning back to reread it, change a word or two, some commas—always the commas—or scratching out an entire phrase. But with unwonted certainty. That's got to go, I said, that doesn't work. I reached the end in a deplorable state, it must have been two or three in the afternoon, and while I bit into a peach to hush the body that enslaves me, I started crying from weariness or satisfaction with what I'd done, grief over Guim or unbalanced hormones. The tears are a distillate, liquid emotion, concentrated. They must be consumed responsibly. I should store them in a flask, a secret potion I can drink on those days when nothing matters, and I live like a numb stone rolling down a hill.

After a little cheese and a long nap rocked by the trickle of the spring, serene and now thinking of nothing, I recopied the story in a clean draft, filing down the details. And more than anything else, I felt proud.

I put off the moment when I'd have to go home as long as I could. What a drag, finding Guim there and having to repair yesterday's catastrophe!

It was getting dark when I arrived. Not a trace of Guim. But there was a note from Manel: he needed to talk to me, it was urgent, serious, I should call anytime, no matter the hour. I decided the urgency could wait until tomorrow, it must have something to do with my mother, and not even the thought that something might have happened to her, and she could be in the hospital convinced me to get my car and go look for cell service to call. Whatever it is, I can't do anything about it, and in my state, I need rest.

I crawled into bed a wreck and, before falling into the abyss of sleep, I thought about Guim and my panties, which were determined to tell me nothing, and I resolved that tomorrow I would go to Vilamitja, do the test, and call Guim to try and reconcile, but without humiliating myself. Tomorrow.

THAT DAY

The madwoman of the woods, you know her, no?
In her eyes you will see cries
sharp like sheathes of chestnut.

At seven I was awakened by knocks on the door. I woke up instantly, disturbed. It must be Guim, he's back. I hopped up, the floor was frozen. I almost went to the door naked, I even thought it might be a good idea, sealing the wound with a roll in the hay. Fucking cauterizes everything. Luckily, my head was faster than my body. You can't just show yourself to him with your flat belly out in the open, it would be a provocation, boycotting reconciliation. I threw on a T-shirt and ran to the door repeating that I needed to keep my cool.

I opened up and there was Manel.

The note, I didn't even remember it. Paralysis. Me there in my T-shirt, which hardly covered me, nipples poking through it like the tips of umbrellas, obscene, showing him my bare feet, standing in front of him with my pussy uncovered, what if he could smell it like an animal in rut. And then: look who just shows up here on a Saturday at seven A.M.! I couldn't find the right gesture, the opportune word.

"Remei," he said in a deep tone I hadn't heard before.

Me mute, with my fuses about to blow from the surge.

"You didn't find the note, Remei?"

Me immobile, a statue of lava solidified on the outside but burning within. Come on, spit it out and leave. I should slam the door in his face before it's too late, before he tells me things I don't want to hear, before I find myself taking care of my mother. Close the door, pack my bags, get the hell out of here.

Disappear, *zub-zub*. Then I told myself this might be a dream, obviously I was dreaming. The infraction, the argument, the note, all of it was a dream. Wake the fuck up, Mei.

He takes a step forward, edges into the house, me still petrified. He extends a hand to grab my shoulder; instinctively, I jerk away. My eyes are pinned to his ugly, too-small hand, the hand of a mangy doll he's held out in the air to try and catch me.

"Something's happened, Remei. We've been looking for you since early yesterday morning. Your husband's dead. Thursday morning, he missed a curve on the highway into Barcelona. Ten miles from here. His car was destroyed and he . . . I'm so sorry."

He takes another step forward, arms open to hug me. What the fuck is he saying? Wake up!

"If you need anything, just tell me. The funeral is today at four in Collserola."

Guim, dead? Is that what he's saying? That you're dead? Collserola, did he say, Collserola? There's a stone inside me, it won't let me breathe.

"What are you saying?"

"Guim's dead, Mei. The car was destroyed. I'm so sorry. You want me to take you to Collserola?"

"Collserola? I'm the one who decides when and how the funeral will be."

"You weren't there, and his family . . . there's a protocol. Your mother says the body was in such bad shape they couldn't put it off any longer. You want me to stay here with you? You want me to take you there?"

I say nothing, I shut the door in his face, I sit on the ground. My body diffuses, it's no longer part of me. The world, too, has ceased to exist. I think nothing, I feel nothing. I'm numb. I've departed reality and lodged myself in a parenthesis of eyes that won't stop weeping.

I drag myself back to the bedroom, open the closet, grab

the green sweater, your favorite one. I put on the black panties, wear my mourning on the inside. I sit on the toilet, wipe, stare at the unsullied paper.

What now, Mondo?

I brush my teeth with a lead brush, look for my keys. Your glass is still on the living room floor; I grab it like a sacred chalice and lick the rim with closed eyes. I see the copy of Durand's *Le Nuagier* you left on the table, a sheaf of spiral bound A5 paper. I put it in my bag, have the hunch that it's indispensable, that I can't go without it.

I leave, take the stone steps slowly, fifteen, reality constant, horribly immutable. Gravity's changed and I can't move my body at its accustomed speed: every gesture stretches on as if it would never end, as if attempting to force me backward rather than forward. I start up the car. Maybe it's my turn to crash today.

The rumble of the road is a jackhammer trying to shatter the walls of the bubble I've crawled inside of. Bars appear on my phone, messages flow in. Too many messages. Silence. Finally, the main road, I glide over the asphalt. Right, curve, hill, to the left the woods I used to wander with my father foraging yellowfoot mushrooms.

Father, what do I do?

Another long straight stretch, I wish it would never end. I enter a curve. Did it happen here? I slow down, twenty-five mph. At every bend I scrutinize the trees, the gravel, for signs of the accident, blotches of dried blood. I want to stop and stretch out on the ground, cover myself in moss and wait, I don't know what for, just wait. I carry on. I need to get to Collserola. The hum of the motor, the wheels advancing over asphalt. Don't think of anything else. The hum and breathing.

But the air in the bubble is unbreathable, dense and saturated with a voice that reminds me that I threw him out. He drank a bottle and a half of wine, the Bordeaux he had brought for me, and I told him to get the hell out. He's not dead. I don't believe it.

I pass through a town, yellow light. A chunky woman crosses the street unhurried, hair pulled back in a bun, dyed blonde, slight hobble. She looks at me and chuckles, death come to earth to look at me up close and mock me. The light turns green. I gun it.

The road winds down along the side of the mountain. I've constantly got my foot on the brakes. I should lift it up and take the plunge, but I have the feeling the bubble would save me. I'm numb even to death. I try to think logically, but logic no longer makes any sense. I should eat something, I tell myself, it'll be a long day, you're pregnant. Maybe. But how dare I be hungry? How dare I do anything but remain here immobile, splintering myself against reality?

Still, like a scoundrel, I get out at a gas station and buy a Coke and a packet of crackers. Yellow wrapper, garish letters. The cashier is bored, wants to chat me up. I cut him off: "My husband just died and I can't even pick out the coffin." He freezes in an oafish smile. I get back in the car, turn on the radio, it offends me. Normality, I'm looking for fragments of normality, I force myself to chew the crackers, hold onto the slight burn of the gas in the Coke rising into my nose.

I turn onto the highway, it won't be long now. I don't want to think about getting there. An Italian song comes on. I've never known the name of it, but now I'll have to look for it, I need to know: I'm weaving memories of your death, funeral garlands. I turn it up and start singing at the top of my lungs. It's turned up so loud that no matter how I shout I can't hear my voice, and I shout harder. Lose my voice before I show up, be unable to talk, even if I wanted to. *Con lui volando lontano dalla terra, dimenticando le tristezze della sera.* And then, for the first time, I realize oodles of people will be waiting for me there at the funeral home. Mom, cousins, your parents, Carles. *Con la luna ed il mare.* The mere thought of it is dreadful.

I head toward Collserolla. I want to turn back. Why do I have to go there? It won't change anything. But I need to see him.

I park at the funeral home. The funeral home I didn't choose.

In the sky, a fabric of clouds covers the blue like a winding cloth. I need to know what those clouds are, what they're called. I need a new redemptive word. More garlands. I take out Durand's bible. I page through it quickly looking for some black-and-white photo that corresponds to reality. There it is: cirrostratus. A glass of milk spilling across the sky, solar iridescences that augur the coming of depression.

I have to get out of the car, but I don't want to. I stay inside, still, one hand stretched flat beneath my bellybutton. I'd like to shrink too and slip into a yolk sac. At the door, people I don't know smoke and laugh in black clothes. Laugh. I clutch my knees in my hands, close my eyes, and bend forward in the seat, the steering wheel presses into me. I wish I were deaf, blind, mute. Open the door and get out, how terrifying. You have him inside you, I repeat to myself, you're carrying him inside you. It's eight days now. I look ahead. Don't look back.

I grab the handle and pull. There you go, get out now and make it to the end of the day. And then a tomorrow will come, and after it another. I stride across the parking lot in my green sweater, I wish I were camouflaged against the mountain that surrounds me, but the lot is grey and hard like the cubic prefab building that awaits me.

In the entrance is a list of the day's dead and the rooms assigned to them. It looks like a wedding reception, but the banquet consists of flesh eaten by worms. A guy with a solemn face stands guard. What's it to him, playing sentinel in a ship of the dead, all he's got to do is concentrate on looking morose the whole goddamn day while he's thinking about the evening's game or his tax return or all the ways he'd like to break it off inside the widow now walking through the door.

Hall 3. I follow the arrows, crossing the Styx alone and arriving in the other world. Don't-look-back, don't-look-back. I see Carles further off in an armchair dicking around with his phone. If only the satellites would stop working right now, the power plants collapse, everyone shut down, the world stopped in its tracks.

When he sees me, he gets up and runs toward me, eyes burning. He hugs me. I don't want to hug him, not him and not anyone. I don't want to see him, not him and not anyone; they can all fuck off.

"How are you?"

I don't answer. What could I answer? Then he starts blabbing, it's not fair, I can't believe it, what a tragedy, dammit. Sobs.

"I want to see him," I say, but he blocks my path.

"You can't, Mei. A car crash, you know how it is, it won't be pretty, his face . . . the coffin's closed."

Bullshit, I want to shout, Guim isn't dead, you all want to punish me, put one over on me, and that's why you won't let me see him. But I say:

"His hand, I just want to see one of his hands."

Carles hugs me again and whimpers. I'm dry inside. Death has charred me and left me like a desert.

We enter the hall. Your father is sitting in a corner, he might as well be a wax statue; your mother throws herself at me and I hold her, mute. The bubble's membrane makes everything slightly distant, reality attenuated. Your mother cries, talks, touches me, but I don't listen: my eyes are pinned to the godforsaken sarcophagus they insist on telling me holds your body. The sarcophagus they didn't let me choose. It's protected by glass. I'll grab a chair and crack the glass, split it open, and run away with you, death nipping at our heels. Don't-look-back-don't-look-back.

Carles comes back over and tells me they've agreed to let me see a hand. "They agreed," as though they were doing me a favor, the bastards, as if I didn't have all the right in the world to see you dead and disfigured if that's what I want, the scum, hiding behind their protocol without even the decency to wait for me to decide things. Protocol, what protocol? Protocol for disemboweled bodies that are rotting too fast.

Your mother says she wants to come in with me.

"Later," I threaten her. "I want to be alone."

A man in full uniform—white coat, languid posture, grave expression on his face—lets us into the backroom. He opens a little door and slides through the cart with the coffin. With the help of a woman, he profanes it. It gives off a strange scent, of rot masked with talcum powder. There's a lump covered by a sheet; at the height of the face, yellow spots smirch the white.

The man pulls out a hand. Your hand. It's yours. The square polished nails. The scar on the little finger. I grab it. It's soft, more like spongy, resembles silicone. I rub it between my two hands to warm it up, to combat the eerie cold. I'd like to cut it off and put it in a jar of formaldehyde so I could stroke it when I miss you, sleep with it, lace my fingers between yours, put them inside me on cold nights.

"Feet," I tell the death agent, and he obeys.

We return to the hall. I emerge from the corridor, sit in an armchair, close my eyes. No one come over. The passage of time has changed and I don't know anymore if the minutes are seconds or hours. I try to concentrate on the hiss of the minutes dragging past, deformed by the gravity of the black hole of death. In the background, a whispering of voices. They don't dare approach. I hear people arriving. Steps, tinkling keys, sobs. The symphony of death sounds insultingly quotidian. Where is the double bass?

Soon some are talking of lunch, what are they thinking. But the hallway is empty and hushed.

And the hours pass. Like seconds. Like centuries.

Until a man's voice announces we may pass into the chapel.

And then I hear those heels I know so well and my eyes open without wanting to. Yes, it's her.

She walks down the hall resolute, in full mourning, hair petroleum black, both hands clutching her purse, nails painted. Impeccable. She's seen me and examines me with the same repugnant paternalism as when I was a little girl. She hurries toward me. The expansive wave of her perfume precedes her. I get up like a robot. She embraces me, and the scent she gives off asphyxiates me.

"Honey, we've been going crazy trying to find you. What a tragedy, my god, what a tragedy. He was so young, so sweet. I can't believe it. How are you?"

I persist in my silence. I have too much to say, or too little.

"Remei, honey, say something. I know it's a tough time, when your father died, even I . . . But you need to let people accompany you, there's no point in keeping it all in and trying to be strong. Come, let's go to the chapel."

She takes my arm and we walk down the hall at the head of the retinue, dragging a chain of mourners behind us. It's a cold, square space, a fridge full of grieving humans. The chaplain asks me if I'd like to say a few words. No. I don't want anyone to talk. But he does, one dull phrase after the next. It would be better if he'd shut up. The torment is interminable. With one hand in my purse, I grasp your nebularium.

Then the procession continues, on to the crematorium. They tell me I can pick up the ashes tomorrow, that would be easiest. I insist on waiting. They insist on what's *easiest,* because I'll have to wait three or four hours. I win. Three or four hours, so what? I don't have anything else to do. Now the future has vanished and everything is the present.

People say goodbye to me; some give me nasty looks, look past the tacky green sweater, accuse me secretly of your death. And they're right. But everyone acts solicitous. *If you need anything,* your cousin says, but all I need is for her to disappear. *If you want to stay at our place*, your mother offers. Carles hugs me. He tells me you called him not long before dying.

"We'll talk," he threatens me, and I have the sense that he's looking at my belly, I have the sense he knows I killed you, that I threw you out, but I say nothing. "I can wait with you," he says, and I don't know if it's a question or an affirmation.

"No," I tell him. "You can go."

Now it's just my mother.

"I'll wait with you," she informs me. "You don't look well."

"I'd rather you go."

"You can't stay alone."

Since she's determined not to respect my will, I decide not to speak a word to her.

And then comes everything she's said to me, rooted out of me, things I don't want to remember, words I've burned, thrown to the wind, because they were rotten and full of grubs, the way your body would be in days if we weren't burning you right now. And it didn't stop until I shouted:

"You want me to tell you something? Fine! I'm pregnant, and I want to make it perfectly clear to you that you will not meet your grandson, that you won't get one glimpse of him, because I don't ever want to see you again, you miserable bitch."

Sometime before ten. I go up to the apartment clutching the urn so it won't fall from my hands. Under my feet, the mottled grey marble of the stairs extends like a sea of cinders. Cinders all round and me immobilized by the vomit of my private Vesuvius.

The key slides into the lock, a nail piercing my stomach. I imagine you slumped on the sofa, the floor lamp lit, reading a novel by Humbert. The green of the upholstery always made you look good. You'd look up, smile, close the book. I've been waiting for you a while, you'd say, you're the sexiest bowlegged girl I know, come here, we've got work to do, and you'd have that sly look on your face you used to get when you wanted to eat my pussy.

But the sofa's empty. I shut the door quickly behind me, to keep grief from following me in, but the monster creeps in under the crack. I leave the urn on the end table and stretch out on the sofa, obeying my imaginary Guim. I've got all night. I've got the rest of my life.

The next day's come, May 22, an impossible day, day of Saint Rita, patroness of lost causes, anyway who remembers saints' days anymore? The saints are dead, too.

I wake up and refuse to open my eyes. As long as they're closed, everything might just be a dream. But noise comes to me from the underworld, buses, cars, a barking dog—what's it saying? I don't understand—a horn, the urban melody composed by all the miniature Sisyphuses pushing along a world all too big, the sound of the stone rolling back down over and over, an interminable eternal return.

I'm exhausted, my vertebrae ache. I don't mind it. Cutting off a leg to stop feeling the ache in your head: I told myself that three days ago, with a still-living Guim waiting for me in the dining room. Now you're waiting for me dead in the urn on top of the table.

I sit up. A spot of blood on the sofa. It's shaped like a brain, but missing a piece. A brain with a bite taken out.

I lower my pants. My panties, red through and through. So now what? Stick in a tampon so no more of it comes out? I need to go to a hospital. Now. Before it's too late. I change clothes. I look for a pad. I shut the door. I fly down the stairs. I catch a taxi.

The urn remained silent on the table, contemplating the blotch of blood.

In the emergency room, nurses with a lack of urgency.

Triage. Blood pressure. Temp. Data. Numbers. And the man who punches them into the computer, the oracle.

But oracles don't exist.

I wait in a side room with a guy with a broken arm and another with yellowish skin who looks like a cadaver-in-waiting. I stroke the Durand in my purse like a person counting the rosary. I couldn't read it if I wanted, right now I have too many clouds inside.

García, the nurse shouts. More cripples come through. Gonzálvez. I count the floor tiles several times, as though the number might change between one count and the next. Solana. Afraid of change. Al-Maiouf.

And finally: Sala.

I follow him down an endless hallway, immaculate gateway to heaven. We step into a consulting room, he pulls the curtain.

"Undress from the waist down and lie down here, the gynecologist will be right over."

I obey. Blood drips on the ground.

I stretch out and put my feet in the stirrups, splayed like a chicken soon to be quartered. A man, half-bald with glasses, comes in. They're always men. Almost always. Why? He dons an affable smile to calm me down. They must have told him I'm a hysteric.

"Let's see," he says, sitting on a rolling stool and bringing the echograph closer.

He grabs what looks like a dildo and tells me to relax. Relax, he says, the joker. He sticks it inside, it's cold. He maneuvers it like a crank, it's a lantern inspecting the far corners of the uterus. The doctor doesn't look at me, he only has eyes for the black-and-white screen. He says nothing. Say something, damn it! He keeps scrounging around. Only a minute has passed, maybe, but I can't take it anymore.

"Did I lose it?"

He takes the thing out.

"You can sit up," he says.

He removes his glasses. A bad sign, I think, he's taking them off to look more human, more friendly. Don't be paranoid.

The verdict: "You weren't pregnant."

"What do you mean? As of today, I was nine days late, and I . . ."

"I can imagine the delay threw you off, but these things happen. Especially in moments of stress or change. It could also be the first inklings of menopause. You're still young, but you never know."

"I lost it, that's what you mean, right? You don't want to tell me, because you think the idea I was never pregnant will be easier to accept. It's that, isn't it?"

"I'm very sorry, but you have never been pregnant. There's no visible embryonic residue."

"Maybe it all came out. If I lost it, how the hell would you see anything?"

"I'm telling you again, it's impossible. Don't ask me to go into technical details, there's no point. I'll prescribe you a mild sedative, you're dealing with a major blow. It'll do you good. You need a few days to take all this in, it's not easy."

"Don't treat me like I don't know what's inside me. I had a boy, damn it, a boy. Technical details . . . yeah, right!"

"I understand your frustration, I understand you need to blame someone, but it's not going to help. I'll be right back with your prescription."

And he leaves me there, cunt dripping over the fabric of the chair. I dress. Sweater inside out. Dumbass!

I emerge from the bay in flames, the world moving in slow motion. I hear the doctor from a distance:

"Wait, Ms. Sala."

I stop in the middle of the hallway and yell that he's a lying son of a bitch.

Once outside, the asphalt drowns me.

162 Days Earlier

I haven't left home. I spent much of the morning sitting on the couch, next to the Bordeaux-colored blotch, hands on my skirt, as if in a waiting room. But I'm not waiting for anything, my name's not on the list. My phone is on silent, messages and calls keep pouring in from those taking pity on me. I don't want to talk or read idiotic messages full of emojis. Silence is better company.

I'm tired of looking at the blotch, or rather of the blotch looking at me all the time, impertinent. A pail of water, soap, brush. I scrubbed in a fury, but the spot was still more stubborn than I. I took the cover off the cushion and left it soaking until it goes away, even though labor under the moronic certainty that if I do get it out, it will come back after a few hours, same as in that horror story.

I've cleaned up the kitchen, where your teacup was with a few crumb-strewn plates, vestiges of your last breakfast. I did a load of laundry with the clothes thrown around the house (why did you have to leave everything just lying around?). I could have thrown it all out, but I thought it best to wash it. I'll fold it, put it away in the dresser, and only then will I decide what to do.

On the nightstand, the second set of glasses you used to wear for reading. I put them on. At 20/50 the outside world looks blurry and vertiginous, it's hard to look—in other words, exactly how I feel inside. I didn't take them off. On the bed, the brown sweatshirt you used to wear around the house, the *gui-miferous* scent beyond the grave stunned me. The green sheets too are impregnated with you. I was trapped in the cobweb of memory until I managed to free myself from its threads. I slung away the sheets and the pillows, the sudarium of our matrimony. I stuffed them into a bag, walked outside, threw them in the trash bin.

Outside, the sun shone far too bright, as if the glasses also magnified the light; everything was diffuse patches of color, people without features, faceless masses strolling about. I hurried back inside, as if the light were chasing me down to kill me.

At some point, the doorbell rang. I stayed still. It rang a second time, longer now, someone was holding down the button. Then, Carles's voice.

"Mei, open up, I know you're in there."

I don't move.

"Mei, if you don't open up, I'm just going to use my key."

I ran to the door, drew the chain, and opened it a crack, taking off the glasses to avoid questions that don't have any answers.

"I don't want to talk, Carles. Give me time."

Then he turned stern, serious face, deep tone, same as when you talk down to a child: That's enough, open up right now. And me, voice a thread, No, Carles, I can't, honestly, I'll call you in a few days. And again, the soft supplicating look.

He says you called him, knows I threw you out, knows I'm pregnant. I didn't deny it, I don't want to hear myself uttering the words, then I said to myself, So you were pretending I was making it up and you thought the same and you ran off terrified.

And Carles went on, It's not your fault, Mei, open up, I'm struggling with this, too, we can keep each other company. But I couldn't: if I'm alone, I can keep my sorrow in a cage, but if someone else is here, it will break out of me. I shut the door in his face, with an apology:

"I'm sorry but I can't, give me a few days. Seriously. Thanks for coming. You're a good friend."

I walked to the sink and scrubbed the spot until my hands started to hurt. I hung the sofa cover outside in the light of day, exposed so everyone could see my frustrated maternity.

I went back to the sofa and night fell over me, now my head sizzled, now it was empty, it's better to be there without thinking.

THAT DAY

If you'd stayed hovering over the asphalt, who knows.
But you wanted moss.
Until you found it.

S tubbornly life goes on. I have to piss, to shit, to eat, to sleep. It's so obvious it's offensive.

My calvary began at the supermarket. The fluorescent lights kill the shadows and make it impossible to hide from life, the light exposes you until you're just another package of meat, it's almost a kind of punishment. I traced out the labyrinth of aisles, not looking for a way out, dragging the basket by instinct like a woman condemned to live.

Milk, toilet paper, butter, apples, a dozen eggs, tomatoes, oil, cured sheep cheese, more apples. I didn't see the shelf of dreams or the freezer of candied optimisms. I crossed a man with a cart bursting with frozen meals and beer, maternal longings kick in, make him cannelloni from scratch: to be someone's mother for a while, even a fifty-year-old chrome dome with a porno addiction.

At the fish counter, an old woman is talking with an employee, the blather of machines programed to talk and say nothing.

Such is life, they say.

I walked on to the bakery, the bag weighing me down like a body. Three people ahead of me, and on the counter, the ginger cookies that used to drive you wild. You'd put them in your mouth whole, and every time you'd say, They're the perfect size, per-fect. I looked at them, wondering whether to buy one, even if I don't like them. Too much sugar, I used to grouse, and you'd tell me a little sweetness might do me good. Suddenly, the girl attendant:

"Sorry, do you know what you want or no? Those people are waiting for the baguettes to come out."

I look up. Everyone observing me: the employee, a retiree, and a woman with a newspaper, and especially the girl with the taut skin, pregnant, with an insolent swell she couldn't or didn't care to cover, as if she were showing it to me alone.

They looked at me scornfully. Go on, girl, order, we don't have all day, get a move on, none of us gives a shit what's going on with you outside, what are you doing here? Shut yourself up at home once and for all and don't bother us!

The employee has arched her apprehensively thin brows:

"Do you know or not?"

Me, quiet, pupils all bearing down on me. I recalled Mercè's pleasantness, the air of ease she gave off, and wanted to be shopping there and not in this nasty piece of shit town.

"A country loaf, sliced."

The girl turned around to grab it, put it in the slicer, slid it into a paper bag, and handed it to me across the counter.

"One thirty-five, please."

"And a ginger cookie."

"One?" she asked, as if asking for just one were an aberration, as if I had only said this to fuck with her.

"Yeah, one." She rolled her eyes, and I couldn't help but add, "Look, give me ten if that's better for you."

She passed me the bag with the cookie.

"One seventy," she hissed.

"I told you I'll take ten."

She snorted, put nine more cookies in the bag, and I placed a ten on the counter. She gave me the change and the bag. No one said anything. The customers looked away. The pregnant woman, the little piglet, chuckled to herself.

I threw the bag with the cookies in the trash can at the entrance and shouted, Have a nice day.

The asphalt exuded an odor of piss; here and there, trickles flowed down, spontaneous infectious effluvia. After stepping over all that dried piss, I'll reach the apartment, the soles of my shoes coated in atoms of urine and dogshit and human shit and flecks of vomit from the drunks who maraud through the neighborhood at night and I'll put everything up inside.

Such were my ruminations while I waited for the traffic light to stop the river of cars, enveloped by specters like me that go from place to place and nobody sees them, waiting for the green light. Green, green, green. But this green is dead and mechanical, a hysteric green. In Sorrius the green is alive. Here the specters slip inside you and grope you like desperate zombies.

A siren wails down the road. An ambulance, a cop car, a firetruck. In the city there are always sirens, I'd never noticed it before as I did today. The idea of Guim in an ambulance, silent, driving unhurried because he was already dead, crushed under the metal of the car, and there was no sense in turning the siren on or forcing anyone out of the way. The repetitive sound of the sirens unsettles me, it sticks in me, I hear it from the bed and I'm afraid someone is about to die in an ambulance, or I imagine the police are chasing down a rapist, one of those goddamn reoffenders the law won't allow to be locked away forever.

And I think once again of the house in the forest, the law of the forest, which is different, and has no sirens or zombies or even specters.

A week has passed since they cremated you and stuck you in an urn.

Six days have passed since my vagina started pouring, expelling what I had inside me. Or what I didn't have. I'll never know.

My country loaf is gone, but I don't want to go back out. For now I'll get by on the leftovers I've got here. Apples, salvaged scraps of bread, grilled sorrow.

All your clothes are clean and folded, I don't open the wardrobe so I won't see you there. In the morning I went to your studio and cleaned it up, erasing your most evident traces, putting you away so you won't assault me at every turn. But the urn's still there on the dining room table and every day I put on your glasses a while to see things through your eyes.

Tomorrow I go to the notary to make my widowhood official. The executor will come and I'll give him power of attorney to handle the paperwork. I don't want to deal with it. I don't think I'm capable.

Today I remembered I used to know a Mei who was writing a novel. Who knew a Mila. Who knew a house in the middle of the forest.

How shameful.

The charcoal drawing in the hallway. You made it for me ten or twelve years ago, when looking at each other still threw us into orbit, when we used to stare at each other to study our every gesture, incredulous, afraid it was all a mirage and would vanish when we went to bed, back when you weren't yet aware you'd grow tired of my nitpickiness, as you called it, we could have drawn every square inch of the other— you with pencil and paper, me scribbling with neurons—the slight asymmetry of your cheeks, that insubordinate eyebrow hair, the tenderness you radiated that made of you a luminescent being, capable of brightening all my shadows, that tenderness you devoted only to me; it was then that I taught you the world *luciferous,* because you were my lightbringer and still I could intuit a suffering that would plunge me into hell—love, assassin of quietude, sower of paranoia—but since you didn't believe me, you grabbed the dictionary: *luce, lucency, lucible, lucidity, lucifee,* then you read aloud, *A substance in an organism such as the glow-worm which can produce light when oxidized in the presence of a specific enzyme,* and with that, the declaration of love: You are my luciferin.

But all that came before the you-go-I-don't-feel-like-it, the you-always-beat-around-the-bush, the you're-the-one-who-doesn't-want-me, and the soulless sex we engaged in from pure physiological necessity, graceless, unimaginative, repeating the same repertoire over and over, stale—a quick blowjob, morning intercourse—racing the clock to get it over with, shoddy orgasms to sate the urge to fuck: we fucked the way a person eats or pisses, fucked to survive. You drew me at a time when the possibility of not loving you existed only in an improbable parallel universe, not even Schrödinger would have been able to find our love dead in a box. Our souls were sewn together like Siamese twins, our breasts heaved in unison, daunted and drawn by the existence of the other. You traced out my features in charcoal when we were beings living a science fiction love, and horror, too, the horror that you might grow tired of me and flee from me, back when love was more frightening than death.

I took down the portrait.

I remember the day my mother saw it in the hallway, one Sunday when, how strange, she came for lunch at our apartment, for the first and last time, I'd say. I can't imagine what the motive was. Mother's day? The anniversary of my father's death? You made a parmentier with truffles, I have that engraved in me: inhaling that delicacy and unable to get out of my head my mother's moving phrase and my regret.

She arrived on time with a packet of profiteroles from the pastry shop in front of our place, the same profiteroles my father used to buy on Sundays and that I went crazy for, despite the sempiternal Honey, you've already had three!

We showed her the apartment making irrelevant remarks of the kind you make on these occasions: "And here's the bathroom," as if it weren't obvious and you needed to explain it was a toilet. She walked around emitting oohs and ahs of overblown admiration, like a visitor to the castle of Ludwig II of Bavaria and not a rickety—if clean and well lit—apartment in the heart of Gràcia.

I still see her entering the bedroom: *Oh, the love nest,* and you and I both smiled at that stupid cliché, a smile from the heart, because love looks for excuses to make you smile even when the situation doesn't call for it.

It was then, on the way back to the dining room, that she stopped in the middle of the hallway in front of the portrait and eyed it up with authentic interest, far different from the frivolous interest she'd shown in the apartment's various rooms, and she said that thing so unusual for her, in the voice of someone talking to herself, as though it escaped her or she weren't aware her thoughts were causing her vocal cords to vibrate and articulate a phrase audible to the two of us, an effect that was multiplied by hearing my name coming from her mouth and not the usual wearisome *Honey*:

"How beautiful, Remei. You're so lucky, I'm jealous, really, that you have someone to look at you with these eyes."

How those words turned my mother of stone into a crystal figurine, and they showed her to me in all her solitude, a fossilized solitude that provoked for the first time in my life the strange desire to embrace her. But I didn't. And then the parmentier and the regret and the mother resplendent in her solitude, a two-dimensional cut-out hung where it oughtn't and that would never match its background.

I never invited her over again.

I placed the portrait in the closet, in a pile with all the pages of clouds you were painting for Durand.

JUNE

The calendar's sadism: it's already June.

I still haven't thrown anything out. How can I rid myself of your relics?

In the afternoons, I sit on the sofa and put on loud music not to hear myself. I shut my eyes and concentrate on envisioning the cello's next note, advancing through the partiture, and in this way I manage to silence my head a while.

But sometimes a thought escapes my control and weighs on me. What will you do now, Mei? And I turn the music up even louder. Write? I ask myself. And I start crying because it hurts so bad. Maximum volume. I feel the bass in my stomach. Is that your plan? Write? Or no? Maybe you just want to stay here on the couch and listen to your life drain away? Or will you look for a job at a publisher? Back to the office, clock in, clock out, antlike, push your rock up the mountain, read what others write just to make the hours pass. Then an avalanche of notes comes through, violin strings twisting and carrying you off. I don't have a plan. All plans seem ridiculous, ridiculous like me. Write, I ask myself, how did I ever think I could? And my imbecilic notecards appear to me, stuck to the door of the wardrobe. Cello, I repeat to myself, listen to the cello.

Writing a novel on notecards . . . embarrassing.

At night, Carles came back and rang the doorbell. Since I won't respond to his messages, he decided to stop by. But I don't feel like talking.

143 Days Earlier

Three weeks, twenty-one days stuck in this apartment. I've distracted myself counting the hours, minutes, seconds that have passed with the calculator. More than a million eight hundred thousand seconds. And now one more, then another, then another. Tireless. The Chinese water torture of time hollowing out my soul.

Today my mother called. I let it ring. Also: Carles's daily messages.

I ought to throw out the phone, take my things, and go far away, from Barcelona, from the apartment, from Guim, from myself. Pass myself off as someone else, turn into someone else. But how do you do that?

Someone else. Who.

I've started to read again, whatever, to run away, but the lines dance; halfway through a paragraph my head runs off to dark places and I have to start again. Since it's hard to concentrate, I've sunk into Durand's bound pages. Each is a self-contained world. I dream of a life of self-contained days, unconnected, without the ballast of the past or future, because the future, too, is a burden.

Keep dreaming, Mei.

The part that talks about common clouds is poetic but insufficient: facile metaphors when she draws an association between cumulonimbus shapes and the rage that builds up in us and inevitably empties out. *L'ennuagement de la colère,* she says. For us, non-francophones, everything always sounds prettier in our neighbors' language. I got up and went to rifle through the illustrations and sketches I recently stuffed into the closet in your studio to see if you'd drawn *L'ennuagement de la colère.* And you had. A cloud with the face of a woman. Boor.

But the final section, which departs from meteorological literality, is a filigree. *Le berceau de tes étoiles,* Durand says, and it evokes for me the grotesque sorrow of the spot of semen left in the sheets after lovemaking; *poussière cosmique que te rend aveugle avec son élcat;* the devastation of *la tienne est une naissance sans témoins.* Maybe I was captivated because now I'm the one inhabiting the nebulous, and the (false) possibility of my dust condensing into a star brings me hope.

In the morning, my mother's squawking by the door. With Bach at full blast, I barely heard her, she was just a murmur in the background, the evocation of a soprano practicing Schönbergian dissonance. Before leaving, the soprano deposited several Tupperware containers of chicken with prunes and pine nuts and cod croquettes, my favorite, on the doorstep.

My phone rang in the afternoon, unknown number. I thought it might be important—the executor, the lawyer—but I didn't dare pick up in case it was a trap: Carles or my mother calling from a different phone, or who knows, someone wanting to console me and tell me to keep my head up. As if that hadn't occurred to me. They left a message.

I called my voicemail and Flavi's voice spoke to me unexpectedly. They told him what happened, if I need anything I know where he is, the bees miss me, the woods are precious.

I started crying.

The line at the unemployment office moves sluggish, like a religious procession, and all of us here to take our communion look down at the ground, concentrating on our sins, waiting for them to give us the host so it can melt in our mouths and we can live in peace for another month. The bureaucrat has me sit down without looking:

In Spanish: "ID please."

I hand it over to him. He's wearing a green and yellow shirt with a firework print. The contrast between the shirt and his milky skin is discomfiting, he looks like a corpse dressed up for carnival. Now he glances at me over the top of his glasses with the ascendency his profession grants him, evaluating me.

In Spanish: "You'll get a notification soon for you to choose one of the free recycling courses. Free and obligatory. Remember, if you don't attend, you may lose your right to compensation."

His ungainly hands pass me a sheaf of forms.

In Spanish: "Sign here and here."

He hides one of those hands under the table.

"Lose my compensation?" I tell him in Spanish, condescending to adopt the language of the invader so that he will listen to me with more interest and not make me pay for being Catalan.

The vanished hand doesn't return.

"Obviously. Do you not want to broaden your skill set to find employment?"

His eyes gleam. A repetitive, almost imperceptible movement of the arm. Am I imagining this? Of course I'm imagining
it, but I fling my head back to get my hair out of my face.

"The thing is . . . I'm going through a tough time. My husband . . . I'm a widow now. Is there any way you could . . . ?"

He looks brazenly at my chest. Around me: tables, bureau-
crats, the unemployed. No one's observing us. I bend forward
to make it obvious I'm reading the documents he hands me.
You can see my black bra, the hint of cleavage. I'm prostitut-
ing myself. I drag the moment out. A rebel thrice over: widow,
whore, assassin.

"Sign," he says in a stifled voice. "I'll see what I can do . . ."

I sign.

"You can go."

Go in peace.

Amen.

I begin the procession home with the rest of the faithful, all
of us packed in the metro. I have your glasses in my bag and I
put them on so no one will recognize me. Clark Kent the widow,
but with no cape to take flight in. Everything looks unbearably
like swimming beneath the sea: the lack of clarity, vulnerability
before the oceanic immensity. But the glass protects me from
the shrapnel of reality.

I take the escalator up. Outside, the streets are bars over
the map of the city, and in their cells the inmates scrub dishes,
do laundry, whole families narcotize themselves in front of the
tube, sleeping on fancy bunks, preparing copious suppers, prisoners in the mess hall.

And me in my spanking new private cell, a cell in the widow's wing, where I've just been transferred. Because the wing of
women with children wouldn't take me.

Mother once more at the door, sermonizing in her perfectly tuned cries. Every time I hear her voice, what she said at the funeral comes back to me, all that I feigned having extirpated from myself, all I didn't want to remember, the phrases reborn every morning post-cremation from their cinders with the curse of her timbre, the words I wanted to throw out because they were rotten and full of worms.

But no.

They stayed inside me—who are you trying to fool, Mei?—cancerous words that multiply by the day and eat away at me. Because she's my mother and I love her. Or I ought to love her. But she's always put herself ahead of others—ahead of my father, ahead of me. She deserves to be hated. But I love her, or I'm supposed to love her. Or not. She's always treated me as an object. A valuable one, but an object all the same. So I should hate her. And in the meanwhile I go on hoping that she will magically change—*zub-zub*—into the person I wish she was and has never been. It won't happen. I know. Still, I go on harboring the hope that it will happen. Even now. Idiot.

"Honey, open the door, please, we can't go on like this. Make an effort."

Make an effort, she says, the same phrase as the day of the funeral. The goddamn conversation's chiseled into my head from repeating it to myself so many times. Indelible. And now I'm once more outside the funeral home in my green sweater. Everyone's gone. She and I are the only ones left.

"I'll wait with you," she informs me. "You don't look well."

"I'd rather you go."

And I think she said:

"Deal with it."

Or she might have said:

"I don't care. I'm staying."

Or else:

"You can't stay here alone."

Since she's determined not to respect my will, I decide I won't speak a word to her.

"What was Guim doing on the highway at that hour? And drunk! Mother of God . . ."

I pretend not to hear.

"He was coming from the house, wasn't he? Did you argue? Honey, you shouldn't feel responsible. It could happen to any of us. Married life isn't easy."

Now she wants to lecture me.

"At least you didn't have children," I think she said, or maybe she didn't finish the phrase, *at least you didn't . . .* and left it dangling, to say it without saying it, so I couldn't throw it back in her face. The bitch was trying to make me cry.

"I'm sorry," she might have said, but I'm not sure, at most she would have whispered it.

And me, without looking at her:

"Drop it, O.K.?"

"Come on, make an effort, we'll talk about something else."

"I don't feel like talking."

"How's the writing going?"

"I said I don't feel like talking."

But her, like it's nothing:

"Tell me something. Is Manel taking care of you?"

Hearing that name makes me retch. I will always associate that son of a bitch Manel with your death.

"He's a good man. Did I tell you we used to call him the Rock Hudson of the village?"

"Shut up!" I shout.

"Honey, I'm just trying to help you a little. I don't know why you won't let me. You're as stubborn as your father."

(Maybe she didn't say that phrase about my father, and I stuck it in there because I heard it so often as a teenager. But who cares, who cares whether or not she said it, I thought, we both know she was thinking it. Because being like my father was always shameful and a cause for ridicule).

She takes my hand. Hers is thin. In my head, I see her decades ago, sitting on the bed, rubbing her palms together with thick lotion, looking like a witch.

"Stubbornness won't get you anywhere."

"Leave me alone."

And then everything spoken very quickly, too fast to process, rammed together, badly expressed, badly heard, badly construed:

"What an ingrate you are. Always thinking of yourself, yourself and no one else. What do you think, that Guim's mother isn't suffering? That she isn't suffering as much as or more than you? You didn't even have the decency to come in all black, to show some respect. It's all about what you want, right? Go to the country house and write, you said, and look how that turned out. It's not your fault, of course, I know that. But open your eyes, honey. Learn to live again! You're not fifteen anymore."

Here a cry started rising from my belly.

"Go on, pretend you can't hear me. Just like you did when Guim wanted kids and you were too busy with work."

(Or maybe it was just: Like when you had too much work to . . . and I didn't let her finish).

"You have no fucking idea."

"Idea of what?" And I'd swear she added: *That your book will be the children you never had?*

I get up and hiss:

"Get out!"

She remains impassible. I can't stand it.

"You want me to tell you something? Fine! I'm pregnant, and I want to make it perfectly clear to you that you will not meet your grandson, that you won't get one glimpse of him, because I don't ever want to see you again, you miserable bitch."

"Pregnant, but . . ."

I turn around and walk off, my eyes welling, the walls of the dam burst.

"Come back. I just said that to get a reaction out of you. You need to let it out, crying will do you good, honey. Believe me, I know what I'm talking about."

From afar, I still hear her:

"I don't really think all those things I said. How could I? I'm your mother. Come back, Remei. Sorry."

And I run off. *Zub-zub*, a magic wand to make her disappear.

THAT DAY

Spread your pussy wide and stick the world inside.
Just imagine!
As if the world could fit there.

A month and a day.
Getting out of the shower, I looked at myself in the foggy mirror. Just a blotch with blurred outlines. I guess that's what I am now, a hazy figure. I brushed my hair as slowly as a geisha. I like to pay attention to everything I do, that way I keep my head from straying into questions that lead me nowhere. Here, now. Shower, scrub every corner of my body, dry myself off with soft touches of the towel, comb my hair. Stretch out the present until it won't give any further and slips between my fingers. As long as I'm in the now, I am neither past nor future. The future is science fiction.

The mirror cleared up and I saw myself: hair soaked, skin radiant, but snuffed out on the inside. This body doesn't belong to me. I hadn't looked at myself in days. I approached my reflection and crept inside the pupils, examining myself from inside. It was me. I'm the woman in the mirror. So they say. I examined myself as if I didn't know myself and the hardness in my stare frightened me.

Who am I? I asked. What a stupid question. But I couldn't help asking it. My double in front of me, so insolent. Now that there's no more Guim, maybe nobody knows who I am.

Not even me.

Black hair dripping, eyes like an oil well deep under the earth's crust, mole obtuse on my left cheek, orderly teeth, too small, like milk teeth, delicate ears, their piercings always empty now, two horizontal furrows in the forehead, getting deeper by the day. I felt my face with my hands. My hands, also too small, doll's hands, my father would say.

Is this me? Apparently.

A siren seeped through the bathroom window like a lament, and dragged in the street with it: people, cars, asphalt, the entire city snuck into my bathroom. And me, stuck in front of the mirror with my pupils quivering, dilating, contracting to the rhythm of the siren, while the town stretches out in my bath tub, the taxis and buses flow from the tap, the unbreathable smoke from the tailpipes, the supermarket cashiers blab crouched in the bidet while the dogs lift a leg and spray piss across the walls, the ceiling stamped with neon signs, and the rats, the giant subway rats gnaw away at my toilet paper.

I wanted to stop looking at myself, but couldn't, I was trapped in my image. I'd have liked to enter the mirror and see if the other side was the same or not, if Guim's reflection was still hiding out in some corner, orphaned and homeless. The siren now drifted off, its tone graver, deformed. And life, too: the Doppler effect, tenor changing as it slipped away.

Then the woman in the mirror shouted at me: What are you doing here, Mei? Go! Get away now! Run, run!

And for the first time in too many days, I saw a future. A paltry future, but a future nonetheless.

I stuck a few things in a bag, turned off the light, the gas, the water, emptied the fridge, grabbed the urn, the nebularium, the glasses, and ran downstairs, as if someone were chasing me, myself, maybe; clutching the future I've seen, afraid I'd forget where it was, how to get there. I got in the car and flew through the streets until the city was behind me. The motorbikes and the factories on the outskirts roared with rage as they watched me escape.

The car took the exit toward the country house all on its

own, as if I weren't driving, like a trickle of water that takes the most natural course, the easiest, the only one possible. The forest, deep green, respectfully observed my return. My return, empty-handed, empty-wombed. I had the sense I was picking up the thread I'd abandoned when I left, that every inch I advanced was an inch backward in time, a film spooling backward that would lead me to the beginning.

But of course it wasn't.

The house didn't move, it was waiting for me. My hideout with walls of stone. I left my things in the car and climbed the stairs. Fifteen of them, as ever. My father's voice sang, guiding my steps: fifteen is fifteen. Fifteen, fifteen, fifteen. At the top, the fig tree exhibited itself to me, garnished with black figs like a grieving Christmas tree.

I opened the door. Again, the stench of damp. I slipped into the alcove, touching nothing, an intruder in my own home, and passed through all the rooms, pausing in each as if they were the wings of a museum.

I took photos as evidence of the crime scene: in the living room, the glasses of wine still there; my stupid notecards stuck to the wardrobe; the bed unmade, the way I left it when I went running to the door thinking it was you coming back and instead found Manel; a pair of potatoes rotting in the kitchen, I grabbed them with a plastic bag draped over my hand and my fingers sank into the putrefaction. My frail future was shriveling.

I went outside. A quick look at the sky sufficed: altocumulus. *Le Nuagier* is my devotional. I sat on the top step, the fig tree behind me descrying me through its dozens of sweet pupils. I'd have loved a cigarette. I haven't had one in years, but oh, to suck the filter and fill myself with hot smoke, take one drag and anticipate the next, unrushed. I looked at the pebbles on the ground, some shiny, some dark, all grimy. I grabbed one, tossed it down the stairs, and listened to the plinking as it struck the stone steps. When I was little, I used to go to a swimming hole with my dad and kill time dropping rocks into the water to listen to the plunk when the river swallowed them. To be a stone, to be ingested by life with a resounding plunk.

When I got tired of sifting through memories, I emptied the car and put the urn in the closet. I don't want to have it in front of me all day, spying on me. I grabbed the other things lying around the room. The bottle of wine, the glasses: the murder weapons. When I finished, I fell back into the armchair.

So now what?

My hands were frozen from rinsing glasses and I rubbed them against my green sweater, the same one I wore the day they cremated you. Maybe I need to incinerate this sweater now, too; every time I put it on, the reflux of your memory will rise in my gorge and I'll see your dead hand, your feet, the sarcophagus. *You'll call me in two days when your period comes and you feel like shit.* But it came, and I can't call you.

I made a tea to fill the time with something warm and stood in the door of my work room stirring the cup. I remained on the threshold a while, taking sips of the scalding tea. All at once, something pushed me to go in—my father's hand pushing me to jump into the water. I sat down. I turned on the computer. On the desk, the notepad with the story I wrote in a feverish burst when you were already dead and I didn't know it. I read it. I typed out a clean version on the computer.

It's good, dammit. It's good.

At six I went out. Today is one of the longest days of the year, and the light's generous. In the distance, Blunted Crest looked down from the heights, observed me as I traveled over the roads, a fugitive mouse, on the lookout for a hole to hide away in. I grabbed a sprig of rosemary and chewed it until my breath smelled like herbs.

Here time doesn't provoke me, doesn't force me to reckon with it. I spent the day ordering things, mired in distraction, reading, sifting pointless thoughts, until someone knocked at the door in the afternoon. Three times. The sound of the knocker, gentler and more human than the doorbell, made me anxious to open up. Even if it might be Manel. Or my mother. Or Carles. But it wasn't.

The same old busted jeans. He handed me a book by Palé. A little misanthropic pessimism to keep you company, he said, and gave me a peck on each cheek and an ordinary hug, not the stifling kind anyone else would give me now that I'm a widow. I didn't understand how he knew that . . .

"Manel told me you were back." Then, reading the suspicion on my face: "He saw you come past in your car. The village has eyes, you know . . . You must be escaping the festivities, no?"

What? Festivities? Whatever, yes, I'm escaping.

"Well, I don't want to bother you."

He turned around.

"Don't go. Come in. You want a tea? I mean if you have time, if you feel like it, maybe now's no good for you."

"I've always got time."

He followed me to the kitchen. I put the water on to boil.

"What a pretty house, it's a little fortress here on top of the hill."

"Yeah, a fortress," I repeated.

Something inside of me relaxed when I saw he wouldn't come at me with one of those how-are-yous that strike me mute because they are impossible to answer.

"They say during the Civil War, this is where all the chaplains hid out, from the Republican side, you know . . ." And he gestured with his hand toward his neck like a guillotine, stuck out his tongue, twisted his neck. "There must be more than one bag of coins in these walls."

"Maybe I should give up writing and buy myself a metal detector," I say, without a drop of decency, as if I were still writing. How can I dare make a joke?

I pour the water in the cups.

"Thanks for coming."

"Don't sweat it, it's pure selfishness. A person with a brain shows up here, I want to make sure you won't just up and vanish again. The forest cures everything, you know?" I smile. "I'm serious, it cures you. You know the grotto?"

"The grotto? No."

"Well, we need to fix that right now!"

I put up resistance, more from reasons of etiquette than of conviction. But after fifteen minutes, I was lacing my shoes to go.

We headed left until a mound of soil and fallen trees pushed us off the main trail and we had to take a detour. Flavi told me that the path has been cut off since the landslides in March. March, just three months ago, a lifetime. I stopped listening and followed the detours of memory.

March, Barcelona, Guim.

But I didn't get far, the terrain grew rugged and I had to scramble over stones. We reached a river.

"Is this the Muntanya?"

"No, the Muntanya is over there," Flavi said, drawing an imaginary line in the air. "This is the Roderic, a tributary."

We crossed, balancing over the makeshift bridge of stones, careful not to slip and fall. Where am I? Safe on the riverbank or traversing the falls? I feel like I fell in some time ago.

"It's over there, see it?" He pointed up.

And atop a pile of rocks, I saw an entrance, a stone giant's toothy mouth. The grotto.

It took ten minutes of sweat and clawing to get there. We were panting. We sat down cradled in the stone walls, the rock uterus. Between the trees, I could see a corner of the roof of my house, one of the giant's toenails peeking out from the vegetation. Further off, the belltower with the houses clustered around it, cowed by the menacing forest. The Muntanya as purgatory, a dividing line between two worlds.

"What's that?" I asked, pointing to a new building, funereal, that stood out to the left, a spitball of cement amid the green.

"The sanatorium. You got mentally ill people there, junkies and alcoholics, too. Good people, tough job. Failures and disappointments so dense you could build an acropolis with them, pave the roads with cobblestones of rage."

"You must know a lot about it."

"Sure do. Too much."

I'd have liked to uproot into that phrase, tear it out and polish it until its meaning gleamed, but if he won't dig it up, neither will I. Wretch.

He took some salted almonds out of his bag and offered them to me. We chewed them in silence, with no more noise than the grinding of our teeth, and my tongue gouging the depressions in my molars.

"You tell me something, I'm tired of hearing myself."

He delivered:

"They say at the beginning of the century a farmer got trapped up here in the grotto. Seems there used to be a road that passed by here," he pointed at a pile of stones, "and the people from Castell would come through on their way to

Sorrius. It was a market day, and the farmer, who was dying of hunger because it hadn't rained in two months—the drought of twenty-two, I'd reckon—decided to go down to the square and sell his ox. When he got to the grotto, he stopped to take a swig from his wineskin and catch his breath. He probably sat here right where we are, and the landscape must have been the same, more or less: the church, the Muntanya, the Pobleny mountains."

I stretched out on the ground and closed my eyes.

"I imagine the guy dusty and desperate because look, a farmer's got to be on the verge of despair before he'll sell his ox. But it's better to sell your ox than your lands, right. Maybe he had a pregnant wife or, who knows, maybe he had seven kids, in those days if you got pregnant, you kept it, and the more hands, the better. I see him here, sitting down beside his ox, the two of them with their eyes lost in the horizon, and him taking slugs from his wineskin, even if that hot liquid burning his throat must have been a far cry from the wine you and I drink. Probably he was still asking himself whether it wouldn't be better to sell a plot and hold onto the ox, maybe he did the numbers once more in his head and wound up with the same conclusion: no, best to sell the ox. And maybe he took another sip of wine just then to wash down his disgust.

"Must have been early then, very early, because if you didn't show up first to the market, it was hopeless, and the weather turned bad, the clouds were soon to waylay him and he didn't even know it. Let it be said, he might not have been much of a farmer if he didn't know how to read what was in the off-ing from the clouds; maybe that's why he was starving back at home.

"Anyway: a drop fell, then more, and so on, like a machine gun. The sky tore open and its entrails plunged to earth. Him and the ox backed into the grotto for shelter.

"The farmer decided to wait it out. A summer storm, it'll

blow past soon, he must have said. And the ox lay on the ground there meek as a lamb. But the rain wouldn't stop and he even got the impression it was falling harder and harder. Hours passed, and the farmer, seeing he'd now get nothing for his ox, took the rain as a sign from God not to sell, and started wondering whether to go home or wait for the storm to let up. He wasn't in the mood to walk ninety minutes in the rain, imagine he got sick to boot, but what was he going to do about his boy on the way or the other seven kids he had? But since he'd struggled out of bed at the crack of dawn, he nodded off without thinking any more about it.

"An explosion woke him. The roar of the world splitting open, of life rising up in a tumult. He must have run outside scared, bewildered by the last slivers of sleep, not knowing even where he was, and he found the outcrop above the grotto had collapsed and was blocking both paths to the road. He peered through the curtain of rain that wouldn't stop falling, and thought of his wife, or his children, or maybe his ailing, toothless mother waiting for him bent over the fire. He raged against the rocks, tried to pull them up and open a path, but they wouldn't budge, not even a millimeter. Then, since no one was watching him, he started crying. That's a little poetic license: I like to make men cry in legends.

"They spent the night in the grotto. The next day was bonny, but the road was still blocked. He could have tried coming down the front way, more or less where we came up, but back then there was a jump of more than a few feet to that platform down there, and he didn't have the heart for it. Plus there was the ox: he couldn't leave his meager property behind. Another day passed. The farmer was dying of hunger and thirst, his wine was all gone by now, along with the water and the four dried figs he had in his haversack.

"More days passed, two, four, the legend isn't too clear at this point, and you're probably asking yourself why the hell

no one went to look for him, right? Maybe he was plain un-
likeable, a bastard who beat on his wife and kids and everyone
kept mum, even his ailing mother, and celebrated that he hadn't
come home.

"Then, on one of those hot afternoons when the sun could
melt rocks and even the sanest people start raving, the ox awoke
with fire in his eyes and approached him huffing horribly. The
farmer tried to calm him down, pressed against the wall saying
Down, down, but the ox was no dog and he was hungry and
thirsty and that heat was roasting his brain, and here everything
turns vague, but after a few days they saw the ox standing over
the grotto bellowing, and nothing was left of the farmer but a
skull and a couple of scattered bones."

There he stopped, I hadn't moved.

"I don't know why I'm telling you this, maybe it's not the
best time. Sorry."

The sun was going down.

"I like your legends, they help me get away from things a bit.
Thanks for making me go out."

"You don't have to thank me."

"You don't even really know me. I feel like I owe something
in return. Death, you know, it's something very intimate. People
ask question after question. How are you, what will you do, you
need to keep going, but I have his death branded inside me and
I don't want to share it."

"You don't have to justify yourself. I get it."

"I threw him out of the house, we had a stupid argument,
I know it's not my fault, these things happen. But. It's hard
as hell to find someone who understands you, and even then,
they don't understand you completely, or you're the one who
doesn't understand them." Flavi said nothing. "I thought I was
pregnant, you know? So what do I do with all this now?"

My eyes wept on their own, like a sponge that can't take in
more water. Flavi wrapped his big hand around my shoulder.

I noticed an aroma of cinnamon and nutmeg. My tears flowed without sobs, tears mute and dead. A spur of star anis lodged inside me. The sun was grazing the mountains.

"You wanted to write, no? Write then," he said without hesitation. "You've got nothing to lose."

That night, from the bed, I heard the pop of firecrackers. Celebrating the solstice, blowing it all up, burning it. Razing the earth and starting over from zero. Maybe I should have made a bonfire, too. But my memories are stubbornly fireproof.

After lunch, I sat down in front of the computer. I opened the screen, pressed the button to turn it on, and opened the folder for the project, *Alone*. What a tasteless joke.

I pressed the w, the h, the e, the n. When.

When the road turned into the woods, the wind started to blow as if anxious to hurry me home . . . There followed a thread of words, phrases of various lengths never reaching a full stop, just commas like hurdles for the tongue, words linked to words through relative clauses of relative clauses, connectors and buts and conjunctions and that damned hermitage on top of the mountain I can't get out of my head with the sunken roof and the altar exposed to the elements, waiting for Abraham's sacrifice, and I thought, This is no good, but it's been days since you've written and you need to get the lead out one way or another, start your engines, and another page-and-a-half paragraph, bereft of style and vomited up unceremoniously, but vomited up nonetheless, that's what matters, they say, so they say, what matters is getting on with it, page after page smeared with words, then the revision will come and whatever else, because honestly, I couldn't stop, despite the voice from inside the armoire saying how embarrassing to just let myself go and do something I like, burying my grief so soon, obsessing over my writing, and I looked up, because I couldn't stand the voice anymore that was filtering through the hinges, and I grabbed the urn and took it to the kitchen, so it would keep me company while I eat, while I cook, while I rest, but not while I write, when I need to, when I absolutely must stop thinking for once of Guim's urn and his soft fucking hand, and I turned back to the computer, the keys danced expectantly, and deep down I told myself, you need to finish the cards, order, you need order, otherwise this won't make one bit of sense, but I kept going.

I couldn't give a fuck about order, not now.

The morning was a catastrophe. The sound of shattering woke me at daybreak. A monumental fright. I thought someone had broken in, but I sat up in bed, listened close, played dead, and nothing. I grabbed a chair, the clothing slung over it fell to the floor and formed a figure over the tiles: my alter ego had volatized.

What else.

I walked surreptitiously to the living room, heart in suspense, suppurating sulfuric sweat. I found a gaping window and shards of glass scattered on the ground. The curtains shook, struggling to free themselves and fly away. Then I heard the howls of the wind. The intruder. Worst of all, I'll have to ask Manel to repair it.

Too startled to sleep, I reread what I wrote yesterday. I got two good phrases out of it. At most. So it goes. I've got nothing to lose and nothing better to do. I'll write two hours a day, whether I want to or not. I've done today, but how can I go on if the first pages are worthless, if they don't hold up? How can you build a house without a foundation?

While I made tea, the urn implored me to finish the cards, order my ideas. You've always been meticulous, now's not the time to stop. Finally I said, Quiet, Guim, in the voice of an old bag talking to her parakeet.

After lunch, I sat in the armchair, Dad's armchair, which I now pretend is mine. In front of it, the painting with the two sunflowers interrogating me, on the ground, the worn rug with the labyrinthine edging. How many hours on that border, circling through the volutes with the toy bus my father brought back for me from London, or piling up blocks of wood with letters and numbers on their faces.

He would sit in the armchair, reading or knitting—scarves, always scarves—and I would show him one of the blocks with the letter D. He'd say *dimwit* and I'd respond with a laugh that dinged like a bell. Then it was my turn. F. But no normal words occurred to me, only impossible ones—fadument, flumerous, fustical—then finally I'd blurt out *flute,* lips pursed, disappointed because the word wasn't funny and all I'd wanted was to impress him.

Next came X, and he said *Xana.* I accused him of inventing it, you're a cheater! He put down his knitting needles and leaned over to me slightly:

"In Asturias, a *xana* is a little witch, a fairy that lives in the forest. Go on, your turn."

And when the W came up, I heard the door open and my mother's high heels tormenting the tiles. She always stuck her head in the dining room with the basket in hand and a reproach on her lips. Have you done your homework, honey? Comb your hair, honey. Honey, clean up. Honey, set the table. Honey, you need to sit up straight. Honey eternally on her lips, as if she'd forgotten my name. Sometimes she'd look over at my father from up high, from her lacquered-fingernail Olympus, and scold him:

"Really? Another scarf? We'll have to open a stall at the market soon. Don't worry, I'll say I made them." And without waiting for a response, she'd vanish into the kitchen.

And me there with the W block burning in my fingers. Dad's eyes expectant, waiting for a word, but at that moment there was only one, and eventually I spit it out: Witch. My father laughed, pretending he hadn't gotten the allusion. But hadn't he? Really?

I went to the kitchen to get the urn and huddled back down in the armchair, surrounding it with my body like a pearl, the sunflowers gazing at me all the while. Father, why did you leave me when I was just learning to walk alone? And you too now, Guim.

The chair's wings and arms enveloped me, and I enveloped the urn, and the urn rested against my vacant uterus, and the four of us were in the house, a weird matryoshka doll. Me, trapped among all the dead with an ox that wants to devour me.

128 Days Earlier

In the morning, I gathered my courage and went down to the store. Sooner or later I'd have to, it was better to get it over with. When my phone got service, the messages started pouring in. Carles, he never gives up. Your mother with her French accent, broken. My mother, how dare she!

Mercè was in the doorway smoking. My Mercè didn't smoke. They've switched her out. I want my yokel, not some sooty battleaxe. When she saw me, she tossed her cigarette, metamorphosed into the her from before, and came toward me, open armed, limping slightly.

"Oh, dear, how terrible, how horrible, and so young. You and him both, so young." She takes me in her soft embrace, the last missing doll, but this Russian girl stinks of nicotine. "You've got to be brave, look ahead, you've got your whole life before you, dear, if you need anything . . ." The hug, still soft, has turned cloying like cotton candy. "Dear, you're a bag of bones, you need to eat, how else will you keep your strength up? I can feel your ribs! Are you sure it's best for you to be in the woods all alone? And with no TV! You ought to go back to the city, with your friends, go out, see the shops and lights, people, life, the movies, concerts, you'll wither here, honey. Think it over."

She pulled away from me to dry her humid eyes with a corner of her apron.

"Tell me, though, how are you?"

I thanked her for the words of encouragement and mumbled something about carrying on and how life keeps going; the thing I was expected to say.

"First your mother, widowed so young, and now you. It's not right! God always seems to punish the good ones. Because your mother, she always was a good one. And generous! The hoops she jumped through to be able to take care of Miss Antònia when she had the detached retina! You don't remember, of course, you hadn't even been weaned yet. Imagine a woman with a child so small, and every three days she did her shopping for her, and on Sundays she took her a roast. I can still see her coming late to Mass on Sundays, dish in hand. And your father refused to set foot in the church . . . even on the days when she sang there."

She stopped talking, waiting for me to chime in that she's right, to take sides against my father. Me mute. I didn't want to get into an argument about my mother and father, it would have gotten ugly. She went on:

"I'd have loved to have a mother who could sing like that."

"I'd have been happy enough to have a mother who sang to me."

"She got lucky with all that with the Minipimer and the dubbing," and as she said this, she looked up at the framed poster, as though venerating a virgin. "I bought two, one for me and one for Manel, who was about to marry the older daughter from the Grau house. 2800 pesetas each, with the mincer attachment and everything. Each time I used it, I'd remember your poor mother. And when that sassy Fina ducked out of the wedding, I had no choice but to hold on to Manel's. Between the two of them, I must have spent fifteen years using your mother's Minipimer."

"So how come you never married?"

"Taking care of Manel is already half a marriage, the last thing I needed was to make more work for myself, in my day things were different, I didn't want to be more of a slave than I already was. But hey, that's enough about me."

She went to the back of the shop and brought me a pot of macaroni I accepted to keep from offending her. I thought it strange she was limping so much.

"Damned osteoporosis. Four years ago I broke my hip, and when the weather changes, I still feel it. A hell of a thing, the way your bones shrink when you age. Be smart, don't skimp on the yogurt and cheese."

I thought that infirmity suited her: she's so soft, her body refuses to give her hard bones the way God intended. She informed me that my mother called to find out if I'd returned to the house. I didn't respond. On the counter, I saw half-finished embroidery and thought once more of the scarves.

"Mercè, could you do me a favor?"

She nodded enthusiastically. I thought she'd be ready for whatever I asked of her: turn back time, read Reiker to me out loud, make my mother disappear, resuscitate the dead, bring me back my child, my husband, my father, mix a potion so I could forget it all, an incantation to turn me into someone else. But just:

"Next time you go to Vilamitja, could you buy me some knitting needles and a couple of skeins of thick wool? One green. Forest green. And one grey. Don't worry too much about getting the colors right, it's just to kill time. No rush."

"You got that from your father, right?"

Before leaving, I told her the gale had knocked the panes out of the window in the living room. At the very least, I got out of calling Manel.

THAT DAY

You wanted to be the procuress of literature
and you're no more than a bootblack of language
working the streets for two bits.

127 Days Earlier

Before lunch, I sit at the computer. The momentum from three days ago is dying down. I'm a pilot losing thrust against the friction of life. I need to write out in the void, where nothing is there to stop me.

I smirch a few pages. I've promised myself I won't let a day pass without working, but everything distracts me: the breeze entering the broken window, the ray of light impertinently projected over the notecards, the buzzing of two flies roving like two gossips at the door to church, the stone on the wall with its snail shape, an itch on my ankle, in my nose, on the edge of my soul.

Finally I get up and warm up a dish of macaroni.

I return to the computer. I see the story on the desktop. I turn on the printer. I print it. I bind it with a paperclip. I put on my shoes and go outside. Embarrassment consumes me before I reach the spot and I want to turn back—where are you headed, cretin?—but I keep going with the nine sheets in my fingers and the note stuck to them.

I find a white van parked on the edge of the road. What's it doing here, now that the asparagus and mushrooms are out of season? What's it doing here at four in the afternoon, in this inhumane heat? Because it's hot, too hot for late June. The road leads into an open field. It's an oven. A crematorium.

Guim.

I don't have water with me, and my mouth is dry. After a

while, Flavi's shack appears, a mirage in the middle of the coals. I creep up to it.

I'm so thirsty. The sound of the running faucet escapes from the open window, the clank of plates and glasses. I crouched in the entrance. A drop of sweat drains between my breasts. I slide the stack of papers under the door. The water doesn't stop flowing. In twenty minutes, you'll be home and you'll have as much as you want. My thirst is burning. I stand up. Flavi turns off the tap. He's coming toward me. I flee. But ten steps in:

"Mei, wait!"

I turned and saw him with the papers in his hand. Me red down to my pinkie toes. Incandescent, scarlet. I laughed.

"I feel like an idiot."

"You're right to," he responded. "Come on in."

I obeyed, abashed.

"Tea?"

"With honey, please. But a little water first, I'm parched."

He passed me a glass of water.

"A few days ago I wrote a story and I need someone to read it and tell me what they think. But I'm wickedly ashamed. It could be absolute garbage. It probably is. Garbage. I should have tossed it. You need to be frank, tell me what you think, no mercy. If you want, I mean."

"I'm on it," he said, sitting down on the sofa.

And me, No, absolutely not, take your time with it, read it later. And him, If you want honesty, this way you'll get all the honesty I can muster, there's no faking or ducking you now, that's a guarantee.

I wanted to disappear.

"No, please."

But Flavi had made up his mind. He motioned for me to be quiet and go get the tea, and he added:

"Hypertrophied embarrassment is an evolutionary error.

Grab a book in the meanwhile. Next to the fridge there's an anthology of Ferrer I've been rereading."

I got up from the sofa. I couldn't stand the idea of seeing his face while he read my story, which now struck me as absolutely devoid of interest. A piece of shit, I told myself, it's not ripe, it's worthless, worthless, you fucked up, Mei, you should have revised it further. What were you thinking, faker, imbecile. You and your cheap enumerations.

I waited in the kitchen in front of the kettle, scrutinizing the spice rack. Oregano, rosemary, some other herb I couldn't identify. I saw him from behind, reading me. The bastard, he's got to know he's torturing me. Who is he, anyway? Why did I give a story to a guy I don't know from Adam?

I poured the boiling water into the cups. I took care to make no noise so as not to distract him. I flipped through the Ferrer anthology, it had been years since I read him. *Què és un home? Una mà al pit i l'altra al ventre d'una dona.* But I was incapable of reading, my head was over on the sofa, with Flavi. I closed the book. In a bowl, papers with a doctor's scrawl. The phone number of a certain Manel. The same Manel? There are lots of Manels. Over there, each page turned augmenting my humiliation. Then a giggle escaped him. Is he making fun of me or what? You should go right now, he'll come find you if he feels like it.

I took refuge in the bathroom. I pissed meticulously, as if my life depended on it: unbuttoning my pants, unzipping, lowering my panties to my knees, categorically parallel, letting the stream out, carefully tearing the paper, not ruining the edges, folding it into a perfect rectangle, wiping off, repeating the whole process backward, drawing out each step. And the image of Flavi on the couch with my dumb story. I washed my hands looking at myself in the mirror, so little you could only see bits of yourself, or else you had to stand too far away. On the shelf, his toothbrush, blue, and a tube of toothpaste. Behind the door, an orange towel.

I couldn't resist the temptation of opening the medicine cabinet. How vile. And what a bad idea: now I don't know what to do about what I saw and shouldn't have seen, I've always been a bad liar. Next to the razorblades, acetaminophen, ibuprofen, and other medicines I've never seen in my life, between the band-aids and rubbing alcohol and nail scissors, amid the trappings of a vulgar everyman's life, I found something that maybe isn't what I think, because what the hell do I know about all that, anyway, apart from cliches absorbed from the movies, but it did appear to be that thing I wished it wasn't and now I can't ask, now I'll have to pretend I don't know, and in reality I don't know because I can't be sure those objects mean what I think they mean, however much everything seems to say that yes, they do: because what else could they be if not, the baggie, the rubber tie, the syringe? Was that why he knew the sanatorium *all too well?*

I touched nothing to keep from displacing even a millimeter any item that might give me away. I shut the door to the medicine cabinet cautiously, like someone finishing a house of cards, afraid that with a touch of my fingers it would collapse noisily and Flavi would learn of my turpitude.

I carried the cups from the dining room to the table by the sofa. I sat down and looked at him. He didn't seem to notice and wasn't discomfited, though that's what I was going for. I examined the crooks of his elbows, no bruises, no track marks. Maybe the movies overdo it and you can't always tell, or maybe I'm going off the deep end.

He's reached the last page. So I'm out. Get up and go. Tear the papers from his hands and burn them. This story's going nowhere, you twit. I took a sip of tea, but I couldn't swallow the ridicule, it was stuck in my throat, nor could I rid myself of knowing what I shouldn't know and what could just as well be my imagination. My hands were sweating.

Now he'll tell me it's a flop, or worse, he'll look elsewhere and say, Oh it's good, and I'll be able to tell he didn't like it at all, that he's just saying this from pity, because he knows I need encouragement right now. You can't tell a lonesome widow what she's written is a piece of trash that makes you want to hide your head in shame, right.

"Don't look at me like that. It's good. That much I'm sure of. The language is impeccable, the adjectives surefooted, free of excesses, the metaphors sculptural, you can read it at any number of levels, the protagonist is believable, not at all dull, the end with the fox tumbling over the cliff, that hits the target. Maybe the digression in the middle is a bit too long, and the beginning doesn't suck you in, but honestly, you did better than I thought."

And all I said in response was Thanks, while I repeated to myself, This guy told you to write and he didn't believe in you one bit. You don't know who he is, you saw what he had hidden in the bathroom. Don't listen.

I've just sat at the computer with my cup belching steam. I've got a few ideas I like, I was turning them over at midnight, when I woke up and couldn't get back to sleep. Today's going good.

But Manel's voice erupts through the window.

"Come, Truffle!"

I stick my head out cautiously and right away pull it back into my shell. I saw him coming up the stairs carrying two panes of glass. Not today, not now.

I remain there in the middle of the living room, immobile outside, seething within. So now what?

Manel knocks at the door.

No, no, no.

I remain there still, unable to decide. I could open up and blow him off with some excuse—mourning, my period, a migraine—or maybe start crying so he'll see it's a bad time. I could tell him I'm about to go out, leave him alone to fix the window. But no, not now.

He knocks again.

No way I'm opening. I don't want to.

I hear the sound of keys.

It can't be. He's coming in. What do I do?

I run toward the cellar. I scutter down the stairs. Irregular steps. My feet too big. But I don't kill myself. Downstairs, I emerge in a dull light. I squeeze against the wall. My hands are sweating. In a rush, I left the door open. He enters. His greasy dog will sniff me out, will find me, what do I say? Go upstairs and say you were getting something. Manel's steps in the doorway. He says:

"Stay here. Lie down."

He opens a door. Pisses. In my toilet. A pup marking its territory. He doesn't flush, doesn't wash his hands. He'll be scattering particles of his dick all over the house. On the doorknobs, the window, my desk.

Now he comes this way, he's seen the open door, maybe he's got tools down here. What are you doing, idiot? I should have hidden in my room, I would have been safer there. You're too slow, Mei. But now it's done. The dog didn't come in, you've got a chance. I sit on the cold ground between the piles of cardboard boxes, slide my knees inside my T-shirt, and my mother, Honey, don't do that, you'll stretch it out.

I hear steps, he comes close warbling a Cuban song, *Oh my seagull, flying circles over the sea.* Now he is coming. I hold my breath, my jugular is thumping. He goes to the dining room. *And driven by the wind, you fly until you reach the sunny shore.* Metallic noises. Tools. He must be installing the panes. I don't move a millimeter. *Shore of sweet memories.* Ah, the Cubano, right.

How long does it take to change two windowpanes? And the measurements, how does he know the measurements? He must have come yesterday while I was at Flavi's. Of course. How many times has he been in here without my knowing it? I should change the lock. I don't have the balls. My tea steaming on the table, he must know I'm at home, he'll come looking for me. Maybe not the lock, but I can install a sliding bolt, yes, I'll do that so he won't come to the house when I'm inside. I could just pop up, pretend I was outside and didn't hear him. But I'm barefoot and a bad actor to boot. So? I don't owe him an explanation. You just go and stand up to him. Hammerblows.

What if he comes in at night and spies on me while I sleep? No, no way, but who knows . . . For a moment, I see myself from without, curled up here, and the desire to laugh overwhelms me. What the fuck are you doing, Mei? When I tell Flavi, he'll crack up. I must be an idiot. But I can't reveal myself now, what would he say? Hey, Manel, what's up? You know, I was just hiding out in the cellar, but I got over it. Yo, Manel, you like creeping into my house without my permission, right? Manel, drop the bullshit and show your cards. What do you want, Cubano?

A sliding bolt. Later.

This is taking forever and I give in to this absurd torment I've concocted for myself. Taking advantage of being trapped, I make a list of ways to occupy my time. Writing, I've got that taken care of. Finding a still spot in the Muntanya where I can swim, going to look for fossils and adding to my collection thirty years later. Making fig jam; they must be ripe now and soon it'll be too late. Make a scarf when Mercè gives me the yarn; I should go down to the shop and see if she's got it. Read. Visit Flavi. Make a pile of croquettes. Masturbate—how long's it been since I touched myself? I might have to put some work in to get the hormones flowing. Have a wax: why? For what? For whom?

A commotion interrupts the mental list. Son of a bitch, he says, and I fret over whether he's broken the window frame. I can see him now coming to the house at all hours, trapped here with me and the irreparable window. Condemned, the two of us. Me hiding away and him pissing in my toilet, on infinite repeat.

I need to do something to kill time. Kill time, the most horrible murder of all, my father used to say. The boxes, why not? I open the one closest to me, very slowly to keep from making noise, as if I were handing a bomb. And when I see what's inside, I realize it actually was a bomb. A cardboard bomb full of mincer attachments. I count them. Nine Minipimers, still unused.

The outmoded typeface and the tones of the photo catapult

me back to the dining room in the apartment in Horta. Mom, me, and her macrame buddy Lina, who was a seamstress and always wore flashy shirts with shoulder pads fit for a rugby player, the three of us on the brown three-seater sofa. In eighty-two, everything was brown, the color of shit.

"Will you put it on, for God's sake," Lina grumbles, taking a sip of coffee just after.

My mother dawdles before getting up and walking to the television-altar. She takes the VHS tape out of the case; she only ever grabs it with her fingertips, she must think it's made of porcelain, or that manhandling the tape will spoil it or dispel the sacred aura she's endowed it with. She puts it into the machine she's bought for the lone purpose of watching herself time and time again performing her cathode *zub-zubs*, no matter that she pretends she bought it for us both, on evenings when *The Twilight Zone* and *Mike Hammer* aren't on, we die of boredom. She got an account at the video store, but she's never rented anything. Sometimes I think she loves me but doesn't know another way to show it, and I even feel sorry for her. So it goes.

The point is we only ever use the thing to play the tape of the ad, always following the same ritual: the friend, the coffee, the three-seater sofa the color of shit, the insistence, the video, praise, replay. It's like going to Mass without ever leaving home. Except that we still go to Mass, too, every Sunday at noon. We adore ceremonies.

Lina is excited. Having a friend who's on TV makes her feel important. Through affinity. It's almost as if she herself were the figure in the ad. She sparkles. A zealot aroused at the sight of a miracle.

And then: the images seen a thousand times on the Telefunken that was a gift from my grandparents. Her made up, splendid in a red apron, cracking an egg or chanting Valdino's allegro with her celestial timbre—how I've always hated Valdino, and how I hated myself when I found myself humming it without meaning to outside or on the bus; I had it in my head, *earworm*, the idea fits, a parasitic larva that bores into your brain through the cochlear nerve and colonizes you. Then comes the disgrace, her—how poorly she acts—pretending the camera's surprised her. Her hair is so black. The close-up shot of the mayonnaise being whipped followed by images of the mincer attachment kneading pink meat was nigh obscene, the static lines were like a prototype of the skin flicks cut through with static you could just barely pick up on channels you hadn't paid for in the old days. And with frame change, her: *zub-zub*. The mincing sorceress. Amen.

After communion, Lina, like all the friends who came before her and all who would come after, would ask, in exaltation, to see it again. My mother would rewind: the VHS hummed like a pesky fly. Me in the meanwhile mute, condemned to the armchair; I can't leave, It's bad manners, she scolded me the day I dared stand. You can't get up halfway through Mass either, you must observe the sacred ceremony. The two of them on the sofa, pressed in close. Their sofa, my armchair, two religious dogmas in opposition. And Lina:

"You must be proud to have your mama on TV, no?" her voice high, the way nitwits do when they talk with a child, as if they were deaf. I could tell her I'm on my period, that I know when people are in love they lick each other between the legs, that she shouldn't disrespect me. But I smile, the same way I still do now when obscenities you're not supposed to utter pass through my head. The day they extirpate my smile, it'll be the apocalypse.

"And all thanks to a friend of Tomàs's," when she says my father's name, she always pauses so the silence will crush us and adopts a slightly twisted pose: she must think this makes her more of a widow, reality weighing down on her and forcing her to walk through life hunched over. "Yes, it was an old friend from college who works in advertising now."

["Neus, I was looking at you just now and telling myself you'd be perfect for an ad we're working on. What do you think," the man must have said over lunch on the first anniversary of father's death, leaning in toward her, maybe.]

"You look so gorgeous dear," says Lina, repeating the same thing as the others. Always the same words. *I believe in God, the Father Almighty, Creator of Heaven and earth.* The liturgy. So gorgeous, so gorgeous, so gorgeous.

"Mom, I have to do my homework . . ."

"Don't be impolite, honey."

"You have a very pretty mama, you know?" I notice an incredulous tone in Lina, she doesn't believe a runt like me could be born of a woman so exuberant.

". . ."

"And independent!"

"A single mother, I've never had a job, you know, and the pension only stretches so far. Probably he felt sorry for me."

["It's an ad for a Minipimer. They pay well and they'll give you ten or twelve of them for your friends. I'll call you to confirm," he uttered—who knows?—with a hand on her knee, and she did not proclaim: *Lord, I am not worthy that thou shouldest come under my roof.*]

"You look thirty years old, you're so lucky."

"Don't exaggerate, Lina."

"I'm not exaggerating one bit."

And always, as New Year's came into view:

"Honey, you need to go confess before Christmas."

But maybe she was the one with things to confess, not I, so she could stride spick and span into the new year.

"You look like Hedy Lamarr, and with a voice to boot. Have you shown it to Maite?"

O Lamb of God, that takest away the sins of the world, have mercy upon us.

"Poor Remei is the one who's suffered most."

Eyes lowered, hands folded chaplainwise, a moment of prayer for the orphan child.

"Hum me a bit of that Mazzolo, Neus."

We praise thee, we bless thee, we worship thee, we glorify thee, we give thee thanks for thy great glory.

"It's Valdino, not Mazzolo, the *allegro* from *In Bloom.*"

"Your hair's so black!"

"*Zub-zub.*"

"What a good mother, what sacrifices, what a hard life, how I admire you, envy you, really, with that smart little daughter who's all day reading, even if she is a little scrawny, and then you: so gorgeous, so gorgeous, so gorgeous." She doesn't say this aloud, she shouts it with her eyes.

"No, for now there's no more ads. But I'm dubbing a few things," and she pronounces *dubbing* with an expert tone as though she's devoted her entire life to it.

"Honey, rewind that and put it back in the box."

Our Father, who art in Heaven. That must be the only truth in the entire rite. If that.

Lina left in a daze. And the day after next or the following week would come Carme, Mariàngels, Maite. And me in the armchair, ever in the armchair, the good daughter. May you go in peace.

I close the box. Better never to open it again. Manel is still up there fidgeting.

Immobility and silence turn me drowsy. I rest my forehead on my knees, close my eyes, my hair cascades down. When will it end? I submerge myself in the dullness of time stretching on. I'm a machine on standby. The sound of the hammer in the tool box awakens me. My ass and my spine ache. I need to piss. I don't know what time it is. What day it is. I'm going.

The hammer again. This will never end. I'll wind up pissing myself. How long have I been here? An hour? Two?

He passes by the door, entering the kitchen. I hear the faucet. He must be drinking water. He's thirsty, me too. Walks whistling back to the window. Everything hurts. I need to piss. I consider just doing it: who cares, when he leaves, I'll clean up, end of story. But what if he does find me? He'll see me all covered in piss, tell my mother, they'll think I'm a madwoman.

After an eternity, he finishes, drags things from one place to another. He turns back, moves something—my stuff? What the hell's he doing? He goes back to the kitchen. Indecipherable noises.

If he touches the urn, I'll kill him.

Now, finally, he's leaving. Or not. He goes to the other end of the house. To the bedrooms. I think. But I'm not sure. Could be the vestibule. Shove off for once!

He must be in my room, or the one next to it, my room when I was a kid. I listen closely. A moan? Maybe I'm wrong. I already know what the urn will call me: Paranoid. Maybe he's just looking at the other windows, I try to convince myself.

At last, when it no longer seemed possible, he left. I got up like an arthritic grandmother. I went to piss without touching any of the door handles. Awaiting me in the toilet was the yellowy urine he left behind as collateral. I pissed on top of it to reestablish my claim to the territory. And flushed.

On the kitchen table, a note and a bag.

> *Remei:*
> *I came to fix the window. I'm leaving your order from Mercè here. If you need anything, just ask.*
> *Manel*

Not one misspelled word, weird.

I opened the bag. Two sets of knitting needles, four skeins of yarn. The perfect colors, I couldn't have done better myself, I'd have started second-guessing and would have wound up with something less fitting. I left it all there and put on my rubber gloves.

I ran the sponge over all the doorknobs, the faucet in the kitchen, the glass in the sink, the window and the new panes, the pen beside the note, the urn, which looked at me indulgently. Then I threw out the sponge. Stiff, the sheets on the bed, bearing the outline of someone sitting down, maybe it was me when I put on my panties in the morning, but then I remember that moan I'm not sure I heard. I tore them off the bed and stuck them in the washer.

By now, it was three in the afternoon, and my big ideas for the morning had vanished. I should have just opened the door for him. I finished Mercè's macaroni and went to the hardware store in Vilamitja.

Chrome, deadbolt, key, no key? A universe of possibilities exists to keep the outside world from coming in. I was looking for an old-style wrought iron sliding bolt, I told the employee. It's odd for a stranger to tell you what you need: why can't everything be as easy as entering a store and asking?

I was imagining a lock like in a medieval castle, but they only had a basic one in wrought iron, the Black Castle Deadbolt Latch, so I took it: ten centimeters, it looked like a mini machine gun. I wasn't sold on the electric drill, despite the necromancer's insistence: I didn't want to tell him I had enough holes in my life as is. Eventually I gave in and bought a hand drill. I did allow him to give me detailed instructions about the installation of the device that would protect me from intruders. Now it strikes me I should have asked him if he perhaps had a sphinx on sale.

At nine in the evening, after more than an hour breaking my wrist with the goddamned spinning crank, I had the lock in its place. I opened it and closed it four, five, six times.

Zzz-crick-crack-crick-crack-zzz.

I found a certain pleasure in the smoothness of its action and the dry sound of the barred door.

Zzz-crick-crack-crick-crack-zzz.

Nobody's getting in here.

A t ten in the morning, it was eighty degrees out, but the stone walls kept me cold and the Black Castle kept me safe from undesired intrusions. A little fortress. Finally. My temple, my prison, my oasis.

I spent the day at home, in panties and nothing else, breasts dangling and hairy legs on display. At the computer, I revised the first few pages, serving my daily self-imposed sentence with an unmistakable feeling of fruitlessness.

Then, sitting in the armchair, I started the scarf. One loop after the other, the needles gliding through. A third-rate spinning jenny. In, out, twist, pull, and back. How I struggled to unearth what I already knew. So many years! And what a surreal image, me there naked and sweating with a thick ball of wool in my lap.

And now and then a cold tea, a crust of bread with honey; go out nude to the fig tree and let the forest stare; feel the soft figs, black whale's tears, pull one down fat as the palm of my hand—a drop slips down its flank like a lactating breast—tear the streaked skin and sink my teeth in the redness of the pulp; wet the nape of my neck with the ice-cold water from the well; go back inside, latch the door, open the window. The sharp air surrounding me.

I stretched out on the rug while the sun filtered in and licked my breasts, hand in my panties quivering until it provoked a groan. And I stayed there, laid out on the ground, with the acid mixture of a longing to cry and to laugh unrestrained, on the verge of gutting myself like a ripe fig.

The Day Before

*You'd rather they'd chopped off your hand
than wander with these doll's hands through the world
every goddamned day you have left alive.*

A t midmorning, Flavi rescued me from my sterile peni-
tentiary, which today (too) has served for nothing but
to blemish a page with mediocre words. I opened the
door and he informed me we were going on an excursion. Go
put your shoes on, and I hurried to obey as if I'd been waiting
for him for some time and I suppressed the drone of the story
with the medicine cabinet and the syringe. If you're not certain,
there's no point in ruminating over it.

I asked where we were going and if it was far, but he wanted to
keep me on edge. In truth, though, not knowing where he was taking me and putting myself in his hands amused me in a puerile way.

"What do you have in your bag?"

And him:

"Everything in due time."

Seeing I'd get nothing out of him, I changed the subject and
told him about Manel's visit two days ago. From a distance, the
entire scene looked even more ridiculous. But why didn't you
come out of your hiding place? Flavi asked me as the two of us
cracked up.

Then he said out of the blue:

"Manel's not a bad guy. He's got a good heart. He just wants
to help you."

"You want to help me, too, and you don't stare at my boobs."

He acted like he hadn't heard me and took a few slices of
melon from his bag.

"Want some?"

I sank my teeth in with relish and the sweet juice dripped down my chin. Help, he says, help. And I wanted to reply, He comes into my house whenever he feels like it, grabbing machines or taking measurements, who knows how many times he's come in without my knowing. He goes through the rooms and rummages in my things. And that moan, which I did hear, even if my brain tried to convince me otherwise to mollify me. I see him now, sitting on my bed jerking it with his crusty hand, picking my panties up off the ground and thinking about my mother. Super best friends indeed! The local Rock Hudson. Help me, huh?

But all I said was:

"I don't like Manel, I don't trust him. How well do you know him?"

"Pretty well, we play chess every Thursday. He's good, the bastard studies openings and gambits on the net and he can whip my ass. He hasn't had it easy. His parents died when he was nineteen and he had to take care of Mercè, who was just eleven. He always dreamed of traveling, and he only ever left Sorrius once, to go to Cuba. But as the lady said, for some people a single memory lasts a lifetime."

"Cuba? I thought they called him the Cubano because he had a thing for habaneras."

"He went alright. It was in seventy-three or seventy-four. Can you imagine? He'd never even left home, and there he was in Cuba, a hillbilly clutching a glass of rum and a woman before a deep blue sea and the silk-white sands, taking a bright-colored car to Matanzas or Cienfuegos with a black guy playing guitar in the front seat, orishas on every corner, him belting out his verses under a colonial-style colonnade: *With the equator's circle cinched / around the little world of her waist / the black woman, the new woman / strides forward in her serpent robe.* The bright lights of communism, before the planned economy blinded everyone with utopia. You should hear him talking about Mariela's sunburnt skin, devout as a poet."

"In other words, he went there to fuck, right?"

"Jeez, you should listen to yourself. Let's talk about something else."

We walked an hour and a half, now sheltered from the searing sun beneath the shadows of the trees, now its victim, with our drenched T-shirts clinging to our backs. We left his house and the beehives behind us, Blunted Crest, and the sheep pen of the stymied traveler. And always more woods, more brush, more insects. Cicadas intoning incomprehensible elegies.

We hugged the right bank of a river with already weary steps, until finally he proclaimed:

"Voila, the Red Gorge."

In front of us, the river opened, forming a little lake edged in a strange red, like an open wound between water and land. On the other end, large smooth stones the sun tried to melt.

We sat on a kind of beach of tiny gravel. I grabbed a handful and threw it in the water, and it sank with a merry clatter. In the background, the incessant murmur of the water.

Soaked in sweat, I was still panting from the heat and the walk. Flavi stood up.

"Shall we?" he asked, nodding toward the water.

"What? Swim?" I asked, incredulous.

"Obviously. What else?"

"I don't have a bathing suit."

"Me neither," he said, laughing as he took off his shirt to reveal a torso of prominent ribs and the occasional badly placed hair.

"I haven't shaved."

I wanted to disappear for saying something so stupid, for even thinking it.

"Me neither!" he exclaimed with a laugh.

And without further ado, he took off his remaining clothes

and with two long strides jumped in the water, showing me his meager bottom with its high bones and sunken cheeks.

Why not?

I stripped off my shirt, my bra, my shoes, my socks, my shorts: I undid my ponytail and shook out my hair; I ran my thumbs under the waistband of my panties and stopped, What are you doing? and right afterward, Fuck it! I took them off and ran in. One, two, three, go.

The ground disappeared.

My whole body sank underwater. The entirety of me pricked, my hair floated in slow motion impersonating black algae. The cold rose up my spine to my brain and crept in, awakening me from the lethargy I've been living in for too long.

When I raised my head from the frozen current, the light seemed rawer, the colors riper, the air clearer, and I shouted like a savage. The frozen current passed between my legs, nudging me along, the way bleach carries spots and filth away. Outside and inside, everything so limpid.

"See how the forest cures all ills?" Flavi said.

"What's it going to cure you of?"

"Not now, Mei," and he dove down.

Emerging from the water, my body was resplendent and new. I hurried to wrap myself in the towel he handed me.

"You hungry? It's getting close to four."

From his bag, he produced all sorts of things: vegetable couscous, hummus, olives, goat cheese, two glasses, a bottle of red wine. I ate like a starved beast. There in the shadows, the wine slipped down with ease and warmed my belly and head.

"If it wasn't for you, I'd end up like one of those dry sunflowers so full of seeds that they can't even lift their head to look at the sun. Thanks."

Flavi shrugged and shoved a handful of raisins into his mouth.

"With its Gothic name, this place must have one of your legends behind it. The Red Gorge! Something bloody for sure."

"There is a legend, but maybe it's a bad time to tell it . . ."

"Come on, don't make me beg."

"It's just . . ."

"What? It's about a woman who gets her husband drunk, throws him out, and he crashes his carriage and dies?" While I said this, I filled my wine glass to drown the insolence of my words.

"As you wish . . . centuries ago, at Castle Clarafort, there lived a count and his wife, the countess Brunisenda. You know the castle? Well, the remains of it . . ."

I shook my head.

"It's on top of that hill, you can't see it from here, the tower collapsed. I'll take you. Anyway, Brunisenda had a taste for breast and thigh meat, if you catch my drift. Her father wouldn't let her go to the convent as she wished, who knows if it was penitence or her predilections that drove her or to find her coreligionists, because lesbianism was forbidden back then and they say the convents were where the action was."

He stretched out. I did the same.

"Her father married her off to a count, a fairly decent guy for the time, but still, a man, and he wanted descendants. She was still a young thing, no older than twenty, and only had eyes for a maidservant she shared her secrets and nocturnal spasms with, and there was no way she was going to let a stinky, whiny monster show up and rain on her parade; they'd have had to take on a wet nurse, and the more people were there, the greater the danger.

"Every night, the count made her lie down on the bed and open up and undergo the fertilization ritual. She must have admired the details of the canopy amid her intercrural reveries about her beloved. Every night the count dipped his wick and every night Brunisenda played her role of chaste lady who withstood it only to bear offspring. Maybe it would have been better for her to just get pregnant and have the kid, but you know, people are how they are. Or maybe the legend errs here and Brunisenda liked meat as well as fish and was hot to trot every single night.

"One thing's for sure though: she didn't want children. So she followed the prescription of a sorceress from the forest, and every month, when her breasts began to feel tender, her lady friend prepared a potion for her, and in blackest nights they'd come down to the gorge, where Brunisenda would release her blood into the water.

"Things went on like this for two years, and the count was well pissed with this defective lady they'd palmed off on him. He brought in doctors with their philters and unguents. The count started tossing and turning in bed, more and more exasperated. What would he do without heirs? His entire existence would be futile. He wondered whether it might be prudent to look for another women who could give him children he could raise as if they'd come from Brunisenda, but his religious scruples wouldn't allow it. Then, one night, a light turned on: maybe the problem was the ritual itself, maybe when he penetrated her punctually each day he was doing so at an inauspicious, infertile hour.

"He ran off to his wife's room, but he found no one there. He walked back and forth throughout the whole castle, shouting for her in vain. From the tower, he saw a lit torch in the middle of the forest. Shaken, he imagined she was kidnapped or worse, and grabbed his sword and ran to the gorge. When he got close, he hid out behind a large boulder. He saw his wife nude in the water and the lady with the torch in her hand, she said, *That's it, it's all out*, and gave her a kiss on the lips.

"The count, seething with rage, ran over to the two women and gave them a smack that knocked them to the earth. *Animals must live like animals* was his verdict, and the next day he had them chained to two trees, far apart, so they couldn't touch, and there he left them to die on the edge of the water.

"And they say that even now, every month when the moon begins to shrink, the edges of the pool turn red from the blood of Brunisenda, who continues to menstruate underground."

He stopped talking for a moment, before adding:

"But nowadays the people in the know say the legend's false and the red comes from some algae or other in the river."

I wanted to pour myself more wine, but the bottle was empty.

"Brunisenda, what a pretty name."

On the way back, I almost killed myself descending the slatey slope, but made it out with no more than a twisted ankle. Flavi walked behind me pontificating, Careful, that slate is tricky, it's ungodly slick, didn't you notice? It's unnatural! I like imagining it's the fossilized scales of some paleolithic fish, a colossal fish, but the scientists stubbornly contradict me; they've got no sense of poetry, they say it's a metamorphic rock, clay transformed by the effects of extreme temperature and pressure. The same happens to people with temperature and pressure, right? They flatten us out until they turn us lethal. Now that I look, from behind I can see the scales hidden in your hair, vixen! As the poet said: *grisalla de pensaments, de somnis*. It's a metaphoric stone, not a metamorphic one, they don't have a clue!

With the excuse of my twisted ankle, we stopped at his house.

"Don't be headstrong, let's have a drop of ratafia, it's the only bottle left from last year. I've got the new vintage out sitting in the sun."

And I, not daring to tell him I couldn't care less about ratafia, wound up giving in, even if I was still a little woozy from the wine, he was too, because he absolutely insisted on reciting me poems by some Italians I've never heard of in my life.

He stood up straight, and with a glow in his cheeks, filled the dining room with luminous words. *Un bubbolio lontano*, he said, stressing the Italian diction, mouthing consonants so expansive I could have reached out and touched them, consonants you could make a mattress of and lie down on for a century. It didn't matter to me what a *bubbolio* was or wasn't, those b's exploding from his lips carried me away. And then *Tacciono i boschi e i fiumi . . . e ne la notte bruna . . .* He fired unsparingly, a goddamn Kalashnikov of verse. Ratatatatatatata: *illuminami dal tuo buio.* Brighten me with your darkness. And me: *I la foscor s'il·luminà de sobte perquè érem dos a contradir la nit.* And him: Hush, hush, let's get it straight, two decasyllables: *Tota la meva vida es lliga a tu, com en la nit les flames a la fosca.*

The ratafia dwindled, all at once it wasn't so bad. I got up and summoned that fragment of the streets covered in moss from that book of Palathy's I kept on my nightstand for so long and read like a missal to ease my mind. I recited it in English with closed eyes:

I dipped into the streets paved with moss. That green, its ancestral peal tolling for me, summoning me. I couldn't help but lay down in that lushness, though it suffocated me like a thick second skin. And I remained there, waiting for something that would never come, until the night became irreversible.

But it didn't stop there, we were absorbed in this strange duel, taking turns unveiling resplendent words and laughing or hushing or grumbling at the other's selection.

At one point, I went to look for the copy of *Solitude* I had seen on his shelves that first day, and opened it to the last chapter:

"The hours, imperturbable, had rolled meekly over Mila, always seated and immobile, like a vigilant statue, in her puddle of sun . . ."

"Stop, that phrase is fucking painful!" And then, in a

borrowed voice: "*The hours, imperturbable, had rolled meekly over Mila.* What a droopy phrase, for Christ's sake, she was just raped. What could be meek about those hours! It needs something more visceral. Let's hear it, Mrs. Literati, what would you put there?"

I drank my glass in one sip.

"The hours flattened Mila like a steamroller, the stone minutes hurled themselves undeterred over the precipice of life."

"Not bad, but a little pompous, maybe, no? Come on, let's make a clean draft, Víctor Català-style."

"Don't blaspheme," I replied, but we read the three pages of the last chapter recomposing them aloud (for that alone we earned our place in literary Hell) until we reached the moment where the inflows of solitude crystallized bitterly into fate.

It had gotten late. Before leaving, I went to the bathroom to empty out and yes, to take a look at the medicine cabinet too. The sight of the syringe didn't have the same effect as the other day. I opened the baggie, it was empty. Who knows, maybe he broke a leg and had to inject heparin. Or whatever else. You and your ideas, Mei.

I'll walk you back, he said, but I told him no, the ratafia had cured my ankle and I could go for a stroll on my own.

I floated home in a haze of ratafia and the dust of ideas, repeating to myself that this was all that life was, bathing in the gorge, laughing, reading, sharing a bottle of wine, no need to overthink it. The beasts of the forest shifted as I passed, but I wasn't afraid. Not at all.

I climbed the stairs crooked, making the usual tally of the steps—fifteen, no more, no less—and when I saw the fig tree, the idea overtook me. This was the moment. I went inside and down to the cellar, same as I did every day, not thinking of that time when I was a girl and I hid and I heard Mom talking with a man and laughing like a cockatoo. The narrow irregular steps didn't make it easy for me. I found the basket and the fruit picker.

With a guileless smile, I started feeling the figs and picking the ripest ones. Then, time to stretch my arms and test my aim with the picker, even if I wasn't in the best condition for acrobatics and everything danced a bit, the branches and the leaves shaking against a sky still deep blue despite the hour, the waning moon like a sidelong smile in a hazy profile, me struggling to pull down a single fig and the aroma sticky and everything so pretty and so simple.

The basket was soon full to bursting and the branches still heavy with fruit, but I lacked the heart to make marmalade as I'd planned: the ratafia had put my last neuron to bed and everything was a dense fog.

I left the basket in the kitchen next to the sink. From the corner of my eye I saw the crack shaped like a swallow bat its wings, but when I tried to look closer, it fell still.

The urn scowled at me, Some nerve you've got, I know what you're up to.

I slid the bolt. Zzz-crick-crack. I lay down in bed without undressing and fell asleep right away.

JULY

I got up at eight with cottonmouth and a hammering in my head. All day, this insatiable thirst. I gorge myself on water and it doesn't go away even when not another drop will slide in. It hasn't rained for days. And the heat at all hours. If it goes on like this, I'll dry out, too.

Morning fog. With the diurnal excesses of the thermometer, these clouds form that rest their feet on the ground; fog, *l'aveuglement dans la brume.* Maybe having your feet on the ground means not seeing past your own nose and it's only when we rise that we gain perspective.

Morning of rituals. Tea, honey, novel, scarf.

The figs were waiting for me on the kitchen table. I don't have enough sugar, cinnamon, or lemon. How the hell did I think I'd make marmalade yesterday? I almost giggle.

I make an excursion to Can Boronat to buy what I'm missing. The steering wheel burns and I lick my paws like a dog. Before reaching the road, I cross a white van, its posterior is almost like a hearse. The sun is shining in my face and I can't see who's driving. Is it the same as the other day?

I park in the village and leave the windows rolled down. I give Mercè back her Tupperware dish, thank her for the yarn and needles, buy three or four more things. I do it all with a far from customary serenity. I don't expect more. Expectation is a bad attitude. While I grab some apples, she enthusiastically recites yesterday's episode of *Criminarium*: it's about a beggar they found dead and castrated in Manhattan. I could put a Mercè in the novel, render her a bit of tribute.

Once back, I decide to pick the ripe figs, now that the world is once again clear and stable. I grab the fruit picker and the basket, which I emptied out in the sink. Crick-crack-zzz. Blinded by the sun, I approach the fig tree. It's picked clean. Nothing but a few runty fruits that still need to grow. What?!

My fig tree despoiled. There were still many figs left yesterday, I'm sure of it. Where are they? Who . . . ? Am I really sure? Everything was a little blurry. I go back inside and look at the figs piled in the sink. Too few. I go down to the cellar. What if I left them there? Nothing. I go outside. I look for evidence around the tree.

Was it Manel? But when? The white van? Flavi? Why? Were they snatched in the half-hour I was gone? How did they know I'd go out if I didn't know myself? Manel—he's watching me. Or the white van. Maybe it's Manel. Who else? Who knows about the existence of this fig tree in the middle of the woods?

I look all round.

Maybe the thief is still nearby, maybe he had to hide when he saw me coming. The trees and the bushes have eyes. I hear nothing apart from the cicadas laughing uproariously. I examine the branches. The odd white drop still wells from their wounds. Maybe they stole them while I was asleep, having breakfast, knitting. This last possibility strikes me as most dreadful of all.

I go inside. Zzz-crick-crack. I grab the figs, wash them, slice them. Behind my back, the urn whispers to me, Watch out.

Two days caged up at home, but no one comes by to throw peanuts at me. Even when I put on your glasses, I can't see the world through other eyes.

I grabbed a towel and two apples and headed to the gorge, head full of Lila and Mateu. I visualize them over and over arriving at the shelter, with the battered red car packed to the roof and emitting mechanical whines when it hits the potholes. She cranes her head and sees nothing but the piles of bags, suitcases, and junk concealing what they're leaving behind, the impossibility of looking back, of turning back. And now one bump and another, and a pit, and Lila's breasts ache from the tossing and turning, her period's on the way and they're swollen. Then the house on the hill and the ruins of the Romanesque hermitage, with a ray of sunlight falling on the stone altar. What the fuck is that about? The ray of sun is a cliché. Ixnay the ray of sun.

I pass by Flavi's house. Four days without a word from him. I stop. I want to knock on the door and invite him to come with, but I don't want to be pesky, who knows what he might be thinking. I could stay here a while and pretend we were just bumping into each other. Nah. Leave him be. I take off my backpack and drink a drop of water. Thirst, the whole day long.

Come on, shoulder to the wheel.

I continue toward the gorge in the baking sun. Now and again, over the rocks, I see a lizard toasting itself. What's the boiling point for those creatures? Some lift their heads when they hear the crunch of feet on gravel, others run away when my giant's shadow blankets them. I could stretch out on a rock, too, remain immobile waiting for another colossus to pass, awaiting a step, the simmering that will evaporate me.

And Lila? When does she decide to evaporate?

The gorge continues where it is. I sit on the pebble beach and pull the apples from my bag, one green, the other red. Choosing, always choosing: what weariness. I wish I was a river finding its path without ever deciding.

I hurry out of my clothes looking around warily and get in the water. Again, the frozen volcano spurts up my spine and my entire body erupts. The cold kills everything, especially pernicious ideas, wicked weeds that ferment in my mind.

Death from cold or from heat, which do you choose? Raving and mummified like a cat turd under the mortal sun, or abiding in a blizzard till your neurons and mitral valve are frozen? When I was little, I used to ask myself which was better. Now I know: no doubt, the cold. The cold pushes me forward.

To keep the current from carrying me away, I grab a root floating in the water and play dead, my two breasts buoys. The forest noises reach me, attenuated like a memory. The sun's flares prevent me from opening my eyes, and behind my eyelids rises up a blackness wounded by light. Water, sun, the root that holds me in place, and nothing more, just me, a lizard in the water.

I seem to hear a chime of jingle bells muffled by the density of the water, and as always, that terror that appears in my belly with that sound. Grandma. I was so little! Sometimes I think I must have dreamed it.

All those years without thinking of it! But the chime has brought it back and I see her now as I haven't seen her for years. All in black, wrinkled, hands folded like chicken wings and covered in dark blotches, rotting hands, and her rancid scent, more like dust than grime, all of her ancient, contracted, shrinking a few millimeters more every second, constantly on the point of disappearing.

One day, while my mother spoke with the caretakers at the center, she left me alone with the mummy. I was sitting in a chair next to the bed and looking at the ground, studying the movement of my swinging legs, moving them back and forth. Anything not to look at that peering oldster. And she said:

"Hear that?"

But I didn't hear a thing.

"They're coming," she whispered to me, "they're coming. Jingle bells!"

I listened closely, nothing.

"They've got them tied to their ankles, strings of jingle bells tied with the hair of the dead. And now they're coming to get me. They'll come for you, too, just you wait."

She closed her eyes and shouted, Come on, I'm here, coooooome, with long, ululating oo's.

I swung my legs back and forth faster, it was as though something were pulling at my ankles trying to strip off my shoes. And the old woman, Come get me, I'm not scared, coooome. She grabbed my wrist and I heard a wave of jingle bells, a sound that grew stronger till it was a deafening cascade, and my legs up and down, fleeing without moving from the spot.

I tried to wriggle away from the cadaverous hand that was squeezing mine with a force unusual in the dying. I shook my head, because I felt the hairs of the dead braiding themselves into mine, while my grandmother went on shouting, Get in here, you fools; and I closed my eyes tight to avoid seeing anything, but the memory of the light made me see shadows, quivering spots, and I shut my mouth so no one would shove a jingle bell inside. That was when my mother came in and asked, What the hell's going on in here?, as if I'd been playing with my grandmother and she'd gotten riled up on my account. And I answered:

"The jingle bells, Mom, it was the jingle bells."

And that dull clanking, I didn't know whether it came from outside or in. Maybe it was Guim's ghost, come to contemplate my nudity in the light of day, or the countess shouting to me from under the earth. Maybe someone was coming for me. Algae will twist around my legs, one of Brunisenda's thousand-year-old hairs, and the current will drag me away. My head will smash into a rock and the river will run redder than ever.

Then one, two explosions.

I stick my head out of the water and the jingle bells are louder now, realer. I'm paralyzed. I listen close, my pupils dilate, I flare my nostrils, just one more animal, immobile in my makeshift burrow, listening terrified to the sound of humans. Another shot rends the expectant silence of the forest. The jingle bells of dogs approach, angels of death on the trail of agony. I wish I was a lizard and could crawl into a crack in a hot rock.

My head's exploding. I want to climb out of the water, wrap myself in my towel, and run away without looking back, but a hunter will appear before me in the brush and will find me undressed. In a flash, I remember the naked madwoman they shut up in the asylum. Manel found her. Maybe he'll find me too and say I'm mad. Maybe she was just out walking and he drove her insane.

"Manel's got a good heart, he just wants to help you," Flavi said.

"Stop with your nonsense," the urn insists.

And my father:

"My little forest witch."

I don't move. The water covering my flesh is the best camouflage.

At last, the jingle bells vanish. The forest respires.

THE DAY BEFORE

Eight, more than half.
And up there, the redhead and the negative of a Malevich.
What does the flesh of a fox taste like?

Today I finished the scarf. I looked at it. The end where I started is a calamity: irregular stitches, some too loose and some too tight. I pulled on the thread and undid the whole thing. What pleasure, feeling the knots go back in time and having the entire skein again.

Starting over with the same material and doing better. If only it was that easy! That's what I should do with my novel. Throw out what I've written up to now and start from zero, with the cards, my skeins.

With this objective in my head, I've devoted the entire morning to revising and organizing them, to finishing the ten or twelve that were missing, hanging them up and taking them down, this one here, this one's better there, that one's out.

But deep down, I feel like an idiot for believing that I'll make a better novel following this method. Recipe literature is born dead. Three twists, stir well, and when the plot begins to brown, add some contradictions to your characters until the dough gains consistency; then, don't forget to decorate it with adjectives and parlor tricks so no one notices it's going nowhere, and you can plate your soulless literary fetus and hope an editor will adopt it. And there are editors by the dozen who want only dead children; they're less work, and as long as they're handsome and sell, who cares if they stink?

Before lunch, I stood in front of the wardrobe invaded by the platoon of scenes and we stared at each other as the stifling heat coiled in under the roof tiles, dripping. One of us has got to die. And it ain't gonna be me. Now, now I'm ready, but for today, I've had enough of the novel.

And yet I noticed I had an itch to write, a tingling in my fingers, a prick in my right earlobe. I opened a new document and scratched and scratched until my skin tore away. I emerged with a story about the gorge and hunting dogs and all that frozen water overflowing until it submerged the entire forest.

When I saw a blanket of sheep's flanks advancing to the watering hole with Manel rising above them like a hayseed Aladdin, I hurried from the house to avoid the possibility of a visit. But when I shut the door, the doubt: what if he comes in while I'm out? I balanced a pebble on one of the door panels.

I walked up through the woods. I found clearings and depressions, hundred-year-old stumps, crooks of perpetual moss, and a puddle with a family of salamanders—yellow-black, like Barcelona's taxis, our city, another life, another Mei, you. I crouched in the shadows of a tall pine and opened the tap of time until the glass seemed about to run over and I went home.

The stone on the panel hadn't moved.

Down from the house, a train of excrement attesting to the passage of the ovine troupe.

A week it was since I had word from him. I don't think that's normal.

He showed up at one. Like it was no big deal. I tried to pretend I felt snubbed that he'd vanished without explanation. He excused himself with various nebulous, unconvincing alibis: something or other about the apiculture society, doctors, family stuff (to myself, I wondered: which is it, then, beekeepers, doctors, or family?), he'd had to go to Barcelona (me, nodding with a pasted-on smile, like: To the city? For a week? So where'd you stay?).

"You want to come over for lunch?"

Inside, divided, a Mei who would say yes without thinking twice, another desiring to castigate him, as if depriving him of my company were a punishment, how vain!

No need to add I slipped on my shoes in a rush and took off with him. We ate outside, under the cane roof of the porch. Sans wine this time. Better. After all these days alone, it would have inflamed my verbal incontinence.

I didn't talk to him about the figs or my novel or the scarf or the Cubano. Just you. When we met, your red sneakers that made me laugh, the scar on your little finger, holding your dead hand, the precision of your drawings, the orderly little apartment where we lived our orderly little life, the child we wanted that never came, your mother and her French finickiness that made me feel boorish and insignificant, that winter years back when we went to Finland and you broke your fibula, your exultant whipped potatoes, truffle, and poached egg, life as a couple like a train taking the same route over and over, without a driver present toward the end, the last day we made love, sex, sad at times and at others effervescent, how you held me around the waist as we walked down the street and it forced us to step in time so we wouldn't bump hips, Carles, who was always hanging around the house and who calls me now and leaves me messages, and the bitch that I am, I avoid him, and how the urn tells me things, how I don't know what to do with it, all the memories, and I don't know if it's better to suppress them or wallow in them, because there is no middle ground.

Flavi listened to me patiently, his nose like a classical statue's pointed at me, until at last I trailed off and let him open his mouth.

"A few years back, a good friend of mine died. He lives in a corner of my mind, he's always with me, but I hardly ever think about him. He's a shadow I carry with me, but I rarely take note of it. It takes time, though, to learn to live with a shadow."

Since the pointless notion of the syringe is still agitating me, I almost asked him what his friend died of. He must have been a junkie like him, right? Of course not, no. What am I saying!

We made an herb tea. Before I left, I apologized, abashed, for my unchecked loquacity.

For eight days now, at last, I am a river.

I descend the slope of life without pausing anywhere, always forward, surpassing one obstacle after the other. A huge rock? Just erode it with geomorphic patience, unhurried, unstinting, every day, all morning, in the evenings sometimes, too, write the first chapter and reread it, erase, find the right word, file down the corners, filter through the cracks in the stone and vanquish it from within, steel myself with patience.

Then continue downward, stepping out for a while in the forest, alone or with Flavi, in imitation of two currents that flow together for a few moments and exchange molecules, looking at everything with new eyes, changing perspectives if the one I have displeases me, finding a slope that permits me to slip elsewhere, folding in meanders or twisting around to arrive back at the same place.

In the afternoon, swing in the hours, knit minutes, and compose the scarf in perfect knots, neither too loose or too tight, work on each section with calm, not thinking of the one before or the one that must come after, or make a tea and curl up in the armchair with a novel by Rezzoli, with the ideas of Teopoldi, and let the water stop and rest a while, not too long, it shouldn't go stagnant and turn green and putrid. Further down now, make a stop at Mercè's shop and vanish in maternal embraces and Tupperware dishes of macaroni. But the stench of nicotine . . .

Not think about the figs or unresolvable mysteries, and if the figs get in my head, pull them up like a weed.

Swallow the contents of the urn and make the ashes form part of me, insoluble.

And again, write in the shelter of the stone walls and barred door, cover the riverbed with words neither too loose nor too tight, aerate the text, give it strength, give it truth, sculpt the water that flows inside me, not despair if it slips through my fingers, never despair.

Trust.

If a storm comes, grow with the new water that falls over me, hurl myself forward more powerfully than ever, rip away what stands before me, or hide beneath the earth, flow through subterranean cities of rock and mud, nourishing myself on minerals, fearless, knowing that sooner or later I will emerge once more in the light and shine brighter than ever.

Once a month, steep myself in my red gorge and begin again, always downward, toward the alluvial plain. Reach it and flood it thoroughly, let nothing alter my course, let no work of man deter me, and the banks lush and verdant like the green scarf I will soon finish.

At the mouth, expand and sink and be sea and ocean, and let the novel embark and conquer some tiny precious world.

I found them a few feet from the house. Flea market sunglasses. Black, with dark, slightly scratched lenses. I picked them up in my fingers like tweezers. I brought them up to my nose and put them on with canine curiosity.

Maybe they're Flavi's, maybe he came by here and stopped a moment to look at my house, the same way I do when I walk by his lair. Or maybe they belong to the Cubano. Or someone else. A ranger patrolling the trails and scrutinizing the underbrush. It hasn't rained for weeks, and everything's so dry you could sneeze and start a blaze. The forests need diligent observation: at 104 degrees, a fire could spread like the echo of a scream at midnight.

The glasses must belong to a ranger. I left them where I found them, but my mind took them with me: at night I dreamed of a squad of uniformed men, all in sunglasses, surrounding the house and talking dirty into their walkie-talkies—put her on all fours like a dog, I'll take the mouth, you take the pussy, her tits'll hang down like a nanny goat's teats—while one of them climbed the fig tree and pulled down all the throbbing figs. Then he threw them to another man at the foot of the tree who stomped them, cackling, till his black boots were covered in red pulp. The sound of the walkie-talkies, louder and louder, mingling with the agitation of the dry leaves. And the cackle turned to the squawking of a cockatoo. My Mother. Fucking. Cockatoo.

103 Days Earlier

It's been two months since you were crushed dead.

I left as it was getting toward ten. Close the windows and doors, turn the key, put the stone on the door. I wanted to go to Gras Spring and see if it had run dry, too. Any excuse is a good one to nestle in the forest until it envenoms me.

Twenty minutes from the house, an impertinent bus started toward me. Through the dust clouds it conjured, I saw a mass of human offspring in ball caps and colored T-shirts: behind the glass, they laughed soundlessly, a pink girl was braiding another's hair, the ones in the back jumped like mad over the seats executing a danse macabre.

Its belly stuffed with backpacks, tents, and sleeping bags, the bus would soon vomit everything up in the tranquility of some clearing. It made me think of a truck of pigs headed to the slaughterhouse. How I hated going to camp, and her, tying my hair back in a ponytail so tight I couldn't even turn my head, All right now, quit your complaining, you always end up having fun.

All of a sudden, going to the spring felt like a drag. The rabble might be camping out on the esplanade that borders it, ready to ruin my excursion. Kids waving canteens under the jet of water, reedy voices piercing my eardrums, whiny snotnoses with skinned needs or shitting behind a bush with a look of congestion on their faces.

My yearning for peace annihilated.

Reluctantly, I aborted the mission. I was fantasizing about

turning to Circe and transforming them to pigs I could make sausages from. I blew off steam kicking a pinecone until I got home, still in a bad mood.

I found a flock of sheep parked at the watering hole, what an impression: for a moment they seemed not to be mere sheep, but all those children transformed by my brainwaves into animals, bellowing at the door to avenge themselves, their ovine eyes mysteriously empty, but over their fuzzy spines rose a man. That man.

"Good day, dear, how's it going? Everything O.K. with the window?"

"Fine," I tell him. "You didn't happen to lose some sunglasses?"

"Don't wear them things, bad for your eyes, mind you me."

"How about the figs, were they good?"

"The figs? What figs?" He responds, smiling to reveal his minuscule yellow teeth, a smoker's milk teeth; he's a good actor, the jerk.

"From the fig tree, what else?" I replied defiantly.

"Somebody got up on the wrong side of the bed, huh? A good rain'll fix that, but if you look there," and he glanced up in the sky, "I wouldn't hold my breath."

Ten or twelve sheep away, I wanted to start the day over, erase the bus and Manel, thoughts that could only obstruct my desire to write. The stink of animals reached me.

"So, you planning on sticking around here long?"

What the hell's he asking now? I don't respond.

"Ten days from now, it'll be August, Xana, you know . . ."

Cheapskate, he's saying it because I only paid him through July. I want to help you, he says, yeah yeah . . .

"I'll pay you six more months. I'll give the money to Mercè, sound good?"

"As you wish. Now if you're thinking of spending the winter here, you should strap your boots on and go looking for wood;

it's cold as a witch's tit and all you've got is that butane heater. Do what you want, dear, but I'd recommend you eat a bit, otherwise a gust of wind will hit you one day and freeze you solid."

"I will," I lied, and carved a path to the stairs between the raw wool, head held high, recounting the steps once more. Fifteen, everything in its place. Maybe I should put some stairs at Lila's house, too: the human slug could crawl up them to her leaving a trail of spittle, sweat, semen.

100 Days Earlier

I went down to the store at one. Sunday. Rush hour. At every corner, old women emerge from Mass after the ritual expulsion from the temple with the May-you-go-in-peace. They fill the streets like a decrepit army, glowing with the pride of religious fervor, dressed to the nines, some hanging on their son's or daughter's arm, eyelids outlined and very black, a contrast to their dye jobs, hair looking like a helmet, their gossip radar registering everything in hopes of detecting whatever will permit them to blather the week away with the rest of the soldiers of God.

They line up at the store to take communion at Mercè's cash register. When I went in, the three who were inside clammed up instantly and turned to me in evangelical poses, all splendid smiles and pious hands. I asked who was last in line and went past them looking for potatoes and some excuse to distance myself from that grubbiness.

I heard them cawing in the background, all at the same time, it sounded like a bunch of deaf people talking over each other. Then they started whispering. And one of them: Whaaaat?

They were talking about me, I'm sure of it.

And I guess the fattest one said, Neus's daughter, and the other, Well she doesn't resemble her one bit, all scraggy and bony and small, and then she added with long-simmering envy, With the presence her mother had! And maybe the hunchback said, What a dancer she was, the mother, I can still see the way Tomàs used to send her flying under the tent! And the fat one, Not just Tomàs . . . and maybe Mercè got a word in here, Being the village bigshot had to be good for something, and she spilled the beans, She's writing a novel. And the smallest of the four, the one who looks like she still rouges her lips, must have remarked in a censorious tone, She lives alone in the woods and she's not married? Well, I just don't know what to say . . .

And maybe Mercè defended me, or recounted the details of my *misfortune*, or maybe not, maybe she's the worst of all and has me well fooled.

When I returned to the register, the fat one, pointing at the cover of the paper with the word *fire* written in giant letters, remarked, upset, Even the papers are talking about it, we're in bad shape, if we don't get a bit of rain, we won't be as lucky as we were last year. And the hunchback, Let it go, Maricarme, don't be a doomsayer, you're always such a pessimist. And Mercè, turning to me, If there is a fire, dear, you better run like the wind, the demon gets round like you wouldn't believe.

The cling of the door cut off the conversation and all five of them turned to see who it was, and so did I, like I was one of them. The mechanic Julià-Joan-Josep came in. First the belly, then the rest of him.

"Morning, girls!"

And all of them giggled at the remark and blushed like teenagers.

"Shoot, we've even got the lady of the forest. So? How's it going up there? You're not roasting without AC?"

What do you know about if I've got AC, I should have said, but I limited myself to convention:

"Fine. Getting by."

"The other day I went by there and I saw everything was dry as a bone," he says, and I think *by there?* What the fuck were you doing *by there?* And the lost glasses, of course, the glasses. "We better start praying for rain."

"That's just what we were saying, if there's a fire, she better get running."

And while all of them started blabbing once more on the subject of fire, Mercè:

"That'll be thirty-twenty, Maricarme."

And then: It must be him, he's the one who nabbed the figs. He's got a van, too. What color was the van he took me to the house in? White? Was it white? The scum. Lady of the forest, says he.

So when it was my turn and the old ladies were scampering through the streets putting the word out about how Neus's daughter's writing a novel and lives alone in the house and is so skinny she doesn't look like her daughter, I told Mercè someone took my figs, leering at the mechanic to see if he'd react, and then I added:

"You think Manel might have taken them?"

"Figs? I doubt it, he's been grossed out by them since he was a boy. But don't let it get to you, the same thing happens to us, every year someone steals our figs."

The mechanic remained impassive before my polygraph test.

I paid and was opening the door to leave when Mercè stopped me:

"Oh, dear, I almost forgot."

She ducked down and reappeared above the counter with an envelope in hand.

"A letter came for you."

When I saw the handwriting, I knew who it was. The twirling capitals, the letters antiquated, like a monastic manuscript. I even thought I caught a whiff of her pestilent perfume, which had impregnated the paper.

I left the letter in the passenger seat and it pestered me the whole time, ready to pounce.

I'll get home, tear it into little pieces, and burn them, to avoid the temptation to tape it back together. She's dead, the bitch. I don't want to hear a word she has to say. The letter must be full of barbs. I won't allow her into my home, into my life.

And then, maybe not, maybe age has softened her heart and has magically turned her into the person I need her to be, *zub-zub,* or the clarity of age has come upon her, maybe in time to the approach of death remorse has weighed on her and she's deigned to ask me forgiveness for what she said to me the day of the funeral, for all she didn't give me when I was a girl because she was too busy doing her eyebrows, her nails, depilating her reputation, filing her dignity, exercising upon my father and me her subtle tyranny based on continuous contempt and occasional scorn, always in an apparently inoffensive tone, that way of hers of making us feel we owed our lives to her, that without her we'd be nothing, that we'd be worth nothing, that we owed her gratitude, should forgive her for not loving us enough, for being who she was. How I'd have liked for her to beg me and to tell her I don't want to forgive her, or can't, or just not answer and leave her hanging with her pointless penitence.

Then I told myself: I'll open it.

And like a flash, of course! She still thinks she's going to be a grandmother and I won't let her lay a finger on my son. She needs to butter me up so I'll let her back in the door. Let her believe she'll be a grandmother and will never see the kid. The idea brought me the sterile consolation of vengeance. But no, that would be stooping to her level. Being like her. I'm not like her.

With the bumps in the road, the letter danced on the seat, it seemed alive and anxious for me to read it.

I brought my groceries inside. While I put it all away, I left the letter on the table, next to the urn, which shook. Toss it, I told myself, protect yourself. But I sat down in the armchair.

Remei,

Bad sign, no *Dear Remei,* no *Hi, Remei.* At least she didn't call me *honey.* And the ends of the R twisting into a spiral. You should tear it up right now, burn it like you thought.

Since you don't respond to my messages and I guess you don't even listen to them, you're forcing me to write you. Your attitude isn't just a burden for you, but for everyone else, too. I suppose sooner or later you'll grow up and put an end to this childish stubbornness.

Childish stubbornness, you say. That's you. Some nerve.

I went to your apartment a few times in case you'd come back. You have important mail: two letters from the DMV and one from the revenue service I didn't dare open. Sorry for looking in your mailbox, but if you're not there, some-one has to. If I don't send them, it's for your own good, I think you need to make an effort to face normal life again. Come to Barcelona. Talk to your family and Guim's. Look for a job.

Yeah, for my own good, it's always for my own good. Like when you made us go live in Barcelona *for the girl's education* when it was obvious what you wanted to do was strut around like the queen of the city.

The other day I got a real surprise. I was dying with worry. It had been so long since I'd heard anything about you! Especially with your condition! So I called Manel.

Manel. Good old Manel. This time, you really should stop reading, ball it up.

But I couldn't.

The poor thing had no idea what I was talking about. "Pregnant?" he asked. You made me look like a numbskull. Manel assures me you're even thinner than ever.

Here I got up from the chair, I couldn't take the immobility anymore, and I went on reading while I walked back and forth in my too-too-narrow cage.

Mercè told me the same thing. She says she's never seen you so haggard, "you can see her ribs and her belly goes in instead of out. Three and a half months, impossible," she kept saying, "are you sure you heard her right?"

So Mercè's talking out of school too. We were standing there face to face and she didn't say a word. Hypocrite. Maybe I should be running from her and not the fire. And inside, the fire kept spreading.

I'm your mother and it is my duty to help you even if that implies telling you things you don't want to hear. You can't understand what a mother feels. Don't take that the wrong way.

The cunt.

But did you really think I wouldn't find out? The very day of your husband's funeral, you were thinking how best to do me harm, instead of accepting the pain, the reality. If your father was alive, it would break his heart to see you acting out like this.

How dare you mention my father and pick and choose his

thoughts for him, you, who never understood one thing about him.

But I am your mother and I love you and I suffer, because to do something like that, you must have been desperate. Maybe you really thought you were pregnant and you convinced yourself of it to not have to look life in the face. You're really scaring me, honey. Something's wrong with you, you need to come back to Barcelona, trust me, isolation in that house up there will drive you crazy, it's not good for you. You can come home. I know sometimes we don't get along, but we're blood. Let yourself be loved, honey.

I hope this time you'll respond to me. Don't make me come up there.

I love you,

Your mother.

I tore the paper until the labyrinth in the rug was coated in bitter confetti. If I go outside and breathe, my breath will set fire to anything it touches.

Come.

If you dare.

Come if you dare, I went on repeating when I got up after a restless night. I need to get rid of her however I can, kill her in my mind, extirpate her from me.

So I went down to the cellar. It's a putrid place, the damp still nests there even now when the heat is cracking the ground. A dark spot descends from the roof, throwing a shadow. Right away I found the rope, the saw, and the axe. For once I'll listen to Manel.

In the fall I'll need wood, so I'll go cut wood.

I walked into the forest squeezing the axe handle, it's slender from wear, it feels like human skin. First I gathered kindling, broke it, piled it up, bundled it; the twigs were so dry, many snapped in my fingers. I scratched my hands and legs on the spiny stems that cover the earth like a pelt; you could make a soup of them and drink it and shred yourself within.

Then I stood over a broken branch almost a palm in diameter and sank the saw in, pushing it down and up like the bow of a violin, but the music that emerged from it was strident, a disconcerting symphony. Here and there it got stuck and struggled to pull it from the guts of the wood without splitting. My sore arm obliged me to stop, and I stepped away then and gathered another bundle of twigs. Then back to the saw to narcotize with every stroke the image of the perfumed cockatoo, immerse myself in the head of Lila and the disenchantment that will grow in her like an embryo.

Zig-zag with the saw till the cleft was deep enough, then grab the axe and chop away with questionable aim, definitively amputating my mother in doing so. Everything was me, and the crack, and the crackling, the lament the wood enunciates as it's riven, and you think to yourself, Now, now, but not yet, wood is hard. Turn the log a bit, attack the flank, the dry blows of the axe thundering through the forest.

Two hours I was there. The bitterness my mother had suffused me with I expelled through my pores as sweat. I made a couple of trips back and forth with the bundles and the dismembered branch, and even then, I stayed a while outside the house, splitting it into logs. That was easy, a few blows and it splits along the grain. I struck it and it cracked suddenly and remained there gutted on the ground, showing me its viscera, and everything was the scent of wood, the odor of vegetation.

Under the shower my sweat—liquified cockatoo—drained away. As she coiled in eddies down the drain, I could still hear her shouting: Honey! Honey!

And at eleven, I was cleansed inside and out, ready to write without rot.

THAT DAY

Where are the keys, Mei?
Did you hide them in the woods
or has your own head purloined them?

AUGUST

They say it's good to read what you write aloud. Why not give it a try? I recorded myself with my phone and sat at the table while I waited for my tea to steep in the kitchen, face to face with the urn, I hit play and I closed my eyes.

My unfamiliar voice recited my words. I could feel the presence of the urn before me, taking physical form behind my eyelids. Like that famous cat that's alive and dead at the same time: if you don't open your eyes, Guim might still be alive, an instant of possibility. I saw you in a parallel universe, face sleepy, like you'd just gotten up, the dark frames of your glasses surrounding your still-swollen eyes, lenses magnifying your hypermetropic pupils, your eyes are black like dark chocolate, your hair a little unkempt from the turmoil of the night.

You'd slurp watery coffee—how could you drink it like that!—and react to my paragraphs with a sidelong smile, or frowning with chubby, often stubbled cheeks. And me: You're scratching, go shave, you're grinding on my pussy.

The voice would go on reading, stumbling occasionally over some illegible phrase. I'd never look at you to avoid feeling even more ashamed. With *More tomorrow*, I'd reach the conclusion, and then I'd look up, Yes, and you'd tell me, It's good, Monda, it really is. Because you never would tell me the truth.

My cellphone went silent. I opened my eyes, the cat was dead. The urn said nothing but I tried to imagine it was proud of me.

I printed the first chapter, just six pages. The first ones. Now I need to reach the last six without thinking how, all in, it's nothing more than a verbal exercise, flimsy and gratuitous.

Before leaving, I grabbed a jar of fig marmalade. Between one thing and another, I didn't make it to Flavi's until one. He'll probably start thinking I always show up then for the free lunch.

"It's been a while!" he exclaimed as he hugged me. "How are you?"

"Getting by. I've been working a lot. Here's the first chapter, but I forbid you to read it in front of me. And here's a little fig marmalade to compensate you for your readerly efforts."

"I made some, too. How about this? I'll give you a jar of mine and we can compare recipes."

"You made some, too?" My eyes bugged out, almost scolding him. "Where'd you get the figs?"

"From an apple tree, what do you think! Don't just stand there, come in."

Once more, I entered his den, telling myself, Don't be a dummy, you really think he's the one who stole your figs?

"Vermouth?" he asked, setting two glasses down on the bar in the kitchen.

We sat on the sofa with our dew-streaked glasses.

"How you handling things?"

"I don't know. As best I can. I've got him in the kitchen. Sometimes I think I should stuff him in a wardrobe to keep from seeing him all the time, but it'd make me feel bad. And when I see the ashes there on the table expectant, all that comes into my head are cliches. That his life was pointless, that all lives are pointless. That we're just here to kill time. That he passed through the world without leaving a mark. Now he only lives inside me and when I die he'll disappear with me, so I have the duty to keep him alive. If we'd had children . . ." I broke off, Flavi said nothing. "And then my head fills with metaphors, as if there were any truth in a fucking metaphor, esthetic truth maybe, what the hell is that. I tell myself, the army of memories drives onward, but the soldiers of survival will destroy it ruthlessly. All day with this exhausting battle against memory in my head, and all the while learning to master the art of war, pushing along the hours: breakfast, write, lunch, sleep. For what? Life: a tedious etcetera."

"When I had the accident . . . I never told you about that, did I?"

I shook my head, and inside: Tell me!

"Look . . ." He pushed the hair up from the nape of his neck to show me a scar that ran halfway up his head. "The grimy life comes with a price. The accident . . ."

"No, tell me now," I said, cutting him short. "Whenever your life comes up, you always duck me. Are we friends or are we not?"

"Of course we're friends, but some things are hard for me. I'll tell you another day."

I grunted.

"The accident left me bedbound, I couldn't even talk, I broke my jaw. Every Thursday my aunt Loreto came to see me. She was a strong woman, I miss her, family, you know . . ."

"Family? I don't miss my mother. Quite the opposite."

I seemed to notice Flavi looking at me with a bit of surprise, as if he knew the cockatoo wasn't dead, but he went on:

"Aunt Loreto always came at three-thirty on the dot, she was kind of German in some respects. She'd sit on the edge of my bed and wouldn't stop talking till it was time to go. She'd tell me about life, her life, her neighbors', her parents', mine. One day she said to me, You know what you should hope for out of life, kid? What the poor have and the rich need. And she left me laid out there without telling me the answer. I spent hours thinking about it while I studied the ceiling and the patterns on the blue bedspread, trapped in my mute immobility. And she was right. Boy was she right."

"So what was it?"

"I'm not going to tell you, think about it a bit. What the poor have and the rich need."

I turned it over a bit.

"I'll go make lunch."

I said no and left despite his insistence that I stay. Sitting down at his table again would have been exploitation. I invited him to lunch the day after tomorrow.

"Are you vegetarian?"

"I eat meat, but I try not to overdo it. Whatever you make will suit me fine."

I t was early in the afternoon. I was sitting at my computer furiously attacking the second chapter. A flash from a nuclear bomb entered the room. We're in the heart of the dog days and it still hasn't rained.

I'd opened the window and the front door to get a little air flowing through, but all that blew in was a burning breeze. I don't feel at ease now if I don't lock the bolt, but if I close the door, the gathering heat will burn me to a crisp.

I heard the crackle of leaves over the cries of the cicadas. From instinct more than curiosity, my eyes looked outside. A bush at the foot of my house shook. I remembered the fox I saw back when I was still in that other life, the life that had a Guim and an apartment in Barcelona I would have to return to. You could give it something to eat, make it your friend. Bond with a wild animal.

I held my hand over my eyes as I watched the bush, and then I saw a shoe, grey and roundish, digging around the branches at the base. I squinted to better focus, the sun blinded me, the bush was too far away.

Go outside, I told myself, grab a log and go over there. But I remained close to the window. It stopped moving. Maybe it was a stone, not a shoe. Grey, round, why not? Maybe putting your glasses on here and there is ruining my eyes.

I sat at the desk, but I couldn't stop glancing over at the supposed shoe, waiting for it to budge now that I was no longer looking at it. My eyes were used to the gloom inside, and it got harder and harder to see the bush clearly.

It moved.

Then the thing I'm not sure whether or not I saw moved so fast and shined so bright. A fleeting mass amid the leaves, a febrile quiver that might have been a hoopoe, a sparrow, or him. *Him.* It was facing me, and for a fraction of a second I thought it was a man with leathery skin. But that was just an instant— two seconds? three?—and it disappeared again.

I ran to the door. I grabbed a log. I ran down the steps. My heart thumping frantically. Brain stopped. All I thought was: Go there and cave in its head.

I reached the spot. Nothing. I looked around, brandishing the log in the air. Nothing but the cicadas' cynical cackles. I glared at the bush, looking for the stone, the shoe, a viscous tip-off. Nothing.

I realize just then I've left the front door wide open. I take the stairs two by two. The hammering of my pulse deafens me. I go inside, lock the bolt, pass through every room, log in hand, look under the beds, behind the doors, down in the cellar.

In the kitchen, the urn. Calm down, no one's here.

It was getting late: I should have started the chicken and *samfaina* earlier, it always tastes better after it's rested for a while. For breakfast I scarfed a piece of toast with Flavi's marmalade. Inside, the grrrr of comparing it to mine, seeing if it was too similar, made with the same figs, even if I know otherwise. I do know otherwise. It's better than mine, it has a provocative piquancy to it.

At the shop, Mercè all smiles, same as ever, but I don't buy it anymore. At a minimum, I now know she's talking to my mother behind my back, but who knows whether she isn't also slagging me off to all the old women in the village. How dare she go on playing the role with me, Dear, you look good, would you like a chicken, dear? That really is something. Having someone for lunch, you say? It wouldn't be Flavi, would it, I heard y'all are getting along? Obviously the scumbag with the smoker's milk teeth cued her in. "He's a good boy, a little bit of a scamp, not quite together, you know . . . You seem a bit sheepish, something going on? This week they ran a special on the fire in Montseny, made me miss my episode of *Criminarium*, I'm in despair. It's a mess though, this thing with the drought. Here, dear, take a bit of lamb, house specialty."

I refused, I hate lamb, it stinks.

"You've never had meat this tender in your life, you'll see."

I repeated:

"I'm really not a lamb person, sorry."

"It's because you've never had the good stuff. Here," and she foisted on me a packet with chunks of the lambs Manel raises. I saw the yellow of nicotine on her fingers, betraying the rot she carries inside.

I shut myself up in the kitchen and enclosed myself in parentheses empty but for knives, pots, and wooden spoons. Clean the chicken, quarter it, salt and pepper. No Cubano, no novel.

Skin the wings, slow-cook it, cut the onion while my eyes sting like memory. No figs, no Guims.

Cover it up, and then the cheeky red of the peppers, the aubergines, the tomatoes. Nothing else. My hands sliced, soaked a moment under the tap, rubbed themselves off on a tea towel.

At twelve-thirty, it was all ready.

I saw the packet of lamb on the table. What would I do with it? The urn licked its lips, probably dreaming of aioli and roasted potatoes to accompany it. I always told you lamb stank, you didn't care, you loved lamb, you didn't know what I was talking about. I wrapped it in two plastic bags and tossed it in the fridge, I won't want that stench around me, and when I shut the door, I thought again about the fox. Seems we really will become friends.

I went to change clothes and get rid of the Lady Samfaina perfume. I couldn't avoid the temptation of the bed, the frame sank as I threw myself over it. I traced out the mazelike volutes of the bedstead, like when I was little and Dad didn't want to wake up. I remembered that morning a few months ago when I came here for the first time, the vertigo, the feeling I'd thrown myself off a cliff and had no idea where I'd land. And you, who were still there. But now everything feels more solid than before, the earth I tread, the light that enters through the window. I'd have slept a half-hour, but I couldn't, Flavi was on his way and I didn't want him to find me dozing off.

I dressed as a person for a change: green linen dress, the

one with the straps, and sandals. I even put on the red button earrings you gave me centuries back, in the Pleistocene if not before. But I looked basic, pat, they don't suit me anymore, and I did like them once, the person I was before liked them, the one who died during the meteorite of your accident.

Three knocks on the door. I opened. Two kisses on the cheek, me on my tippy-toes as always and him crouching down a little.
"You look nice!"
"I'm tired of feeling like a wild boar dressed up to run through the forest."
He handed me a bottle of white wine. In the other hand, he held my eight pages covered in notes written in pen. My stomach clenched.
When I went inside, I slid the bolt behind him and he gave me a strange look.
"It's habit," I said by way of justification.
I opened the bottle of wine, turned away a bit so the urn wouldn't see me, and grabbed the two glasses you brought with you that dark day in May.
"I made a little potato salad to nosh on. But when I went to mix in the mayonnaise, I couldn't get the Minipimer started. Do you have one?"
Bad juju, that word in his mouth.
"Wait," I told him.
I went down to the cellar and brought back one of the untouched Minipimers.
"Keep it. Don't ask."
He sat down in Dad's chair. How odd, seeing him there, out of place. I couldn't find my place, either.
I couldn't hold back:
"So? What did you think?"
"Well, it's hard to judge with so few pages, a novel has a long trajectory and it's hard to get a sense of one with so little."

"Yeah, yeah, great, but . . . ?"

"The language is great, it shows craft but it's not overdone, it's not too simple, not too recondite. The first person I like, it always helps bring you closer to the characters, to get into their skin, but there's a danger there of falling too much into the I, wallowing in it, you have to watch out for that. And the owner is a little flat, you give away too much for this to just be the first few pages, it lacks subtlety. I think you need to tone down her aggressiveness a little, the reader's still getting their feet on the ground."

I shrank progressively, concentrated on holding a natural smile so my face wouldn't betray my disappointment, my disappointment with myself. What the hell did you think? That he'd come here and say you wrote a fucking masterpiece?

He continued:

"Maybe it's a little short for a chapter, but like, that depends on how you structure the novel, I mean there's thousand-page-long Russian books with teeny tiny chapters that work just fine."

What you wrote is shit, and he doesn't know how to tell you.

"What you need is some punch. You need to trap the reader right away, pull the string a little tighter. Look, the first line, for example . . ."

I prayed, Don't read it aloud, do not read it.

"'When the road turned into the woods, the wind started to blow as if anxious to hurry us to the hermitage.' I don't know, are you sure? The first sentence is important. So, I mean . . . Starting a novel with *when* . . ."

He thinks I'm ridiculous. You are ridiculous. The first sentence, the very one I've rewritten a hundred times. Shame burns my cheeks.

"But whatever, it's just a matter of refining the tone. All you can do is write, if you write the tone will hone itself, and then you'll rework the beginning. Because there's good stuff here, the initial situation is good, you generate expectation and the characters have legs. It's got something rezzoresque to it. The Rezzo of Sorrius, they'll call you."

Fucking pity.

He stopped talking, took a sip of wine. I had to say something, somehow conceal the immensity of the blow, make it to the chicken with *samfaina* and put a good face on the whole thing.

"I appreciate you being so sincere."

"If I'm supposed to lie to you, we might as well drop it, no?" He handed me the pages. "Here, I wrote some comments so you could see specifically what I'm referring to, otherwise it's all a little abstract."

"Thanks . . . I guess," I burbled with a granitic smile.

I needed to change the subject.

"Listen, a while back the mechanic told me a story about a crazy woman running naked through the forest ten or fifteen years ago. Manel found her, he said. Does that ring a bell?"

"Yeah, Renata."

"Renata?"

"She lives in the sanatorium. It was nine years ago."

I nodded for him to continue.

"She got out. She said the staff at the center wanted to kill her. She's paranoid schizophrenic." He paused. "Sometimes, though, she's the most lucid woman I've ever met."

"How do you know her?"

"We can go see her one day if you want. You'd like Renata, but it's crushing, setting foot in that place. When you come out, you really think life has no point . . ."

"How do you know her, though?"

"I worked a while at the sanatorium. I'll make the mayonnaise and we can sit down, O.K.?"

"Worked there how?"

"That's why I came out here, but it was a different time. I don't like to talk about my life, I'm sure you noticed. Where do you keep the tablecloth?"

With that question, he put an end to my failed interrogation.

While we set the table, I got him to confess his marmalade has ginger and a generous pinch of salt. I took note for next year.

I like watching his lackadaisical movements, he acts as calmly as if the time he inhabited were endless, always with extreme delicacy, smoothing the tablecloth out with his hands, laying out the flatware, which in his hands looks like something from a dollhouse. One day I'd like to see him on edge, or in a bad mood, even furious, just to confirm that he's human. I told him that out right.

"I'd say it's not worth it, right?"

The guy's an ascetic. But an ascetic who's wild about my chicken with *samfaina*. Between it and the wine, I was starting to get over the shock of the first chapter.

When we were making the coffee, he asked me:

"Hey, Rezzo, what's your name?"

"What the hell? You know my name."

"I mean your surnames."

"Why?"

"I don't know . . . it's just weird not to know at this point."

"At what point?"

"Listen, if you don't want to tell me, don't!"

"Sala Munt."

He leaned back and repeated with his eyes closed:

"Mei Sala Munt, Mei Sala Munt, Mei Sala Munt . . . It's pretty, it sounds like a mantra. Mei Sala Munt. Or like a greeting in Arabic, As-salaam-aleikum, peace be with you, *meisalamunt*."

"Apparently Mei means pretty in Chinese, so I've been told, I don't know if it's true."

"That makes you twice as pretty, Re-Mei."

"You?"

"Flavi Ferrer de Porumb," he said, stretching out his hand.

"Pleased to meet you." I took it and kissed it as if he were a young gentlewoman. His skin smells like honey. "Your name sounds like a Germanic incantation. I'll utter it when I want to ward off the wild beasts," and as I said this, I thought of the bush shaking yesterday.

He burst out in a laugh. Making him laugh makes me feel important.

He left as it was getting dark. I gave him a long, tranquil hug. At the last second, I obeyed the impulse to kiss him on the neck. Right away, I regretted it, and in a chipper voice, I blurted out, See you later! as if I hadn't done what I'd just done.

At nighttime, I left a lambchop on the doorstep.

I was in the dining room in Barcelona. I couldn't stop walking back and forth over the zigzag of the parquet, to the wall, then turn, then back to the front door. I liked it, it was a game, even if I was trapped in a cycle and couldn't escape. Guim wasn't there, he didn't exist, he never had.

I heard a noise outside and was certain it was the postman delivering a subpoena. I'll get it now, I thought, because I knew he didn't dare knock and would pass the citation to me under the door, as he did every day. I ran to the door and opened it wide and there, on the floor, I found a fox drinking milk from a bowl.

Its pelt was orange and so immaculate I felt the irresistible urge to touch it, even if I was sure it would bite me. I crouched slowly to avoid frightening it, my knees were crackling. It looked up, and I realized it wasn't a fox, it was Ester, she'd dyed her hair fire-red and she said, like nothing was out of the ordinary, like she wasn't there naked in front of me on the landing licking out of a fucking bowl, You want to go for a drink on the beach? I put a leash on her and she ran through the street on all fours, her buttocks obscenely spread. And no one looked at us.

I woke with a film of sweat on my chest. How long had it been since I'd thought of Ester? Why did I stop seeing her? Why did we abandon each other? Laziness? Lack of interest? I guess. And that unbearable boyfriend of hers. How long ago was that? Five or six years? Why did she suddenly come back to me now? I could call her, but what would I say? Who even knows where she is right now, maybe I wouldn't recognize her anymore, or maybe she wouldn't recognize me.

Where are my friends?

Today, again, a lambchop on the porch. It must be the fox that's eating them, no?

Lila's finally met the shepherd, I was waiting for them to find each other.

She has little hands, doll's hands, like me. I imagine them kneading bread, sinking into dough white like her, ductile like her, with a tenderness at odds with her husband's distressing sponginess. With time she'll grow thinner, her body will turn wiry, legs sinewy, flesh haggard, all of her will exsiccate.

The shepherd has big hands, and when he walks, he grips his crook on account of his left knee, broken years ago and badly healed. He's thin already. When he meets Lila, the sun is about to go down and the shadow of his immense figure, a bit bent like his crook, covers the hill like a blanket.

She goes back home with the bunch of asparagus he gave her, and from the vestiges of that encounter, she will build the fantasy of a heartening future.

At night she will dream, but what do I do with the dream? Do I put it in, or no? Vulkanov said making your characters dream is gratuitous, a magic trick fit for an amateur. Is that what I am, an amateur magician?

I write the whole scene, but I can't stop thinking I should redo the first chapter from top to bottom. I can't stop hearing Flavi, it's just a matter of refining the tone, what you need is some punch, there's a danger there of falling too much into the I, wallowing in it, start from the top and once again, it's worthless.

Mei Sala Munt, it's worthless.

August 10. Today you would have turned forty-four. *And many more . . .*

You would have come to the house to see me and I'd have ridden you on top of the labyrinth of the rug. I'd have taken you to the gorge. We'd have gone to Vilamitja for dinner. You'd have made me laugh.

But you're dead, you bastard.

I finished the scarf and imagined giving it to you. But you didn't like scarves. They're annoying, you used to say.

I swam alone in the gorge. The water was icy, but the sun burned, and inside, too, there burned a corrosive ember.

I've got no lamb left and I haven't seen the fox once. Maybe it wasn't her.

80 Days Earlier

The heat lingers and it seems it's melted time. Whatever. All the days run together. But the novel's moving forward. I've got thirty pages. Thirty.

This evening Flavi came by to chat a while. He brought back the Rezzoli and gave me a Hathaway I've never read. He insisted the day after tomorrow we go for dinner and to the dance in the square for the town fair. I agreed, what a horrible idea. I'm supposed to go pick him up at eight. Why did I say yes?

The town fair dance, the image of my mother dancing under the tent when she was young. I won't dance.

I put a lambchop on the doorstep. Mercè gave me a good price.

I've got thirty pages. Thirty.

A FEW DAYS BEFORE

Meat or fish.
The doubt will nestle in your intestines
and if you tear it out, it will kill you.

At four in the afternoon, it started to pour, the sky discharged forth with fury what it had been saving for weeks. Mammatocumulus clouds suckling the earth, Durand would say. I watched from the living room window. The woods in shadows, dampened by a muffled light, received the storm with gratitude. I too was grateful, because the Mother of God of August must have listened to my prayers and compelled the aborigines to cancel the town fair banquet. So I told myself as I slurped my fuming tea, relieved to have freed myself from the evening's theatrics.

From time to time, the thunder tore through the sound of rain and resounded like roars beyond the grotto while the thirsty trees stretched their arms to the sky for nourishment. I imagined the fox crouched on a boulder in the gorge filling its open mouth with water, ribs visible through its soaked fur, and at its feet, the Muntanya rumbling downward.

I went outside in my underwear and let the rain feed me a while. Immense drops on my face, on my shriveled nipples, down my back and creeping between my buttocks. Gooseflesh. I'd forgotten how the cold felt. I stretched out my branches and the water fell over me in torrents, washing away the moss that had grown on my bark.

When I went inside, I was longing for a fireplace with a fire burning at all hours and the scent of wood and smoke that clings to your hair. I had fantasies of thick pumpkin purees and the refuge of midafternoon darkness. I wrapped up in a towel and, without meaning to, fell asleep in the armchair with the droplets plunking off the roof tiles like thousands of fingers drumming out a lullaby.

I woke up a quarter to seven, disoriented, stiff from the contortionist's posture I'd fallen asleep in. The sky had gone quiet. I stumbled over to the window. Outside, the sun shone implacably, same as it has the entire past month, not a single laggard cloud.

I wasn't sure whether the storm had been a dream, I opened the window. A rivulet ran down the shutter and wet my bare feet. The Mother of God of August is a nasty sadist, she likes to play pranks.

I had an hour left to get dressed and pick him up, an hour to find a Mei capable of walking onto the square with him and letting herself go.

The lambchop outside, the pebble on the door panel. I took the stairs down two by two to make time run faster.

On the way my stomach ached slightly, the same way it did when I was a girl and I had to go to the pool and I still was convinced I'd drown there. I knocked on his door with my sandals and my toes covered in mud. His inviting, familiar smile opened up.

"Here's a present, if you don't like it don't wear it."

I passed him the scarf.

"Oh, I love it, thanks!" He kissed me on each cheek, hand on my waist. "But I can't break it out in mid-August! You got a plate, a glass, and silverware? I forgot to tell you."

I shook my head, hopeful, as though that might save me from going.

"I figured, I already packed enough for both of us. Shall we?"

We got into the car.

"I've been thinking about your aunt's riddle, what can we

hope for out of life: misery? The poor have it and the rich need it . . ."

"That's a bit of a negative conclusion, the best we can hope for in life is misery! Here, I'll give you another clue: the dead think of it."

"Hmmm," I grunted. What was Guim thinking about then?

The bumps in the road jostled my boobs and made them ache. My period's coming and they're weighing down like ripe fruit.

"We've still got time to bail," I proposed.

"False!" he exclaimed, taking from his pocket two tickets to dinner and waving them in the air. "Come on, it'll be good to get out of your shell a while."

"Yeah, maybe."

Unusually, he wasn't wearing threadbare jeans. Did he spruce up for me?

"Hey, you didn't happen to lose some sunglasses a few days ago? I found some close to home and . . . I don't know, it wigs me out to think about some stranger passing through there."

"Sunglasses? Me? No way. I like my reality unfiltered. Always. Where'd you find them?"

"At the foot of the oak by the turnoff, the one that's split."

"I mean, that's not exactly close to your house, that could be someone going to Rocatallada spring, the path up starts right there. They say the spring never dries up, and with the drought and all . . ."

"Yeah, I know it, I went up there one day. Go ahead, tell me the story, I know you're dying to."

"To tell the truth, there isn't one. You'll have to make it up. You could do something crazy and become Wild Mei of Rocatallada."

The parking lot in front of the shop was packed. As soon as we turned onto the small street leading to the church, we could already hear the hum of people chatting and the distorted soundtrack.

What the hell are you doing here, Mei?

The square was garnished with colored banderoles and flanked by monumental speakers. In the middle, twenty long tables covered in paper. We left our stuff on a spot that was still free. I shivered when I considered who might sit next to us.

On the steps of the church, a group of prepubes showed off their cellphones and bellybuttons, arrogant and naïve. Here and there, huddles of blathering oldsters, the women in summer dresses, low heels, and cheap perfume; the guys smoking with a beer in hand and loud laughter bellowing from their lips. I didn't care to imagine what sort of trash they were talking. Not a single person appeared interesting.

We opened a path to the bar with our empty glasses, feeling everyone's eyes on us, things whispered into ears. A woman with a hand's length of cleavage served us pestilent wine from a ten-liter jug, the kind that have a handle attached. I took a long sip to fire my courage. They called it wine but it could just as well be Drano.

We squeezed in at the bar, arms touching, Flavi amused, eyes wandering over the garrulous grouplets, me almost buckling from the tension, donning a desolate smile, I've always been a sorry actress.

Then a crippled woman came through. She advanced toward us, rocking, her arms too long, her hair too mahogany brown, reminiscent of an orangutan. People made way for her, greeted her with claps on the back, kissing her ass, making declarations of feigned elation. She smiled with a mouth full of big, disordered teeth smirched by lipstick, looking like a burst pomegranate. A blushing hillbilly in his Sunday shirt intercepted her. It was all laughter and camaraderie.

With the immobile mien of a ventriloquist, Flavi asked me if I knew her.

"She's the mayor. She's been following me for days. She's an ogre. It's risible, you'll see . . ." He trailed off, the virago advanced, soon she was just a few steps away.

"Well, son, I see you've got some nice company tonight. You must be the famous Remei, no? God help us, the writer who will put Sorrius on the Catalan literary map. A pleasure to meet you, dear."

We shook hands, or rather her damp hand shook mine with the feigned conviction of a president. If she knows who I am, it means everyone does. But I don't know who anyone is, I don't know who this faceless Goliath is formed of the people of the village who talk about me behind my back. Instinctively I pulled close to Flavi, our arms touched, his warm like a baguette fresh from the oven.

"So? Where'd you get off to, son? You saw yesterday we reopened the road to the sanatorium? Just imagine what it cost us! But listen, I've been looking for you for days on account of the honey festival, we're running behind!"

Flavi excused himself. Time was tight, he was sorry, he could give her the information of the Apicultural Association of Catalonia, he wishes he could help, but . . . She cut him off:

"You don't have time! Now there's a good one! For God's sake, you pass your whole day scratching your balls!" She waved her hands, swatting away inexistent flies. And then she added, nodding significantly in my direction, "Or maybe you've got other distractions now?"

My cheeks lit up. I lowered my eyes and swallowed my glass of Drano. The waitress with the sweaty cleavage served me more. Behind me, the push-pull continued.

"Maria Teresa, I'm sorry, but I just can't commit, I told you . . ."

"Fine, but next year . . ."

Then a man's voice joined in and started talking about the new parking lot. It was the mechanic. All those people, and me in the middle, an alien, pickling myself with wine. I noticed from the corner of my eye the spiteful expression on Flavi's face, and the mayor, God help us, and the inflatable man, God nothing, you just have to do the work. And the orangutan, out of nowhere, Listen, you know what it cost to reopen that road to the sanatorium? We can't just do everything!

Flavi's hand tugged at me, and as the primates jawed on, we ran off to seek shelter at the foot of the cypresses next to the church.

"God help us, right? Hahaha! I'm not used to you keeping mum, Rezzo," he told me, and then he raised his glass and exclaimed: "Cheers! May the town fair keep us with our feet on the ground every year!"

We clinked glasses, but I don't think a repeat's in the cards for next year. Who knows where I'll be next year and if I'll have finished the novel. If my unemployment runs out, I may take off for Barcelona. My stomach sank. Next year. An acidic emptiness came over me. Vertigo.

Next year, last year, years, life.

I looked at the square, everyone there chatting, mechanically happy and content. Next to the fountain, Mercè was smoking, puffing petitely, surrounded by churchmarms, ruddy to match the apples she sells. *Dip the apple in the brew, let the sleeping death seep through.* She's a good woman, don't be nasty. I waved back to her and smiled, too.

Some teenage girls were a few feet away, their naïve gazes a contrast to their glaringly turgid breasts. It was just a few days ago I was a teenage girl, what happened? The taste of my adolescence rose through my throat, the first tongue that profaned my lips, that explosion that rose up my spine, when life gave off a painful light you could bite, when falling in love was still possible. Falling in love!

Flavi rescued me.

"That rain today was spectacular, right?"

"I went outside naked and let it fall over me."

"What? Me too, behind the house, in case a car came by and caught me with my wang out." The image of him nude under the rain overcame me, and something inside me contracted. "But hey, careful where you stand, you could get struck by lightning! *Il lampo che candisce alberi e muro e li sorprende in quella eternità d'istante.*"

I replied in kind:

"*És quan plou que ballo sol, vestit d'algues, or i escata.*"

"Look, they're bringing out the platters. Should we go to the table?"

A group of guys and girls who'd only just reached the age of majority sat with us, their heads full of precious chimeras, I don't know if it was that or the third glass of wine, but right away, I started to feel better. The blonde girl next to Flavi is still walking around with her heart on her sleeve, she's started Biology, she's imagining a future she's sure to never see, she'll go to Barcelona, her life will take off; I envied her faith in these promises a little. The brown-haired boy beside me, blustery and cocky in a way I found endearing, served me wine with a seductive air, and I egged him on, occasionally brushing his knee to inflate his gullible ego a bit. But then:

"You've got the eyes of a killer in love," he said dead-serious, even if he might have been joking—I don't know. I cracked up, unsure if I found that sublime or terrifying.

We gobbled down sausages, country bread, and tomato salad, seeming to eat without thinking, and talking uninterruptedly of banality after banality: last winter's snow, the simian mayor, the urban legend that smoking dried out banana skins can get you high—the brown-haired kid insisted we had to try smoking salvia and Flavi laughed, his mouth boorishly open—and whether piercings were sexy or gross. The emptiness of it all was as strange as it was liberating.

The blonde lit a cigarette. How long it had been since I'd smoked! I asked her for one, the taste was repellent, but it reminded me of the preposterous sense of security you feel holding one in your fingers, sucking in, feeling the smoke contaminate you inside. We smoked together while she talked to me, with that enthusiasm common among obsessives, about cannibalism among primates—they eat their children! she exclaimed—and then she gave a detailed account of research at Atapuerca that had confirmed that those who lived there also ate one another. And me, while the smoke and the wine slowly killed me, ruminating about what human flesh must taste like and if inside us hominids who throw parties for the town fair, that atavistic anthropophagic brutality still abides. I'm sure it does.

The blonde and the brown-haired kid walked off with their gang. We said goodbye, me a little disturbed by both of them: in my head there mingled chimpanzees eating their young and psychopaths in love. I imagined them kissing with hot tongues at some club in the village and feeling each other up with the desire of those who want it all. But who knows, maybe now people fuck on the first date. Or maybe they don't want it all because they've come to believe the cliché: you can't have it all.

We went for coffee-and-brandy, No, Flavi, if I have a coffee now, I won't sleep till tomorrow morning. But I drank it anyway. The music came on, and the golden agers gathered on the dance floor, the men grabbing the women around the waist, even pinching their asses. The night gleamed in the deep darkness; the scent of night here, so different from the scent of Barcelona, Barcelona at night, Barcelona in the daytime, and Flavi trying to convince me we should go to the beach one day, and Why not? We can get there in an hour and a half and we can go have *fideuà* somewhere, and me begging him to rent us a paddle boat so we can take off for some secret cove, because it depresses me to see all that flesh stretched out in tight rows on the sand and I can't bear the shouting of their rotten kids, when they're running wild outside it pierces your eardrums even worse. Fine, we'll rent one, but only if you'll build a sandcastle with me, you need to do something with your hands, get out of your head, Rezzo.

Mercè sat down with us, all that dancing, she could hardly breathe. She rattled on more than usual, the changing weather and the dance, bad combo. I gave her two earnest kisses on the cheek, I felt bad thinking ill of a person who'd done so much to care for me, a blabbermouth, sure, and her brother . . . a shadow passed across my mind and I asked about Manel. Sick, she said, he really hates missing the town fair, he loves to dance, when he was young, him and your mother . . . The thought of the cockatoo made me jump up like a spring, I need to go to the restroom, and I left with a big smile so as not to offend her.

Flavi came to find me, Hey, let's have a gin and tonic, it's the town fair. And me, Are you kidding, I can hardly see straight! And all at once I had a gin and tonic in my hand. The music was playing and we got up, my hips were swaying, the rhythm escaped me but I didn't dare abandon myself to it.

And Flavi, Flavi, Flavi.

The animal choosing the music got the bright idea to put on a *paso doble*, and the bee astronaut dragged me out onto the makeshift dance floor, and Please, no, no, don't do this to me, but I was dying laughing, and his white, well-ordered teeth naturally carried the day. He grabbed me a bit higher than my waist, aping the straight posture of the older gents with their drinks and cigars, and we lit up the dance floor with our bodies that looked tender alongside those caper-cutting retirees.

Then a classic rock song came on and I didn't need to be asked, I was having fun, all those years without dancing, why? Idiot! Suddenly Flavi threw me up in the air, showing off the way people who dance but don't know how to, and a little voice told me I'd pay for that, people would be gossiping about us all month, but whatever, I leapt on him. He grabbed me around the waist, gripping me in those paws that could have held the entire world, Atlas hands that sent me aloft, and then I felt my groin push against his zipper, a quiver ran through my sex, I wanted to get close to him and feel his erection, Fuck, look at yourself, that gin and tonic was a dumb idea.

But the rock and roll went on and with it the smile that had overtaken my face. I wouldn't mind if those big hands got a little grabby, I told myself. People were watching us, we were obviously pretty tipsy, but who cares, now just his hand grabbing my waist, I rubbed a breast against his arm, my erect nipples poked through my dress, he should kneel down right now and suck them, bury his head between my legs, stick his tongue inside, all I wanted right then was his ass, his arms, his big hands squeezing my tits, grab me by that slender neck of mine, please, let the world disappear right now so he can pull down my panties and fuck me no regrets against the centuries-old wall of the church, I'd pull him close so he could push it deep inside.

And despite the eyes observing us, the slack-jaws murmuring, I was getting hotter and hotter, and more and more I wanted to scandalize them, to throw it in their face, to show myself off more obscenely, spinning and dancing, legs, arms, breasts, hips shaking, exorcising my yearning while my pussy started to thrill against the crinkly border of my panties. I could feel my gaze burning and that forgotten force that swells you and turns you into a being impossible to wound.

Then a drop fell, two, too many, and the music turned calmer. The master of ceremonies started gathering his things, Nina Simone's voice echoed off the church's counterforts, I too remembered the faces of every man who put me here, and one day I *shall be released* too. And Flavi said, Should we get out of here?

I would have stuck my tongue down his throat to the uvula then and there, but just:

"Yeah, sure, let's."

We got to the car just as it started pouring. Maybe in the end the Mother of God of August isn't as big a bitch as I thought. Dummy. Fervid, we ran and stumbled, constantly on the verge of slipping or falling, it was the gin and tonics' fault. We had twenty minutes of country roads before us and a craving for flesh that was metastasizing uncontrollably inside me: the epidemic of desire.

Every time I changed gears, his knee a few inches away. Pull down his zipper, jack him off, I couldn't think of anything else. We drove into the woods. The night was transparent black. The violence of the rain on the roof of the car spurred me onward. I slowed down to keep from smashing into a tree.

Drinking and smashing into a tree. Beat it, Guim.

Flavi whistled, looked out the window with his prodigious eyes, capable of seeing in total darkness. The windshield wipers at max speed swishing away the water that fell on us as it had in the afternoon. In the afternoon. I imagined him nude behind his house, his tight butt, his skin slightly saggy from the years, as if he inhabited only the instants when I see him and then were only a warm breath circulating through the forest. Him under the rain, dick dripping water. Kneel before him and drink until my thirst was quenched.

The sky went on ejaculating without restraint. Stop the car here, right here, get out, let him do you in the mud while the rain lashes you, ride him on a patch of moss, let go, suck it till he weeps, rub yourself against his knee like a bitch in heat while you suck one of his balls, then the other, while you lick the tip greedily and then fill your mouth, make him moan, make him lose sight of the world. Turn in the damp darkness, open my legs till he rips me apart, stick it in me till he splits me in half, fill me until this night became irreversible.

I couldn't even talk, my entire self was stifled, burnt with delirious desire, boom-boom, my vagina pounding, tick-tock, a time bomb counting down. We got to his shack. Now, dammit: jump on him.

"Shall we strip down under the rain?" Voice trembling a bit.

And him, with a cackle:

"Shit, now?"

We got out of the car. I pulled him over. He looked at me sternly.

"I'm afraid I'm out," he said with a sad smile.

"Fine. As you wish."

We were both soaked, the water evaporated when it touched my burning skin. I wanted to kiss him on the cheeks and say goodbye, but his neck, the scent of honey! I put my hand under his shirt, touched his back—skin, bone, muscle—my pussy dripping. I pulled into him, my chest exhaling vapor, I licked his neck, put my lips on his mouth, tried to open it with my tongue.

He pushed me away softly.

"Hey, Rezzo, easy, I'm not like that. It's complicated."

He gave me a humiliating kiss on the cheek and left me standing under the rain."

"Be careful!"

The night swallowed him.

I could have shouted loud enough to tear open the world, and inside, all that burning, desire and now rage, humiliation. What the fuck are you doing, Mei? The water went on falling imperturbable, but it was incapable of diluting my dishonor.

I got in the car, took off with a hand stroking my slit, and with every jostle, the image of him ramming me, the fire inside and my hand implacable, now inside my panties, brusquely shoving its way between my lips, and more jostles, deeper in, all of me liquid, boiling, spilling from my cunt, my eyes, melding with the rain in my hair. And a derisible, impotent orgasm, as if my vagina were a black hole and wanted to suck in the whole world, but just wasn't strong enough.

I'm not like that? Like what? What the fuck are you saying? You're not the type who likes to fuck, you're not the type to throw yourself at the first person who comes along, you're not the type to light a fire and then run away and let it burn everything down? Coward, bastard, idiot!

I parked at home. The jingle bells murmured, a pickaxe echoed, and the current come down from Blunted Crest curled around my ankles.

From the foot of the staircase, I saw something higher up. I climb three steps and see the black outline of the fox clear against the black background: avant-garde in a state of nature. But she is there, I see her, she looks at me, I'm sure she's looking at me. You know I'm the one who feeds you?

I tear off my dress. I confront her nude, animal to animal. We stay there taking each other's measure, eyeing each other up without seeing.

A bolt of lightning strikes and engenders a crystalline moment where we see each other pupil to pupil. She hurries off; from within me erupts an interminable birthing cry, my throat burns as it flees.

Come back soon, I beg.

The pebble is no longer on the door panel. But who cares. Shame and rage consume all.

I stayed in bed for hours, incapable of setting foot back in reality, squashed against the mattress by the blanket of humiliation. The sun crept in, shifting the shadow of the curtain, everything else was immobile, even me, as if immobility made me invisible to the eyes of the world. Not moving allowed me to disappear, to not exist.

I recalled the night before in flashes, and with each image came a jab of impotence. That bit on the square, showing off in front of everyone. Dancing. Dancing! And then, from the kitchen, there came the caustic rattle of the urn, which knows all, which saw it all through my eyes. Piglet, it said to me, you've already forgotten me?

Going back to Mercè's shop would be torture. I'd prefer to be mute, cut my tongue out so I wouldn't have to speak. And blind, blind, too, to not see the looks, the gestures, the mockery.

Dead, I'd prefer to be dead.

My lips crashing into his, closed like a fucking lockbox. Me pushing into him, pressing my mound into his zipper. The urn cracked up laughing. And derision. I won't go back in the kitchen, I know it's waiting for me there, sarcastic.

A frenzied bitch in heat. Maybe I moaned, with one of those irrepressible moans that rise up from my cunt. Moans, desire in sonic evaporation. Porno flick moans.

I pull the sheet up to my chin. With every slight movement, the pulse like jabbing inside my cranium reminding me I'm alive, and my head stuffy, full of mucus that drains from my nose. Too much nipples in the air yesterday, too much skin soaked by rain.

Suddenly, I notice the damp between my legs. The red damp. I need to hurry, before it's too late.

I sit up, the world tilts, the floor is cold. I walk to the sink with automatic steps. Maybe that's the key: limit myself to acting like a robot.

Panties already stained. As always. With the spot, the mental reflux: what couldn't be, and that bastard doctor. I wipe. A clot. Red clumps of opprobrium. I go to the armchair.

My nose is running, my cunt is running, my soul is flooding out. Disappearance through liquidation. It's not a bad plan.

I question the sunflowers, awaiting their response with the balsam of an irrefutable truth. Minutes, hours, defying them with my gaze. But they don't console me, the fuckers.

Then a knock at the door.

The automaton rises from the armchair in the T-shirt that hangs to mid-thigh, barefoot. She slides the bolt and finds him standing there with his radiant smile, today he does open his mouth and rubs in my face those perfect teeth he wouldn't let me lick. He hands me a jar of honey:

"Since you told me you were out . . . How are you? Headache, right? That cheap gin is a killer! But we had fun, right?"

The operating system fails to issue a response. The human continues:

"Listen, I feel bad about yesterday, maybe I should have . . ."

The emergency program kicks into gear with spiteful bitterness:

"No need to apologize. I'm the one who should apologize."

"I just feel like I wasn't very . . ."

The automaton cuts him off:

"Let's not talk about it. I'm embarrassed enough as is." It says that looking at the ground because it's afraid of looking into his iris. Fear of sight, does that exist? Opsiphobia, patient zero. "We should probably see each other less. I need to concentrate and work. I'll see you soon."

"As you wish."

"O.K. then," she says in a tone of valediction. She can feel a drop of blood slipping like a grub from her vagina. Plop.

"Sure, right. Come and see me though, O.K.?"

She grimaces, it's trying to be a smile, but affronted melancholy overshadows the expression.

"Bye," she says as she shuts the door without any kisses on the cheek.

She slides the bolt. Avoids the kitchen. From an angle sees the urn, severe, on the table. Returns to the armchair to interrogate the sunflowers.

Salty seeds slip from her tear ducts, unstoppable. Some automat she is.

Write, just write. Thirteen days writing at all hours. I'm not afraid of the blank page, more so of the written page, imperfect, imperfectible.

The fucking first chapter, rewritten top to bottom, has taken on ten more pages and depth. I think. The second and the third are pretty polished, waiting for me to trim them. Four through seven are still raw, but they fit.

Letters and letters coming together and pulling apart. Period.

Ward off distractions, implacable. Disturbances, out.

The shutters always shut, to avoid disruption by any quivering bushes, any fox that might be looking in, any sunray trying to fall on my pale skin and scorch me. Any cloud that might force me to reread Durand.

Go down to the store now and then and buy a few things, eyes pinned to the ground, tongue severed, enter and leave like a shadow.

Cut wood, thinking all the time of Lila, and above all of that primitive being that secretly observes her and rubs her skin as it passes, with evident swelling between its legs and a turbid gaze. The human slug.

Logs and branches. The axe and I have become friends.

Winter's coming, and I'll be waiting.

History repeats itself. One month later.

Again, dress and retrace the route to his shack with my first chapter in hand. As if time could be made to run backward and the same scene could be rehearsed a thousand times. But no, in life there are no rehearsals, every first time is definitive.

Many days without seeing him. I think of him often even if I try to make it seem like I don't. Who am I trying to fool? Me.

I knock again at his door. He opens it back up. The same movements repeated, the two kisses, the look of surprise. But all of it now freighted with horrible melancholy.

We greet each other like whatever, but my eyes elude him, I don't want him to read into them. Acute opsiphobia.

I hand him my papers.

"First chapter, redone."

He tells me to come in, we'll have tea. I refuse the invitation.

His scent! A warm wave drives me, a need to kiss him and bite him to death then and there. Feel his tongue intertwining with mine. My stomach has contracted to an infinitesimal point and might explode at any second. Big bang and remake the universe. I need air.

He insists I come in, we should sit down on the sofa. I can't say anything, if I open the sluice gate of words, I'll overflow. He perseveres with this show of normalcy.

"What, you had to go sign for your unemployment?"

I shake my head no.

"I mean, if you didn't . . . You know, Barcelona is a delight in August: the desolate cityscape, like in a Western, plenty of places to park, the rolling shutters of the shops closed and cockroaches big as your hand taking over the streets. The death of civilization. As though a virus had exterminated humanity. I love it. If you like, I'll come with you." I shrug. He continues: "What do you say we do something this week? Come to lunch tomorrow, and I'll make a rice. Then we can go see Renata. How 'bout it, precious?"

Precious, he says. Precious. The word flips a switch, the sluice gate opens, my eyes cloud over.

"Better if we don't," I say in a trembling voice.

I look at him and we observe each other in silence as a tear bisects my cheek. Flavi hugs me.

"Mei . . ." he says. Him all big hands, me all small. "I'm sorry. Come in, let's talk about it. I didn't think you . . . You're fucking great, it's just . . ."

I give him a kiss on the neck, I can't help it. I pull away and say:

"Some other day, O.K., Flavi?"

And I leave with long steps, anxious, as if it were possible to leave behind the ball of tenderness I have inside me, but it follows me, rolling behind me, tenderness piling up like snow on a hill, catching up to me, turning gigantic. I start running so it won't squash me.

THAT DAY

You can tie a leash around the cockatoo
and walk her naked around the town square.

SEPTEMBER

I have breakfast in silence at the kitchen table. Since that night, the urn refuses to speak a word to me, and the honey tastes bitter. I don't put your glasses on anymore so the patches of color I see when I do won't turn the entire world into a colossal Rorschach test; too many possible interpretations, your vision beyond the grave's no good for me, same goes for your rebukes. In the morning I'm still unsure, but in the evening I'll throw them in the trash without the least trace of remorse, and they'll lie there with the lenses streaked with pesto next to a dirty Kleenex and a rotten tomato.

Today, September begins. I hope for nothing new. Forest, phrases, pages. Nothing more.

I decide to go to the gorge to commend myself to it, soon it won't be hot enough to submerge myself. I grab my backpack and a sack of ideas for chapter eight and I set forth. As I turn the key, a whisper: Take me with you.

I open back up. I go to the kitchen. I look at it there, still, wagging its tail so I'll take it out for a walk. I open my bag and put it inside. I go back out. I turn the key. The stone on the door panel.

I reach the pebble beach with my back soaked in sweat, take off my backpack, take out the urn. I leave it to sun while I undress, watching it, I wouldn't want it to get away. He wants me. Even dead and cremated, he still wants me. A finger disappears between my moist lips and I sink slowly into the hypnotic shimmer. I hide my entire body inside the water and I stay there until my air runs out.

I should put a lake in the novel. A dark, immense lake, full of rotten algae that twists around Lila's feet and drags her to the bottom. To kill her.

I lift my head, take a breath, return to my liquid lair. Over and over again. The pleasure of repetition. Without thinking. But eventually I get tired. I dry off and sit next to the urn.

What shall we do, Guim?

I stretch out my hand and stroke the ceramic with the tip of my index finger. The thin skin of dead ceramic. I bring it close. My hair drips down on it, drops fall down over the surface of the urn, which is bulbous like a human cheek.

I feel a sudden mad urge to be at home, I need to sit down at the computer. I throw on my clothes, grab my things, and take the trail back with long steps propelled by roiling thoughts.

(The lake, Lila, the shepherd).

I don't even see where I'm going, I take off running, I need to get there before all of this escapes me. I chase my ideas, which are running faster than I am.

(The strayed lamb and the slug's eyes, the blood of the lamb diluted in the lake).

I leave the river behind, my desperation drives me. I jump down the slate slope, I fly over the chips and slivers, exactly, I'm not running anymore, I'm flying.

(Lila's dream, flying over the hermitage like a kite, and in the shepherd's hands the rope that holds her to earth).

My foot slips, and all of me flops backward in slow motion. I stretch out my wings to full breadth, my arms flap sterile. I will never dare to be Icarus, he flew too high, the water will soak my wings, a fucking hummingbird flailing underwater. I open my eyes wide, pupils dilating with danger, and trying to see more and better, but the poor things are unable to find anything to hold onto. My hair rises with the weightlessness of the subaquatic world, rebelling against gravity. Deep down, it's always that: the attempt to resist the forces that suck us down, that bend us, that crush us.

Gravity humiliates me, and I fall. A dry thud. Back against ground. With my satchel. A noise of shattering, a crack that splinters time.

I stay there laid out, immobile, staring into the provocative placidity of the sky and the branches that sink into it like claws. A shard of ceramic tries to pierce through the backpack and penetrate the flesh of my kidneys. I don't budge.

Seconds pass.

Minutes pass.

Or maybe time stopped and is waiting for me. When I shift even one finger, it will start over again. A black and white magpie heckles me with a porcine grunt.

I've got no alternative: I get up and open the backpack. Chunks of ceramic and grey dust. Do you want to run away, Guim? Did you want to be free, and did you trip me yourself? Or was I the one who needed to let you go?

Mondo . . .

I sink my hands in the dust. I fill them with you, cupping my hands like when you gather water to wash your face. You run between my fingers.

I dump it all out on the ground, on the traitorous slate. Grey on grey. Hands grey, too, covered in the chalk of death. I bring my index finger to my lips. I lick it. You taste like nothing. I hoped the ashes would melt in my mouth like spun sugar, but no, you've turned to sand; the son we never had could make a castle out of you. I crunch you between my molars, powdered bones, indurate. A beach of Guimean sand, roll around in it. A fragment of you burns as it goes down my throat. What is it? A chunk of your pelvis, your gangly fingers, the eternal smile on your jaws.

I rub you on my arms, sunscreen. You scratch. Rough stone. You will protect me from getting burned. All of me draped in ash, you are my Vesuvius. When the lava chills, I will be a statue. Stop looking back, or you'll become a statue of salt.

I could sharpen flakes of slate and make a refuge where no one could get in without being cut. Live in a slate crystal. I lick my palms. Tongue of ash. Fill myself with sand, live burdened so as not to rise too high.

Enough with the bullshit, Mei.

I gather the remains in my hand, the bits of ceramic come together, clink with an unbecoming joy. Or maybe not: maybe with a joy very much in its place, the joy of liberation. Some particles take flight. Your fog. I inhale you. I breathe you. You smell like nothing.

Nor do you say anything. Have you left, then?

I get up. I kick a big chunk of ceramic. It flies, strikes the slate, splits. I step on you, scatter your remains with my feet. The grey mixes with the black slate. A sea of greys.

I abandon you there, without looking back. You contemplate the sky and the boulders and branches, and you will watch all the clouds pass that you will never draw.

I was writing torrents of words until four in the morning. I don't want to believe it was you who held me back, that abandoning you on the slate I've found the door I was looking for. I don't want to think it, but I do.

Do I?

For days I've been eating leftovers, dry bread, marmalade, bitter honey, crumbs of the future, leftovers of unfinished projects. I don't want to be a slave to my stomach, but I'm hungry. I went to the store.

I drove slowly, dazzled by the forest, when a van appeared, *that van*, the same one, the one resembling a hearse. I slowed down; it accelerated. It was just ten feet away. I stopped. The sun burned everything with a blinding white light.

It passed by me too fast, rumbling over the pits in the road. Who is it? Where are they going?

I saw wavy chestnut hair, a denim shirt. The person turned away from me on purpose (on purpose?). Carles. I think it was Carles. But in a denim shirt?

Is it him? Why haven't I called or written to him? Don't act like you don't know, Mei. You know all too well. Because he's the only one who knows the facts. That you threw him out, that you were pregnant, that you killed him. That's it, right?

He must have been roving around the house for days observing me, moving the pebble, stealing my figs, losing his flea market shades. He wants to drive me crazy because I killed his friend. That's what I deserve, right? He wants me to confess, to have me locked up, he wants people to know, for my mother and Guim's little French mother to know. The urn: maybe he wants to take it away.

After parking in front of the shop, I called Carles. It rang eight or ten times. Why won't he pick up? Is he at the door to the house? And then:

"Mei, I'm so happy you called!"

"Hey, Carles. Where are you?"

Him, thrown off, too thrown off, maybe:

"Where am I? What do you mean?"

He's faking. Is he faking?

"Just that, where are you? I was thinking of you and I wondered where you were. Silly, right?"

"I'm in Mallorca, visiting my aunt and uncle, you know, same as every summer. You could come, there's plenty of room. How are you?"

"Fine, fine."

"How come you never answer my messages?" He pauses, awaiting an answer that doesn't come. "Bah, don't worry about it, I get it. I'd love to see you. I'll go up there when I'm back. I wanted to earlier, but then I told myself you probably wouldn't open the door. Now I see I should have. I'm an idiot. Sorry."

"You know where I'm staying?"

"More or less. Near Sorrius, right? I'd have just gone to the village to ask."

Is that what he did, ask around the village to come spy on me?

"Nah, it's better if you don't."

We both stopped talking. Maybe he is in Mallorca, why would he need to deceive you? What makes you think he'd be stalking you? I remembered him hugging me at the funeral home.

"Sorry, Carles, I don't know what got into me. It would just hurt too much for me to see you now. I'll call you. Take care."

I hung up and entered the shop. Mercè's eyes were beaming, she could easily have been one of those serial killers she admires so. Nosy bitch. I grabbed everything—cans, oil, bread, apples, pasta, rice—to keep from having to come back until autumn. And her with her breast swelled with gossip and the same song and dance as always, Honey, you're not eating, honey, you need to go out, honey, how long are you staying, honey, the fall, the lamb, the macaroni, honey, honey, honey, we saw you dance, you little whore! You want me to tell you the story about the streetwalker they found gutted on the banks of the Hudson?

"Any chance some guy's been around here asking about me?"

"No, sweetie, I'd have told you something like that!"

"Yeah, of course."

While I put the things in the trunk, I saw the swings in the park next to the river. One in the afternoon. The sun baking the deserted village.

I sit on a swing and push myself upward with my legs as though my life depended on it. The creaking chains. The childish dream of going all the way around. Jumping at the top and taking off into the sky.

I was outside with the axe and the saw. The pile of wood is no longer meager but it wouldn't get me through a week of winter. Brandishing the axe gives me balance, the blade's metal conjures telluric forces. The power of the forest flows within me for a while.

I didn't hear him coming, he was on foot. I turn around and find him standing behind a tree. He startled me. I shouldn't have taken him that first chapter. What I should have done is not see him again. I'm consumed by shame. And the longing to kiss him.

Get out of here, that's what I ought to do. But where?

"Would you have me in for a tea?"

I can't refuse him, I can't refuse him anything.

We sit in the kitchen while the water boils. Scent of honey, wooden bones, straw hairs toasting in the sun. I miss the urn on the table.

"So I read the new version, and it's not bad, even if . . ."

"Be honest," I cut him off, gaze serious, battleship pose to keep him from pitying me. A porcelain battleship.

When he finished telling me in gentle words that not a single part of the new first chapter holds up, that it's jumbled, the style baroque and redundant, that it abuses enumerations and adjectives—at this point he read my words aloud while I flashed a stony smile—when he finished telling me the characters are so absurd they try the imagination, or so flat they make you yawn, when he finished telling me, in sum, the first version was better, that I need to let myself go but without losing measure and control, when he finished telling me all that, nothing was left in the kitchen but Mei's shell, inside the humiliation had melted me down entirely. And he still had the nerve to add:

"But parts of it are really good, I swear. Just keep going, get on with it and revise later."

He went to the bathroom and left me there in the kitchen, alone with my dilettantish ineptitude. Get out of here and away from the novel, who are you trying to fool? I repeated that over and over until he emerged.

"By the way, does Manel know about the damp in the bathroom? That needs to be fixed."

"Yeah . . . I didn't tell him yet, it always escapes me." And inside, the entire conjugation: I escape, I will escape, to escape, we escape, we will escape, I would escape.

"The spot is a little creepy, too. It looks like a decapitated woman!" He laughs.

"It reminds me of a chrysalis. I actually think it's pretty."

"I've got to see Manel this afternoon, I'll tell him to come by."

"O.K., thanks."

We remained in silence, not sure what to say. Behind each word and gesture, the weight of the unsaid, the subject we avoided and that nonetheless wedged itself between us.

"Hey, now that I think of it, have you seen a van driving around here lately?"

"A van? No."

"No? Like a white van, long. I keep running into it. I'm worried it might be . . ."

"Long, white? It could be from the sanatorium. I wouldn't worry about it."

I nodded. But.

To get rid of him, I said I wanted to write a while. He left. The scent of straw toasting in the sun, honey hair, and giant hands that will never grab me around the waist.

What a strange blend of aromas—lamb and red wine—trails Manel. He came to fix the damp. I let him in, me in front and him behind, with the toolbox and the eyes magnetized by my ass. Flavi and Guim would tell me I'm making it up. They're not women. I stood there in the bathroom doorway, watching him.

"That's coming up from downstairs," he determined after running his hand across the blackish blot. "It's creepy as hell, the shape, looks like a decapitated woman. We'll have to re-paint when spring comes."

I said nothing about the chrysalis. We went downstairs.

"I'm going to head back up, I've got work to do," I told him, and he smiled sardonically, as if to say I didn't have shit to do and spent the whole day with my thumb up my ass.

But of course, I didn't get back to work. I sat at the arm-chair rubbing my hands together and eavesdropping while he burst into one of his habaneras. *I met an old shepherd out driving his sheep.* Ideas popped into my head about what he might be doing there by himself. When he goes, you'll have to give him your hand, and who knows what he's doing with that hand right now.

I started walking back and forth, from the painting of the sunflowers I now know by heart—I need to take the damn thing down for once—to the armchair and back. I heard the clatter of the tools, and also: *What will the sea be like, big and blue as people say? Is it true it glows like silver in the night?* I couldn't take it anymore.

I found him perched on a box, squeezing putty sloppily into the corner where the damp started. His stench impregnated the cellar, it was hard to breathe. He turned, showing me his yellowish teeth in an attempt at an amiable smile, and said:

"You must be happy, no, missy? I fixed that for you right away."

That shoddy repair wouldn't last two days, but what could I tell him?

"Two minutes, dear."

Dear, always dear. He says it because he knows I can't stand it.

"If you wouldn't mind going ahead and making me a coffee, I'd be most appreciative."

I told him, Manel, I've got a lot of work to do, maybe another day if you don't mind. He laughed, you'd think I'd told him a hilarious joke.

When we were going upstairs, me in front, kaboom! The bag of tools on the ground and him grabbing at my ass.

"These stairs are a doozy!"

Maybe he didn't reach for my ass and he was just trying to get a grip on something to keep from falling. At that moment I wasn't sure, but the more I think about it, the less I buy it. He absolutely meant to reach for my ass. Let's get real.

My cheeks were on fire. I said nothing and I kept climbing with trembling hands and stifling heartbeats. I stood stiff-legged by the front door to see him out.

He took his sweet time tying his boot. Outside Truffle was waiting, groaning uneasily, pulling as best she could against the rope tying her to the wooden bench. She could smell her owner was near. When Manel made it to the door, I had the volutes of the handle imprinted on my palm. He stopped. The dog wagged her tail, impatient. For the love of God fucking beat it for once.

"All right, hon, work hard, and we'll leave the coffee for another day," and he winked.

I start to shut the door, but he still has a foot on the jamb.

"And eat a little more, dear, you're too skinny. A woman should have some meat to grab onto."

To refresh my mind, I went to the grotto and stayed there throwing stones into the void, mesmerized by a robin that studied me from afar, thinking about what Flavi told me about letting myself go.

I am entering the house now. I'll eat a piece of toast with olive oil and salt and work on the scene with Lila and the shepherd on the riverbank, her hand looking for his, and the legend of the spring. I won't go to bed till I'm done.

The weeks pile up like the firewood under the awning. I stoke the fire of the days with branches of dry words and dead pages.

And on windy nights, I open the window, take a deep breath, and imagine the forest brings me your ashes.

When the sun burns too hot, the scent of honey comes to me, fox droppings, the perfume of a cockatoo; the stench of guilt and ineptitude, the stink of facing life in ridicule.

But soon the cold will come, and the firewood in flames.

Twelve days. Twelve. Twelve days with the cellar window thrown open and me, an idiot, putting the pebble in the door panel the few times I go out when anyone—*he*—could creep into my home like a rat through the open window.

Twelve days. Twelve. And the question: Did he do it on purpose, to leave a secret entrance open? Yeah, I know what he'll tell me, the putty for the damp needed to dry. Sure. But did he come in one day? Did he creep into the gap and has he been wandering around my house?

Twelve days. Twelve. And three or four nights back, the night I dreamed about the colossal doors of worm-eaten wooden boards that looked like stone, doors that shrieked like a cat when you slowly crush its head, and behind each door more and more doors, all identical, and the intensity of the shrieks got louder and louder, so strong that I had to cover my ears, one with a hand and one with an uplifted shoulder, in a hunchback pose, because I needed one hand free to push them open; the night I woke in the wee hours of the morning with sour sweat covering my chest, startled, thinking the unbearable volume of the shriek of the oneiric door had pulled me from my dreams, and I sat up with my heart hammering into my ribs; the night I found myself naked there in the midst of the shadowy void, thinking perhaps I was still dreaming, because the blackness was so dense it didn't seem real, a petroleum gloom that stuck to your skin and seeped inside you, lungs full of murk; the night

I heard a noise, the sound of something dragging itself slowly, a lizard from Brobdingnag scraping the tiles with its scaly skin; maybe that was the night he escaped through the cellar window after watching me while I slept, an inch away from my face, engulfing me in his decaying smoker's breath, or maybe from the doorframe, shining a flashlight on my naked body over the worn sheets, legs outspread, cunt offering itself up.

Twelve days, not a single one more. I closed the window and I checked every opening of the house to leave it inviolable.

THE DAY BEFORE

Father.
Skull against the rocks,
symphony of bone on stone,
and a red burst on striking ground.
Father?

OCTOBER

A downpour fit for the world's end. The drops struck the roof tiles, trying to crack them and flood my house. Still, Flavi came by. He comes once a week, I've got him figured out at this point. How compassion repels me. Once again, he's insisted we go to the sanatorium one day to see this so-called friend of his Renata.

"Now that the road's finally open again, it's easy going, you need to get out, take your retina off the screen, your eyes are going to lose the ability to focus more than eighteen inches away."

He's right, the world is a little blurry, but I like it better that way: just now, clarity is too sharp.

"Some roads, it's best if they're never opened," I tell him.

I don't know why he's so interested in introducing me to the madwoman of the forest. What if she went crazy over his scent and his straw hair, if one night she threw herself around his neck or sucked him off the way a child sucks a teat and can never get enough, and now Flavi wants her to tell me the secret so I won't freak out or lose my head over him, with the wisdom of the dead returned from the beyond, or maybe who never did return.

I asked him to buy me a couple of things if he goes down to the village, maybe he could save me the trip, and I got rid of him without concealing my sour mood, faking, actually, I was in an even worse mood than I was, wallowing, but all the while gazing sidelong at those hands of his that obsess me, that I can't stop imagining rubbing my body down with honey. What if it's just that, something that petty and stupid, the fact that I haven't been laid in five months. Of course, it's easier to think it's just that.

I stretched out on the bed and masturbated with my panties still on to keep from burning my fingers on my incandescent lips.

Sometimes, orgasm is tragic.

S ince yesterday, I can't get the sanatorium out of my head. Skipping breakfast, I put on my shoes and took the road to the left. Five months I've been here and I've still never taken it all the way to the sanatorium. First because it was blocked, then who knows why, I think it scared me, or more than scared, filled me with an anguish I couldn't quite bear.

Renata's latent presence disturbs me and I'm afraid of meeting her and of the look, the gesture that will tell me something I don't want to know. Obviously that's absurd, but it's what I feel. Childish fear invades me. Her name's Renata but it could be Sibyl, Cassandra, Pythia. I imagine walking through the woods and she appears unexpectedly, behind a bush, nude, two bags with nipples sagging to her waist, her skin is violet and her knees skinned from crawling on the ground, a scattering of long grey hairs grow from her pubis, her vaginal lips dangle, her hair bugs out, her eyes are unkempt, she drags a strand of jingle bells tied to her ankles and points with a knotty index finger, every joint like a knurl in wood, her left hand holds a chipped axe, and she whispers to me in my grandmother's voice, They're coming now, and before I have time to avoid it, too surprised to react, she grabs my wrist, and when her skin touches mine, I realize she's infected me with an incurable virus, a catastrophic clairvoyance, a knowledge that can't be unknown; I've unwillingly tasted the fruit of the knowledge of good and evil and now I'm condemned. I already told you: childish fear.

That's why I never took the road to the left to its end. Now I do so and nothing happens in particular, it's the same woods as ever. I leave the grotto behind me, I can hear the nearby murmurs of the Roderic. A few feet more and I cross it on a wooden bridge.

There's a cool breeze. In the sky, a bank of high clouds restlessly advances. Altocumulus, naturally. *Nuages élevés, habitat des dieux, une déesse minuscule dans chaque gouttelette.* So it will rain later. I'd best hurry.

Rising up in front of me at once is the ten-foot-high fence around the perimeter. The prison. In its center, a two-story building, new construction of wood and concrete. I can't see inside. Parked at the gate, the white van that pursued me. The green lawn surrounding the sanatorium is so immaculate you'd think no one had ever set foot on it; electrified grass, green lava, a vegetable moat to keep the crazies and junkies from getting out and telling people all the secrets that can only be conveyed by touch. I follow the fence. Grass and more grass surrounding the cube where humanity's castoffs reside. I discover a garden with huge zucchinis and sad tomatoes in the back.

In one window, I see a woman sitting in an armchair, reading. Could it be her? From this far away, I can't make her out clearly, just a somber figure in a sky-blue robe with chestnut hair. Now I regret not asking more questions: What's she look like? How old is she? The white of the curtains and walls hinted at through the glass frame the reigning silence. I watch the woman a while. I wait for her to turn, I want to see her face, but I can't. Maybe she's asleep. I realize she isn't moving. Maybe she's dead. To die reading, seems like a good plan.

Then music rings out, a plangent cello. The notes come to me now formidable, now soft, depending on the gusting of the wind, the highs sharp, shrill. It's as if a record player were turned up to ten and I were listening to it under the water.

The door opens and five people appear, three men and two

women in identical blue tracksuits. They laugh. I know, there's
no law against laughing in a sanatorium, but it shocks me, the
sight of prisoners—disturbed, drug-addicted, ill—laughing, it
doesn't jibe with what Flavi told me. The laughter with the cello
accompaniment has an air of the tragic for me, as if all five of
them were about to die and I alone knew it. They turn toward
the garden, tread the moat of green but do not fall in dead.

I look closer at the two women. One is very young, she
couldn't be more than thirty, no way. The other must be around
fifty, short hair, blondish, brown skin, lanky. One of the men
sees me and shouts:

"Renata, we've got a spy here."

The lanky one turns and starts coming toward me. She smiles
at me as if I already knew who she was, she won't take her eyes
off me, and I'm incapable of breaking the stare, however much
I tell myself over and over, Mei, go, Mei, don't look at her, Mei,
this is your Medusa, that stare will condemn you. When she's
just a few steps away, I take off running. A running statue of
stone. Behind my back, I think I hear a voice.

"Hey, come heeere!"

The further away I get, the more distorted the voice grows, I
won't turn, I won't be Lot's wife.

"Come with us!"

And when I reach the wooden bridge that crosses the river,
I still think I can hear it:

"Meeei!"

The first thunderstrike, and the river murmurs like a passel
of emaciated jingle bell children.

I work better in the dark. No distractions. No weightless backlit particles like fairy dust that can no longer make me fly, no dust bunnies under the wardrobe to remind me of my indolence, no colors. If I was doubly daltonic, I'd write better, see everything in green, period.

Plus, not opening the window kept me from wasting time with the clouds. Now, whenever I open them, the first thing I do is look at the sky: just yesterday, in the evening, there was nothing but harmless stratocumuli out for a stroll, but I second-guessed myself and spent half an hour or forty-five minutes rereading Durand because I couldn't relax until I'd confirmed that they were, in fact, stratocumuli. The wind made them file past quickly, but how quickly, really? And then it struck me how nice it would be to have an antique nephoscope to calculate the angular velocity of the clouds, one of those nineteenth-century contraptions Durand describes (you'd have drawn one beautifully). Contraptions and books to pin the clouds down, but the more you know, the more they escape you.

Closing everything up also insulates me against the gentle noises of the forest, which have ceased to be helpful or agreeable. Now I'm with Lila besieged, with the beast that sneaks his hand under her skirts and slides his fatty fingers underneath her panties to sink them into her, glassy eyes and filthy stare, while Mateu returns from taking a piss behind a pine tree, scratching his balls and yawning, blind. Now the cheeping of a sparrow on a windowsill can no longer disturb me. I can't be a goddamn Snow White anymore or no one will believe what I write.

I sit at the desk in the darkness. The white light of the screen illuminates me. A window onto a more resplendent world. I dive in headfirst and fill that world with words. Oceanic paragraphs, syntactical sierras, piles of word-bricks rising to build a place where one can live.

Three hundred and seven pages I've done.

With this new disposition, time is blowing in my favor. The sun no longer sends rays over the tiles marking the hours insidiously. It doesn't matter anymore whether it's day or night or even lunchtime.

Just me, my QWERTY, the light of the screen traced out in the dark, a reverse black hole. My white hole that engulfs everything.

I heard the roar of a motor. I didn't pay attention at first—for days now, mushroom foragers have overrun the forest—but the mechanical lion came to a stop at the foot of the house.

I opened a shutter in the living room to be sure. The sun told me it was midday; I'd have thought it was no later than ten. Recently I've been a little disconcerted by time, you could say we were playing cat-and-mouse. I could use another one of those nineteenth-century gadgets to measure the angular velocity of time: how quickly does it advance? Now and then I'm certain it's something other than a second per second.

A white and red motorcycle, gleaming. But the driver's not there.

Three knocks at the door.

Me standing in the middle of the living room with the black pants I wear around the house, your wool sweater, hair pulled back in a stopgap bun, heels sticking out of my old lady slippers with the hole in the big left toe.

Three knocks, and a man's voice:

"Mei!"

A familiar voice. Angry? No, of course not.

"Mei, open up, I saw your car out here!"

How do you know if I'm here or not? Maybe I left on foot, I think, I could have slipped and fell on my way up to the grotto.

"I'll wait outside here. I'm not leaving without seeing you."

I don't move a muscle to avoid making noise and giving myself away definitively. I'm a rabbit in its warren. A defective warren, with only one way out. An imbecile rabbit that doesn't know how to dig a burrow the way God intended.

I approach the front door on tiptoe. I feel the presence of Carles behind it. He's sitting on the big slab at the top of the stairs. I don't see him, but I'm absolutely certain. He's rooting through the gravel with the tip of his index finger, drawing circles. Or spirals: yes, spirals, and he's contemplating them as if he wished to fall inside, hypnotized.

It's time to fix this. I have to open up.

"Hey, Carles."

He turns and hops up all at once. He's different, thinner, his hair is close-cropped now. His ears stick out so far now I want to touch them, they're so little, they look like magic charms. How long has it been since I've seen him? When was the funeral? An ice age ago, at minimum.

He stretches out his arms.

"Mei!"

I have the sense he's about to burst into tears. He hugs me. I didn't put on deodorant today, I think suddenly, as if that made any difference. I haven't showered in days, either. Repel him with my animal musk. He smells like aftershave and a civilization unaware of the existence of comforting burrows.

"How are you?" he asks, still immobilizing me in his embrace. "Thin, I can see that much." He feels my ribs. "A little disheveled, too."

He pulls away and studies me like someone evaluating an artwork's authenticity. Is this Mei? Is it a genuine Mei or a cheap knockoff?

"Getting by. I'm well here. I'm writing, you know . . ." If my smile stiffens any further, it will crack. "What brings you here?"

"What do you think?" he asks, half-irritated, half-amused.

"A lot of things, I guess."

"You don't respond to my messages. We haven't heard from you in months. MONTHS!" We? The first-person plural unsettles me. Who is this we? "Would it be so hard to call once in a while, send an email . . . ?"

I cut him off:

"I don't have internet or cell service up here."

"You know what I mean, don't play dumb. Your mother's going crazy, the poor thing. Don't make that face. I know she's a mean bitch, but she suffers, too."

"Is she the one who told you to come here?"

"No, Mei, fuck, of course not. I came because I'm worried to death, dammit!"

"Sure . . ."

After a moment:

"Well, you've seen me, I'm good."

"Good, you say? Come on now, open your eyes. You look like a skeleton. I doubt you're eating. And there's something weird in the way you're looking at me, like you haven't seen another person in centuries. You look dirty, unkempt. How long's it been since you looked in a mirror? Go get dressed, let's go down to Sorrius for lunch. Let me feed you, at least."

"Look, Carles, I'm writing. I'm writing a lot. It's my way of getting past it, you know. Everyone has theirs. You need to talk, me, I need to write. Stringing together words is how I make it scar over. You all don't need to worry."

"Listen, your mother . . ."

"Leave my mother out of it. She's selfish. Period! Don't play her game. You think I don't have a right to hate her just because she never hit me, never abused me? You don't need disasters of that magnitude, sometimes there's something subtle but no less horrible."

"Yeah, but . . ."

"Do you know what it means to spend your entire childhood watching someone treat your father like shit, laughing at him twenty-four hours a day? Do you know what it means to have a mother who never speaks your name, as if the very word repelled her? Do you know what it means for your teenage years to be gray, tied to the house, obeying arbitrary moral codes, feeling guilty for not being enough, always afraid of not satisfying her, fearing the next outburst, waiting for it, knowing you will soon once more be a cause for disappointment? Do you know what it is to grow up with that constant tension? Do you know what it means to feel you're an annoyance for the person who's supposed to love you most in the world? Do you know what it means never to be looked at with pride or love, to be treated like something to scratch off a list: the house, the shopping, dubbing, the girl? Do you know what it means to be fourteen years old and think you never make anyone happy? You don't, do you? Well, if you don't know what you're talking about, then don't come here trying to teach me lessons about my mother, please."

We stop talking. He looks at the ground. I don't.

"Maybe you're right."

" . . ."

"But you're not well."

"Jesus, what is this? I am well, I'm fine, I'm relaxed. And when I finish the novel, I'll be even better."

"What about unemployment? Did you go sign for it?"

"Carles, let it go, all right."

"Did you go there or not? Maybe you can do it online. Don't tell me you didn't go sign!"

"No, I didn't go and I didn't sign either. So what? I just had a few months left and with what they pay . . . Guim had life insurance, you know how he was, Mr. Foresight." It bothers me to speak about you in this ironic tone. "Maybe if they figure out I killed him, they'll make me give back the dough, right?"

"Don't say that . . ."

"It's the truth and you know it."

"You're not going to let me in?"

He didn't deny it, I repeat to myself: he didn't deny it.

"Best if I don't."

"Are you serious? Incredible. Incredible! I come all the way here and you won't even let me in your house? You really are fucked up." He stretches his neck to peer inside. "What are you hiding in there? Why won't you let me in?"

"What are you getting at, dude? What do you think I'm hiding? A body? We cremated the body months ago. Don't be paranoid."

Does he think I've lost it? Does he want to make it seem like I've lost it?

"It's really dark in there. Why don't you open the shutters?"

He's trying to make me doubt myself.

"I work better like that, O.K."

"Let me in," he orders.

I hesitate. I could put on a show and get him off my back. A few tears, a few promises to clean up, come back to Barcelona, all I have to do is play the widow card.

"I don't want to."

Incredulity swells his eyes.

"Be reasonable."

His look turns suddenly hard, his smile can't cover it up. He hates me. For a moment, I'm certain he hates me for killing his friend.

"One coffee. Let's have one coffee and I'll go. I swear."

"Carles, let me do things my way."

"Your way? What way is that? Stop eating till you up and disappear? Turn into a savage in the woods? You know what, I don't believe you. I don't buy it. You're not writing, you're lying to me. Show me."

It's a trap. He wants to come in and once he's inside he'll make me doubt everything. Classic gaslighting. Drive me crazy as revenge. Make them lock me up. With Renata.

"I am writing. I don't know why you're so set on questioning everything I say. It's almost like you enjoy it."

"No, that's not it . . . Sorry. I just think about it all so much. Him. You. The two of you. You loved each other so much!"

"Don't exaggerate, you know it isn't true, the love had worn thin years ago, but you know how hard it is to throw out old shoes, right?" I look at my busted slippers.

"So your pregnancy? What happened with that?"

I squeeze the door handle tight. I look him straight in the eyes, my pupils the size of the eye of a needle.

"Nothing. Nothing happened, as you can see."

I need to get rid of him. Think, Mei, think. Make time.

"Listen, let's do this: you leave, and I promise you in a month I'll send you the first draft of the novel. If I don't, I swear I'll come back to Barcelona. What do you say?"

"Hmm . . ."

"I think it's a pretty reasonable proposition."

Finally, I get it out of him.

"O.K."

19 Days Earlier

I take the basket out early in the morning. The green awaits me. The wind gusts murmur words to me for the novel, for the love of Lila, whom it swoops up inside itself and swallows whole, whirlwinds of bliss and escape hatches, tingles of future possibilities. *Le vent, amant des nuages.* The air brings me honey and cinders of death. Cinders of honey. Breeze of honey's death.

I take the path through the pine woods upward. I cut between the clusters of still-stunted yellowfoots gathering on all sides to welcome me. Once in a while there's one of a decent size. I crouch down, dig my fingers into the moss, and pull it up. It's an extraterrestrial flower. I could put it in my cleavage and dance a tango with the forest.

I reach the depression with the saffron milk caps covered by an autumn sea of damp leaves. I dive in. My feet sink in the spongy earth. It could swallow me up at any moment.

I see three mushrooms at the foot of the thick pine. I unsheathe my knife, cut them at the base. Feed myself on mushrooms, blackberries, asparagus, flowers, figs, river water. Never step on asphalt again. All I need is to learn to hunt and skin a rabbit. It can't be that hard.

I clean the bloody blade, wiping it on my knee. It's nice there in the bottoms, the branchwork of the trees is dense, the sky can hardly be divined through the vegetal mesh. Leaf clouds. I play dead on the velvet moss.

Palathy rises to my lips, inevitable as a yawn or a belch. I recite her haltingly, penance in the confessional: I *dipped into the streets paved with moss. That green, its ancestral peal tolling for me, summoning me. I couldn't help but lay down in that lushness, though it suffocated me like a thick second skin. And I remained there, waiting for something that would never come, until the night became irreversible.*

Three Hail Marys and heaven will be yours, my daughter.

As I stand, a spiny stem scratches my wrist. A seed of blood falls to the ground. There, a bloody milk cap will grow or a tree of fruits with red flesh thick like molten chocolate, fruits the size of a cow's heart and palpitating.

I take the main trail back. Today, too, I pass by Flavi's. I stop to drink water behind the bushes. We're getting to be friends, these bushes and me.

I observe Flavi's shack once more. Grief. Rage. What do I know.

The door opens, and out come those phrases of Valdino I detest. Valdino: cockatoo, the Minipimer, *zub-zub*, destruction, adolescence, father demolished. Driven by the notes, Flavi appears, smiling, and behind him, Manel, his hoarse voice reaches me, I can almost smell the stink of tobacco. Of course, it's Thursday, chess day. They stay there standing by the doorway, I can't hear what they're saying over the music. Valdino, decomposer of my life.

Flavi pushes aside the hair falling in his face, lifts his head a bit, puts a hand on Manel's back. The other says something softly, leaning in a bit, almost as if telling a secret. Flavi cracks up laughing. I wish it were a false laugh, but no, it's sincere, he's not faking.

Did I ever make him laugh like that?

Flavi turns and goes back inside, then comes right back out with a book. He hands it to Manel, who takes it and whirls it like a magic wand.

They shake hands. Manel departs, Flavi goes on shouting to him, Hey, thanks! The other waves his hand and puts on sunglasses. *Don't wear them things.* Sunglasses.

The flames are crackling. I strip naked and sit close to the fireplace. I want to feel the scorching on my skin. I bend down slightly over it from above, arms outstretched to embrace the flames from a distance. They burn.

I stand up, turn my back, and my buttocks light up. I separate my legs, the warmth scrubs my inner thighs. I squeeze a breast as if to milk myself and my other hand sinks inside me, I shake it fast, I want to finish as soon as possible. I bend forward, pussy close to the fire. A tongue of burning air. I see the pile of wood. I could stick a log inside myself, jab myself with the splinters.

I grimace as I orgasm. From pleasure? From pain? Does it matter? Is there any difference?

I stretch out on the ground with closed eyes, feeling a cadaverous cold. Let them find me here dead, nude, lying on the ground, hair brushed, a sprig of rosemary in my fingers and another poking from my vagina.

Not yet. The novel. Finish the novel. There's not much to go.

I open my eyes and I see three hundred and seven pages on the armchair. Shouting at me. I dress, grab the pages and the red pen. I'm unstoppable. At last.

The novel is potent. I don't doubt that anymore. After this, I won't be able to write anything more. Never again. It won't work. I've given everything here. It will be a luminous novel. Just twenty more pages, maybe thirty. Then that will be it, I can grimace definitively and fall into a coma.

At ten, I go down to the shop. From the corner of my eye, I see the inflatable man talking with a customer at the entrance to the garage, but when they see me, they stop, turn, he waves. I don't wave back.

I burst into the shop, the door chimes. Inside, an old church-marm eyes me up, a machine scanning me for factory defects. I bark:

"Good morning to you."

From the shop's innards Mercè emerges, her limp worse than ever. Her bones are dissipating like an effervescent tablet, she'll soon look like a cuttlefish, one bone and the rest flesh and cartilage, a human cuttlefish chameleonically changing color depending on whom she talks to. She comes to the counter cradling sausages like a baby, the meat ropes hang past her arms, slip through her fleshy fingers, resembling a nest of serpents. Dead pigs minced and stuffed in intestines with traces of shit. Sausages without bones, like her. A human-shaped sleeve packed with ground meat. *Zub-zub.*

"Hey, Remei, it's been forever! I'm so happy to see you!" Then, to the old bag: "Twenty euros, forty cents, Angelina. This is Neus's daughter, d'you know that?"

The two of them look at each other with fake, assembly-line smiles and verbose eyes. Telepathic slander. The old woman stares at me a few seconds before disappearing: too many defects for a single unit.

I grab three country loaves, a bottle of virgin olive oil, two pens. That's all I need.

"Let me give you one of these white sausages, dear."

She wraps it in plasticized paper. A severed dong. Then she sighs. Stops.

"Remei, dear, you look rough. You need to comb your hair."

"I was in a rush when I left, and I didn't think about it," I lie. "Next time, I'll pull it back in a bun or braid it real pretty, so I won't embarrass you in front of your customers."

"Come on. That's not why I'm saying it. It's just . . . you look like you haven't washed in a month. Is your hot water working?"

"Yeah. I'll shower before coming next time, too, don't worry."

"Dear, are you O.K.?"

We both pause.

"You need to see people."

"I see Flavi."

"Flavi, Flavi . . ." She rolls her eyes. "I saw you all dancing at the village fair . . ."

"And?"

This *And* could cut diamonds. Mercè doesn't respond.

"You don't like him being my friend?"

"Flavi's a good kid, I wouldn't tell you otherwise, but maybe you're getting too close . . . in the end, he's . . . you know what I'm trying to say. Don't make too much of it."

"You want to tell me what you're getting at?"

I raise my voice slightly as I say this. She flinches. She's afraid of me, my scent's acrid to her, somewhere between sweat and piss. I'll grab one of those sausages and smack her with it till she's laid out on the ground in her white immaculate apron with her Russian peasant face, I'll pinch her cheeks till they're speckled with hematomas.

"What? Say it?"

I'm losing control. Her apprehensiveness only makes it

worse. Next episode: the village shopkeeper found strangled with a strand of sausages.

"What???" I roar. "What the hell do you want to say?"

"You know . . . there's some people who say he, er . . . that Flavi prefers meat to fish, you know?"

I stab her with my eyes. I drop a ten on the counter and go. She's still blabbing. The human cuttlefish drags itself to the door, shouts at me that I'm unwell, threatens to send Manel to watch over me, to call my mother. But I hardly even hear her. The thought whirls in my skull with the vague unmeasured whirling of fever. When my car passes in front of the shop, I see her smoking, nervous as a junkie, with watery eyes. Russian peasant women don't smoke.

Meat, fish, she said.

Meat, fish.

So much for restraint! Swallowing a succulent dick, that's what Flavi likes. Why didn't he tell me? Maybe Mercè made it up. Gossipy bitch.

Meat, fish.

I'm not like that. Like what? He swings the other way. Is that what he was telling me? He's a bastard for not just spitting it out. Coward. Dammit.

There's some people who say Flavi prefers meat to fish, you know? I bring out my linguistic scalpel. Some is not the same as all. Some could mean the wagging tongues in the village, nasty tongues that only utter words incapable of bearing fruit.

I eat meat, but I try not to overdo it. I try not to overdo it. Sly fucker. The poor widow, he must have told himself, you can't disappoint her like that, can you? Let her rub herself raw thinking about me, throw her a line so she can put her life back together and write her little novel.

Again: *There's some people who say he prefers meat to fish, you know?* Say. Saying isn't knowing. Saying could mean talking just to talk, the way a nasty wagging tongue does. Saying doesn't mean certainty. Saying is action, not truth.

Manel? I know him pretty well. We play chess every Thursday. Chess every Thursday? That laughter when I saw them two weeks ago coming out of the shack. The village Rock Hudson. Chess? I see him on all fours on the sofa with Manel railing him from behind and Valdino shaking the walls. *Zub-zub.* The two of them laughing at me. How they must have laughed, the bastards. The writer. Ha! The horny writer who threw herself at him.

Stop, maybe it's all just talk.

Because *There's some people who say he prefers meat to fish, you know?* Prefers meat to fish. A comparative. Does he eat pussy too, then? But at the end, there's that *you know.* But *you know* really means everyone knows. It's just a plea for confirmation of the self-evident. You know? You know? You know?

A few years back, a good friend of mine died. He's always with me. He's a widower, like me, that's what he said without saying it. Yes, now I see him without the cobwebs of reverie. Everything reveals itself fully, like a spot under the sunlight.

I now see the entire village cracking up laughing the day I danced with him in the square, that's why they were staring at us the whole time. It wasn't envy that made their eyes sparkle, it was sadism.

I'm fuming with rage. I want to kill him. Kill. Go see him right now. Not let him open his goddamn mouth. Him with that pious face the whole day long. Bullshit!

No, I can't go there. Not now. I'd make an even bigger fool of myself. And what if it's not true?

I park at the foot of the house. I can't go in, I need to fill my lungs with something that isn't burning. I take off running to the grotto. I scurry up the rocks.

Meat, fish.

Why not stretch a foot out a little further than I should and put an end to this once and for all, tumbling downward?

Once on top, I roar like a carnivore ox, flesh, that's the only thing I need. Human flesh I can devour.

THAT DAY

Copying lines from that woman with a man's name, Mei?
You're a joke.

5 Days Earlier

I think I didn't sleep. I'm not sure. At night, time agglutinates strangely and loses all direction: a minute might be seconds or hours. The constant writhing only reinforces the sensation of infinite repetition—again, face-up, again, face-down—the unspent nanoseconds trapped in the folds of the sheets we keep rediscovering. The terror of eternal night. You should keep still, but time drips on incessantly and slowly perforates your head. Chinese seconds.

And last night, in the hollow of my skull, too many rotten chimeras congregated, and I no longer knew whether what lay in my head were dreams or thoughts or even if I was alive. Darkness, ever emulating death.

I dragged myself out of the bed as the light timidly profaned the darkness. Walking barefoot on the frozen floor confirmed to me I was alive. My bony feet looked like a corpse's, your feet beneath the white sheet. Soulless Guim abandoned in the middle of the forest, he who'd always preferred the pavement. Bitch.

I sat at the kitchen table with a tea. Sans honey. Bitter. Eyes pinned to the sheet of Formica with the furling corners.

Home, cold. Disappointment, hot.

Flavi. How stupid. How stupid indeed. I could slap myself. The cockatoo would die laughing if I told her. But if it did kill her, at least it would have been good for something.

I bit my wrist to appease my rage. Till it bled. I need to discharge this fury.

I got dressed. I gathered all his things lying around the house: books, honey, the jar of marmalade, the plate I should have taken back weeks ago that he'd brought with the zucchini omelet, the hopes I'd placed in him, my charred affections, my disillusion. I stuffed it all in two plastic bags. My disillusion wouldn't fit, I had to leave it behind.

I cranked the motor and departed slowly through the corridor of trees, a hearse bearing the remains of a friendship.

The day can't decide whether to rouse itself, dense clouds, eclipsed light. Belly too empty, head overcast from insomnia, feet unsocked, the shoe leather scrubbing the skin still numb from the cold. All of me possessed by the oneiric sensation of not having slept, when your body won't obey and neither will your head.

I rehearsed what I'd say to him, the indifferent pose:

"I brought your things, don't come back to my house ever, you son of a bitch."

And the way I'd turn, impassive, get in the car, and take off unhurried, in full possession of myself.

And once more from the top. This time imagining how I'd tell him with a contemptuous smile:

"Piece of shit, I brought your things. I don't want to see you again. Ever."

Or I'd grab his package and squeeze his balls:

"You like that, do you?"

I knocked on the door with my fist. Three times. A magpie took off flying, its raspy cry crept into me. I would caw too, if I could.

As soon as he opened up, he provoked me with his big hands and saintly gaze.

"Here. I brought back your stuff," my voice muffled by the knot blocking my throat.

"You brought me back what?" he asked, disconcerted, naturally. He couldn't know that I knew everything, and he went on playing his role.

"Yeah. Best if you don't come to my house anymore."

"But . . . ?" He looked at me incredulously. "Are you O.K.?"

"Perfect, Flavi, I'm perfect. You know what? I figured out the solution to your aunt's riddle. What can we hope for from life? The same thing as from you, right? The same."

He grabbed my shoulder in his giant's fingers, but I pulled away brusquely.

"Nothing, Flavi, we can hope for nothing. Nothing at all. Isn't that right?"

"Do you want to tell me what's up with you?" he shouted. How delightful, making the monk shout.

"What's up with me? Please, drop the pretense. You've been laughing right in my face. Did you think it was funny to watch me fall in love with you? You must have had a hell of a time acting all mysterious and getting one over on us women. Do you hate them, Flavi? Do you hate women? Is that what you did to Renata, too, you bastard?"

"Listen, Mei, I feel like . . ."

"Shut up, I don't want to hear one more lie. Did you and Manel have a good laugh while he was giving it to you up the ass or were you too busy moaning? Look at you, a little lamb that keeps bees. Did he tell you he broke into my house?"

"Mei, enough! You're sick. I can promise you I'm not . . ."

"I told you to shut up. Don't talk to me like you were my father. You all would love to make me think I've lost it. Look at yourself: hiding it from me, letting me throw myself at you. How two-faced."

"Don't accuse me of things that . . ."

"You've really got it down, your little saintly pose, don't you? You're disgusting, Flavi. Disgusting. You're a junkie and a sicko, what do you think, I don't know what you've got in your medicine cabinet?"

"You went through my things? Unbelievable. How dare you!"

I turned and left him hanging. I walked to the car repeating with swollen lungs disgusting-disgusting-disgusting-disgusting-disgusting not to hear what he was shouting to me. His voice reached me tinted with rage, what pleasure. I cackled colossally as I got in the car.

He came in my dreams. The Hamletian ghost of my father. Fortunately the bard isn't my bible. But what he said to me while I slept, even if I know it isn't true, left me unsettled. He was talking as though in a whispering cry, in soundless desperation: Your mother put the water and the sandwich in the climbing backpack. Get it? The backpack with the cord, the harness, the carabiners. Her sandwich, my things, her hands rifling through it all. Understand, Mei? Understand?

The novel wells inexhaustibly inside me. I opened the tap, an old rusty tap, and now I can't turn it off. I will write until the well runs dry.

The well. Lila is at the edge of it, body glazed in sweat and soot, black lard, clothing stained too. How she peeks over to bring up the water. The glistening, soothing thought of getting lost in the blackness, throwing herself inside and banging her head against the walls. A pebble falls in. Plonk. The rough rope tears the calluses from her palms.

She returns home with two full buckets threatening to spill, two lead sinkers holding her to earth. She advances slowly, body straight, to control their swaying. Her clavicle, her wrists, her hip bones poke out with the insolence of a corpse. She's a skeleton draped in a film of skin. She's dry, shriveled, exhausted. The breeze sends airborne the black hairs that fall from her kerchief. Hair of the dead, like hers, still growing after the quietus. She enters the door in profile.

(My fingers type. Assign a note to each letter and listen to the sound of the symphony of words I compose with pauses from the space bar).

She huddles in the fireplace. She wishes she could coat herself in soot and camouflage herself in the surrounding shadows. She grabs the sponge and presses down with desperation, arm outstretched. The black water runs down her arm from her hand and drips onto her skirt. The sponge is a heart with black blood. She squeezes it. Two tears of rage trace a white line through the filth on her cheeks. Through the back window, starving eyes observe her.

(The pages fill up on their own. I think of Carles, who will be here in ten days to demand the novel. I'll crush him with my pages. How many? Right now its five hundred twenty, when I finish it'll be what, six hundred? I'll give him a printed copy and shut the door in his face. I'll shut Carles up. Shut my mother up. Shut up Flavi. I'll shut up the bastards from the publisher who threw me out on the street. I'll shut up the village gossips, shut up Guim and his lack of faith in me. I'll shut up the world. Every page I fill is a small act of revenge).

Night's fallen over Lila. A lightning bolt freezes the hermit-age on the hill. The furious murmur of the rain is like the whisper of a mountain endlessly crumbling. The world crumbling. Lila doesn't hear the creak of the opening door. He creeps into her house leaving a trail of blood. The human slug.

I feel Lila's disgust when she notices his claw on her shoulder, how her blood freezes (the nails long and grimy, the stink of wine on his breath when he approaches to toss her a few coins). She presses into the back wall of the fireplace, looks around, imagined she could flee up the chimney like smoke, then she senses the hairy talon sinking into her flesh and the bitter breath of the beast. She burns, trapped there in the fireplace.

And then all the rest.

(I'm getting close to the end. The last measures of the symphony. I take a break. Straight to the kitchen, chew up a few mushrooms and a bit of dry bread with fig jam, my daily meal.

I get back to it. I open the original. I copy a few literal phrases, a little homage to the great lady).

When the beast is gone, she can't bear to stay a second more in the house. She waits for her husband to return sitting on the edge of the well, her lone companion the offense of time indifferent to everything: the night runs its course. The tame hours flatten Lila like a steamroller, the stone minutes hurl themselves undeterred over the precipice of life.

At dawn, that panting piece of milky flesh appears. Her husband.

"Don't try to follow me. I'll kill you," she tells him.

And the descent begins.

(Now all that's missing is the epilogue, the inevitable twist ending. The rock awaiting her halfway. But it'll have to be to-morrow, my eyes are stinging, my eyelids rebelling.

I lie down).

THE DAY BEFORE

Crouching behind a bush, I gnaw a sprig of rosemary. Flavi is on his porch in the lotus position. The lotus, happy petals that float and never glimpse the depths. I observe him, today too, as if by doing so I could arrive at some certainty, waiting for my eyes to get used to the light he exudes and see further, deeper, down to the rotten mendacity lurking beneath his perennial smile.

I could smack him in the temple with a rock and knock him out. Hypocrite. I squeeze a stone in my hand, if only I could crush it. But I could also throw myself on him and beg him to say yes, he's my friend, he loves me, all that was just talk. Maybe if I hold my breath, I can crush the stone inside me.

I walk crouched over until I'm outside his field of vision. Death caps emerge to greet me, how opportune! I crush them with my boots. I return to the main road. The sky rumbles. Two months ago, deadly drought; now the water reduces everything to mud.

I cock back and hurl the stone. Like my life depended on it. If it goes past the puddle by the turnoff, if it goes past the pine further back, if it goes so far you can't hear it fall, if you send the stone into orbit, if you crack the window of your childhood, if you manage to make it skip fifteen times across the surface of Guim's memory, if you throw it so hard that the velocity breaks it up, if you reach the eye of time and blind it, all will be possible. A bet with myself.

The stone falls discouragingly nearby.

I crouch, grab another.

Gravity laughs at me.

And another.

The stones never run out. Nor my perseverance.

Another.

I hear a thunderclap. The world shakes.

This is the good one.

A thunderclap, an avalanche approaching.

I turn, throw the stone at Flavi's shack, now too far away to reach, and it describes an arch over the trees. I wish it would land on a branch: the stone that never fell to earth, the stone that bested gravity. A mythic stone. A weightless stone.

The avalanche envelopes me. I imagine a wyvern with an open mouth coming straight at me, and me blind, incapable of seeing it. A rundown truck appears in the middle of the road; perhaps it's got a dragon's neck, but from where I am, I can't tell. Liquid light scatters across the windshield, concealing the passengers. The stone strikes the hood and falls to the ground, defeated. The vehicle stops sixty or seventy feet away. The thunder dies down.

I consider taking refuge in the forest the way a hare does when headlights fall on it. The way the fox does. Transform into a fox and scurry off between the bushes. But no, the fox doesn't flee. The fox stops and studies me. Defies me.

I stop and study the vehicle. Both doors open like the gills of a respiring shark. Legs appear under the doors: a man's and a woman's legs. I know them. I think I know them. My fur stands on end, my pupils dilate. Instinct tells me to flee, but my body doesn't respond.

"Honey!" the cockatoo cries as she comes straight at me. Her hair's pulled back, black flakes of petroleum undulating over her shoulders like serpents.

I can't move. Now I'm the stone. Amputating her will do

nothing, the only way out is decapitation. Or maybe not even that, maybe her head will multiply like a hydra's.

Manel checks whether the stone has damaged the hood. He's chewing something. A spring of rosemary, like me. I spit mine out.

The gorgon has reached me. She embraces me. She wants to smother me in her cyanide perfume. I remain petrified.

"Mother of god, honey, look at you! You're a stick, and your face!" While she says this, she grabs my chin and moves my head left and right like a slave trader. "And your hair? Are you not showering? You stink. You've had me dying with worry!"

She hugs me again, she surrounds me with the whole of her body. I'm choking.

"Say something to me."

I wish I could play dead, like when I was a girl and I used to imagine thieves were breaking into the house or someone found me in the middle of a battlefield. Play dead and let the murderers pass me by. But it's too late.

"You aren't well, honey, you are not well," she shakes her head from side to side and sighs. She starts up again, her tone severe: "Your friends think you look off. You need to do something. We need to do something."

My friends, she says. It echoes: my friends, friends, friends, ends, ends, s, s, ssssss . . . Flavi? Carles? I don't have any friends. Apart from the fox.

The cockatoo has one of my hands pressed between hers and strokes me while she observes me with her head tilted, awaiting my reaction. Manel approaches us with cowboy steps. Now he'll take out his revolver and put me down like a lame sheep. He stands close to my mother. Too close. His proximity cuts into me. I hiss:

"What are you doing here?"

"I came to find you, honey. It's no good for you to be here alone. Look at you."

"Look at myself? You want me to look at myself?" I feign a cackle. "What about you? Have you seen yourself? In that skimpy little skirt with your cheeks rouged like a whore, like you're still twenty years old. Is that what a person looks like when they're *well*?"

Manel grabs me by the elbow:

"We know you're upset, but have a little respect for your mother."

I jerk away from his mitt, nostrils open to get in more air.

"Respect? There's a good one! Oodles of respect!" I extend my arms theatrically as if addressing a multitude. "Let's fill our mouths with respect. Till we're bursting." I make a dramatic pause. "But respect for everyone, otherwise it's no good. If you respect me, I'll respect you, O.K.? Now, if you'll excuse me, I'm leaving, I've got things to do."

I pass by with my head held high, but again those greasy fingers grab my elbow.

"Sweetie, you're not going anywhere. Don't be nasty."

"You're not singing *habaneras* today, Cubano?"

"Honey, come on, don't make this hard for us . . ."

"Or what, Neus?" I refuse to call her mother, I call her by her name, I know it infuriates her. "Or what? You'll take me by force? You'll tie me up and stick me on a bus? Come on!"

"Enough, Remei! Do you hear me?!" she shouts.

She has the same face as when she upbraided me as a girl: furrowed brow, furrowed lips, furrowed pupils. And her mouth, an atrophied anus spewing nothing but shit.

"You think you still scare me? Dream on. Leave me be."

I pull free of Manel. My mother bursts into tears. The balsam of each of her sobs. Tremendous.

"Sweetie, you can go pack your bags. Find another house. I don't want trouble in my house. I'll refund the months you paid, but I want you out."

She whines:

"No, Manel, no . . ."

He lays a hand across the cockatoo's shoulders while she looks at the ground and repeats her insistent Our Father:

"She's crazy, she's crazy, she's crazy . . ."

"What are you saying, Neus?" I ask her.

She looks up.

"That you're crazy, honey, Mother of God, you're crazy."

I can see she's scared. Manel's hand has descended to her waist. The two of them there in front of me, squeezed together.

"You disgust me. And you, stop feeling her up!"

"Remei," he says, I think it's the first time he's called me by my name, "if you don't come with us, you're going to force us to call for help."

"Help? Don't make me laugh. Who are you going to call, the fire department?"

"The mental hospital, Remei, the mental hospital," the human turd replies.

"Oh, Neus, if my father could see you, if he could see this, you can't imagine how sad he'd feel. How fucking sad . . . You're sad, but worse than that, you're pathetic, a pathetic woman, a pathetic wife, a pathetic mother. My poor father."

"Leave your father out of this! What do you know about it? Who was he? The man who took off for the mountains, who decided to kill himself instead of putting up with us? Is that the father you mean? Don't make me start talking, dear. If you only knew, honestly, I ought to . . ." she bit her lip, twisted the fabric of her skirt.

And then I saw it all, like a flash that illuminates everything for an instant and then the darkness cannot be the same black it once was because now you know what it's concealing.

I saw how my mother looked at Manel, how they communicated with their eyes in a familiar language woven across decades, how he shook his head while his hand squeezed her waist; I saw Manel's lean frame, a bag of bones; I saw the sprig of rosemary sagging from his tiny teeth, his smoker's milk teeth; I saw his bowed legs and his miniature hands, risible for a man, doll's hands.

Bony, bowlegged, milk teeth, doll hands.

And me, bony, bowlegged, milk teeth, doll hands.

The horror paralyzed me, only my brain continued to function, searching for evidence to deny what suddenly appeared obvious. Dreadfully obvious. How could I be so obtuse for so long?

Poor father, did he know? And her, humiliating him at every turn. The rotten bitch. Was it an accident, up there in the mountain? He was always so prudent, it was strange, too strange. And a little voice muffled by proofs to the contrary went on telling me: Mei, don't overthink it, these are coincidences, you've got your father's intelligence, everyone always said so, she's sharp like her father, they used to say, and your language obsession, your gift, your black hair, like your father. And your mother, too, like your mother.

My disgust flared up.

"You scum, I should stick burning hot needles under your nails, I'd cut your fucking fingers off one by one with an axe just to hear you scream and beg for forgiveness, you pieces of shit, fucking away the whole day long like a couple of animals while my father took care of me. My father, right? Or should I not call him that? My father. You should have freed him, but no, you wanted your upright life, you and your appearances. Strut around like the queen of the city. And torture him, you loved that, didn't you? Pig. Did he know? Tell me!"

"Honey, what on earth are you saying? You're delirious. Of course your father is your father. Manel and I went out when we were kids, that's all. Besides, he was in Cuba when . . . How could you ever think . . ."

"Admit it, goddammit, admit it!"

"This is preposterous, Mei. Manel is not your father. Don't be ridiculous."

"Ridiculous?"

I walked toward her with leaden steps. My body was sweltering, prey to a sudden fever, my dilated lungs exhaled the air of fanaticism.

"Let's go, Neus," Manel said.

They ran to the car, fleeing me.

Fleeing me.

I remained nailed to the ground until they vanished around the curve.

The clouds began to empty out a ruthless rain above me. But the fire was inextinguishable now.

Me, that piece of shit's daughter?

And my father.

My father!

Putative doesn't come from *puta*.

No friends, no husband, no mother, no father, no kids.

The inflows of solitude, as she would say.

The woods. My woods.

A gust of wind gliding between the branches, the balsam of rain, the consoling murmur of leaves; the greens so green and so distinct from one another they each deserve their own name; the knots in the bark and the stumps that measure time's passage in ringed lustra; the infinite stones covering the roads with stars from a terrestrial galaxy, always ready to be picked up and thrown down the stairs, over the path, into the black waters, stars a hand's breadth away; the frozen gorge that always takes you in, the grotto that always shelters you, the Blunted Crest that always watches over you; hares, mice, boars, hoopoes, cicadas, foxes, coarse and honest beasts your only companionship; mushrooms, figs, asparagus, pure water, welling from the belly of the earth for me alone; blackberry brambles that demand a drop of blood to seal your pact.

I left the road, I wanted to return home through the forest.

I took off my clothes and threw them in the brush to feel the leaves scrubbing my skin. The clouds of Venus are made of sulfuric acid, Durand told me so; the rain of Venus chars everything. I want to leave this planet. I took off my shoes and walked on the moss, covered in the vomit of clouds. At each step, the clink of the keys in my hand in imitation of a jingle bell.

The day withered away to offer me the shelter of the shadows.

The wind began to push me as though hasty to get me home, and at last the house appeared on the hillock, big and splendid. I would have run to it, barefoot, arms outspread, nude, but lightning flashed, and I thought I saw a figure atop the stairs. A man.

By now the darkness had taken possession of nearly everything. A veil of rain before my eyes, impossible to make out a thing. I crouched, I felt the soil like a blind woman. I grabbed a rock.

Who was it? Manel, Flavi, Carles, a stranger? Had I actually seen a man?

I advanced cautiously, like a fox, gravels embedding themselves in the soles of my feet and hair clinging to my body, sniffed the air, but all was lewd nature.

A step, the first. I count them from inertia every time I take them up or down to reassure me the world isn't deceiving me, to hold onto the belief that immutable things exist. Fifteen steps. And at the last one, a man waiting for me. Perhaps.

Two steps. The surface is thin, eroded by the licks of time, with the feel of skin, a skin made of stone.

Three steps. At the top of the stairs, the darkness is diluted. I scrutinize it, not wanting to let a single movement, slight as it may be, pass unnoticed.

Four steps. Body alert, every muscle tensed like a bowstring ready to fire.

Five steps. The rain drips down my chin and my cunt.

Six steps. I squeeze the rock, I feel a slanted furrow in it, it seems to be smiling. Cynicism of nature.

Seven steps. A howl gathers in my stomach.

Eight steps. I start to see in the dark, fear sharpens my gaze.

Nine steps. The roar growing within me no longer fits inside and I let it go. An ancient cry rends the curtain of rain—the gravels quake like children on the verge of tears—and sinks its claws into the bark of the pines, climbs to the canopies, slathered in sweet resin, shakes the needles, their shrieking echoes in the wind. In the background I sense a metallic, repetitive clack against the rock.

The blackness shakes, contracts, whirls, something slips off into the bushes, a black mass precise over the shadows. Black on black advancing toward me with an invisible smile.

Ten steps. The rain falls not in drops, it's a continuous jet I must pass through, a wall my body must pierce, the water flows down the steps in torrents, my bare feet want to run.

Eleven steps. My legs impel me upward in flight, soaring over the steps that remain, I throw the rock blindly, hear it tumble to the earth, I regret it, now my only remaining weapons are my fingernails and teeth. Weapons enough, I tell myself, I don't need anything else, I'll tear off his ear in my teeth, a fox devouring a bunny, I'll taste the ferrous tang of blood in my mouth, I'll crush his nuts with my knee, I don't need anything else: fingernails, teeth, intelligence.

Twelve, thirteen, fourteen steps.

One's missing, where is it?

Fifteen. There should be fifteen.

Mind always quicker than body, than word, than reality. The stone and doubt, slippery, they betray me, I slip, the angled edge strikes my ribs, my forehead hits the ground, my ankle twists, I look around, nostrils flared to sniff out the man in heat, I could still bite his dick off, claw his balls until semen bubbles out with every heartbeat, milk draining from a split fig. Incessant pounding of the heart, thunder, the forest's lament, a drop of blood rills down my cheek.

On the steps on all fours, I continue to analyze the darkness, the rain roars so loudly I can't hear my thoughts or fear. Someone grasps my two shoulders from behind, I can't move, a weight falls over me, breath warms my neck, behind my ears, a tongue wetter than rain, scent of lamb, scent of honey, scent of tobacco, scent of the cockatoo's deadly perfume, scent of rancid wine, scent of straw, a voice rough like sandpaper, sweetie, dear, Xana, Rezzo, Monda, Remei, Remeiona, I'm gonna fuck your ass, a warm piece of meat spreading apart my buttocks, I'm gonna stick it in you till you beg me to let you suck it, you piglet, same as your friend, he always used to ask for it, Meeeeeeeei, he says, imitating the bleating of a sheep.

The trees bend down over us, extend me their branches so I can grab onto them and flee, I stretch out my arm.

I can't reach, I can't reach, I can't reach.

I moan. One of the claws pinches my nipple, the voice is suddenly velvety and stings like a caterpillar, A writer, she says, how's that novel coming, Mei? You give birth to it yet? Or will you go to the hospital and have them tear it out of you before it's born? Go ahead and bleat, it turns me on. Beeeeee.

A red-hot cock for branding cattle impales me, pumps me, inflates inside me like a dog's dick, What about your dad, Remei? You want your daddy to come give it to you up the ass? *Zub-zub*. Every two words a whine, he pulls my hair until my head jerks back, Look, Rezzo, look.

I open my eyes, the fox is six inches away, studying me, she approaches, licks my hands as they sink into the mud. I bite her neck, she yelps, she runs, I've got hairs in my mouth, I spit them out, frenetic pounding in and out, a burning pain rages through my rectum, the rain gushes down trying to extinguish it, the voices run together, You threw him out, he told me so, honey, you're so skinny, you need to eat, dicks, sweetie, let's go *zub-zub*, you need to eat juicy dicks until you choke, two at a time, like in that video I used to love, Monda.

A hand on my head and the other kneading my breast, convulsive movements, eyes rolled back, owls hooting, the spiraling dirge of the forest comes and goes like a siren attesting to the catastrophe.

The cock defecates inside me and pulls out right away, without a word.

I collapse on the ground, offering my ass to the air to take away the thick rill gasping out of my hole.

Liquefy me, make me rain, dissolve me into the ground. Infect it, poison everyone, make them bleed to death inside without their knowing. Exterminate the rats.

I abandon myself to the darkness and the rain.

NOVEMBER

Mei Be, Maybe Not

You counted, there were fourteen.
But you can't discount reality.
You never can discount it, Mei.

THAT DAY

It's cold. I wake up quivering. From humiliation. My body broken; my hair and skin handsomely bemired. Dressed in mud, I rise, count the steps. Fifteen steps, it's fifteen again. The light grows. You can glimpse the outrage of time, indifferent to all: the night has run its course, the steamroller of tame hours has already passed over me.

I look for the keys on the ground, on the steps, at the foot of the steps, in the greenery. I try to think where I last saw them. I remember the tinkling in my hands as I walked through the woods. When I noticed the shadow at the top of the stairs, I gripped them tight, they dug into my palm. I look at my hand, not a sign of them. I climb up and down the steps over and over in futile succession.

The sun's now high in the sky. I go to the door, thinking I'll force my way in. The keys are in the lock, moron. I take them out and throw them far away.

I go into the house, the walls are silent, they don't know what to say or how to act. They fear me. The living room greets me with stony silence. I pile up kindling for the fire, a few thinner branches, a mighty log to crown the pyre. My body acts on instinct, with meek movements, as if it lacked the force of culmination, like a ball that rolls and loses momentum an inch before reaching its destination. Failed movements.

Over the fireplace, the pupils of the sunflowers follow me, I feel them on me, they're waiting for me to stare them in the face. They pity me. Sorrow covers me, shovelfuls of sorrow bury me. I approach the painting, buckling under the weight of its compassion.

I give in, I look at the sunflowers. Father?

I should have taken the damn picture down months ago. I grab it. One hand on each side of the frame. I pull it off the wall. With a knee, I knock out the canvas and the backing. I open the window. The sunflower seed stare of my father takes flight and my knee starts to bleed.

The fire's burning now. I curl up in front of it to heat myself. I don't want to get dressed. I don't want to wear a disguise. I gnaw a crust of bread, hypnotized by the flames.

Now what?

I run to look for my computer. It's a foreign object. All white, perfect lines, lights that turn on and off, a miniature spaceship. I yearn for a computer of wood, with keys of stone. I turn it on, but I can't, the screen is a blur. I grab a pen and paper.

Now what?

Now finish it.

"Don't try to follow me. I'll kill you," Lila says, I could say: Don't try to follow me. I'll kill you all.

But he follows her like a dog wagging its tail, moaning for his owner to forgive him.

This canine whining creeps into her, she covers her ears, but she just hears it louder, it's inside her, pitiful moans. If she stops, he'll leap at her and lick her ankles, her hands, her face, with the same tongue that's licked up his own piss and the shit from his mongrel ass. He'll mount her leg and copulate with it.

She takes off running and sings to keep from hearing him. She sings the first thing that comes into her head. A song from Mass when she was little and used to go to church with her mother in her Sunday best. A song from when everything was possible. *Hevenu shalom alechem.* Full-throated. *Hevenu shalom alechem.* He trots audibly behind her. *Hevenu shalom alechem.* She sees a stone in the middle of the path, bright black over the dun soil. It's waiting for her. *Hevenu shalom alechem.*

She crouches. She grabs it. So smooth, so cold, it's perfect.

When she turns, he stops, and they look at each other. What hatred in her gaze. She throws the rock and strikes him in the head.

His body falls back, and his shirt rides up, revealing his stomach. The flesh, distressingly pale, flops flaccid, like fermenting dough, a deflated balloon that will never be blown up again.

Shalom.

She continues down the mountain. No shouts, no gestures, no tears. In her eyes, the unsettling tranquility of deep gorges.

The deep gorges of the soul.

The fire's still burning. Is that it? Was that it? Just that?

Writing. How stupid. What am I trying to show? To whom? Myself, Guim, Mother, Carles, the assholes from the publisher? The world? Or is the idea that I'll endure through my little book? Hilarious! My piece of shit novelette. My legend is another. What clarity, all at once.

I throw the whole thing in the fire. The pages burn eagerly. I incinerate the possibility of making an even bigger fool of myself before life. The nebularium burns too. Clouds of fire, she left those out.

I grab my backpack. I stick a knife inside, a few pieces of clothing in case the urge to dissimulate returns, a blanket, a few jars of the marmalade I hid in the cellar that night, matches.

The laptop is in the armchair. I smash it with the axe. The shards of screen spread like tiny diamonds across the labyrinth in the carpet, leaving the outline of a bug-eyed moth. I put on my shoes. I throw my coat atop my nude skin. I leave the door thrown open.

Already I can hear the legend spreading from one mouth to the next.

Seems she went crazy, they'll say, she was running naked through the forest with an axe in her hand, no one dared go near the area. They sent the dogs to look for her. Here they'll fall silent, make sure there's no children close by, so they won't hear what I did to them, how I chopped them up with the axe and hung their legs and heads from the branches of my trees.

She dug in at the Rocatallada spring, the one that never ran dry. Word is, as soon as you got close to it, the water would start to run red, sometimes black even, and that still today, twenty years after the fact, it's poisonous. Some workers put up a metal plaque there: Not Safe For Drinking.

Nobody will ever know where I had my cave. They'll say I killed my husband, I set fire to the beehives, I killed whole flocks of sheep. The legend will take on a life of its own, will grow: I tried to kill my mother, the village shepherd, an AIDS-infected junkie living in a shack. They'll say everyone left the vicinity, terrified, that every day of their lives they'll think of me. Every day.

The story will mutate like a virus, and maybe it will be Manel I'll chop up and hang from the trees, or I'll humiliate my mother by walking her naked through the village, exposing her flappy skin to the world, without makeup, hair unwashed; I'll exhibit her like an animal at the fair, tied with a leash, a green scarf asphyxiating her, and I'll make her tell, sniveling in the middle of the square, how Manel used to fuck her against the cellar walls. Or I'll kidnap Flavi and won't feed him anything but my pussy until he dies.

I could burn down the house and make the carpet disappear, the bed, the cellar, the land that watched over me when I was born. Reduce my origins to ashes and get rid of the prints.

Such ideas, such possibilities!

She was already mad when she came here, some will say. No,

the others will counter, it was the woods, the water from the spring, the novel, love, solitude.

You don't know the legend of the madwoman? they'll ask.

And I'll be waiting for them in the forest. Alone.

ACKNOWLEDGEMENTS

To Melcior, for boundlessly sharing my love, table, bed, and literature, in other words all the things in life worth sharing.

To Eva, for our matrimonial friendship, her advice, her patience with my deliria.

To those who had the good will to read the earlier versions (you too, Marc) even if often I don't pay enough attention to them (Salvador, Maria: for now this is the best I can do).

To my aunt, who gave me the protagonist's name and so many other things.

To you, who live with your children in the forest of a country we invented twenty years ago, for always giving me the fuel I need and for letting me be part of your lives.

To Juliette, for help with the French.

To the asterisks, for their impeccable work.

To the editors, for believing in me.

To those who read me, because without you, this book wouldn't exist.

To the wounded and fallen, because they helped me and I loved them.

To my children, for everything else.

About the Author

Carlota Gurt is a writer and translator from Barcelona. In 2019, she won the prestigious Mercè Rodoreda award for her collection of short stories *Cavalcarem tota la nit*. *Alone* is her first novel.